WITCHES BREW

PHANTOM QUEEN BOOK 6 - A TEMPLE VERSE SERIES

SHAYNE SILVERS
CAMERON O'CONNELL

ARGENTO
PUBLISHING

CONTENTS

Shayne Silvers & Cameron O'Connell

Witches Brew

The Phantom Queen Diaries Book 6

A TempleVerse Series

ISBN 13: 978-1-947709-21-8

© 2018, Shayne Silvers / Argento Publishing, LLC

info@shaynesilvers.com

SHAYNE AND CAMERON

Shayne Silvers, here.

Cameron O'Connell is one helluva writer, and he's worked tirelessly to merge a story into the Temple Verse that would provide a different and unique *voice*, but a complementary *tone* to my other novels. *SOME* people might say I'm hard to work with. But certainly, Cameron would never...

Hey! Pipe down over there, author monkey! Get back to your writing cave and finish the next Phantom Queen Novel!

Ahem. Now, where was I?

This is book 6 in the Phantom Queen Diaries, which is a series that ties into the existing Temple Verse with Nate Temple and Callie Penrose. This series could also be read independently if one so chose. Then again, you, the reader, will get SO much more out of my existing books (and this series) by reading them all in tandem.

But that's not up to us. It's up to you, the reader.

You tell us...

DON'T FORGET!

VIP's get early access to all sorts of book goodies, including signed copies, private giveaways, and advance notice of future projects. AND A FREE NOVELLA! Click the image or join here:
www.shaynesilvers.com/l/219800

FOLLOW and LIKE:

Shayne's FACEBOOK PAGE:

www.shaynesilvers.com/l/38602

Cameron's FACEBOOK PAGE:

www.shaynesilvers.com/l/209065

We respond to all messages, so don't hesitate to drop either of us a line. Not interacting with readers is the biggest travesty that most authors can make. Let us fix that.

FAE ARE MISSING ALL OVER BOSTON...

And apparently, no one else is suicidal enough to look into it.

Good thing Quinn MacKenna—black magic arms dealer and Fae half-breed— has been searching for a way to earn back some of Boston's goodwill after almost destroying the city...twice. Besides, favors for the Fae usually pay dividends if you play your cards right...

As long as the Fae don't double-cross or otherwise backstab you. But that hardly ever happens...

Thankfully, Quinn has Robin Redcap to back her up—between his skill at navigating Fae politics and his penchant for extreme, brutal violence, it's a match made in Heaven. Or Hell.

But the only evidence they have to go on is a crime scene laden with ritualistic ingredients and blood—lots and lots of blood—leading Quinn to suspect witchcraft.

Except the witches are a tight-knit community who don't appreciate Quinn's intrusion—even when all she wants to do is help. Simply put, what happens in the coven stays in the coven.

The situation grows murkier and deadlier by the minute as Quinn finds herself cauldron-deep in a swirl of betrayal, conspiracy, and vengeance.

Especially when she discovers who is really stirring the pot, and that it might all stem from an unfulfilled promise made by a certain trigger-happy redhead regarding a certain magic-slinging wizard in St. Louis. And the Fae put pretty big stock in promises and agreements.

Double, double, toil and trouble...
This little oath-breaker is in big, big trouble.

CHAPTER 1

*I*n my opinion, there's something inexplicably wrong with your life when you find yourself in a strip club before noon on a weekday. To me, it felt as culturally insensitive as using a fork to eat sushi: just because you *can* do it, doesn't mean you should. Of course, maybe that was only me. It's not like the time of day would make much of a difference to your average person; all strip clubs are kept dark and windowless, which meant most would be hard pressed to tell whether or not it's night or day outside, let alone guess the hour.

But if you knew what to look for—if you'd been to enough clubs enough times to sense the sun creeping up on the horizon in a windowless room like a hand reaching out for you in the dark—you'd recognize the symptoms. You'd notice the energy of the club was calmer, somehow—the girls less inclined to hustle, their breaks longer, the drinks thinner. The customers would appear likewise changed, their gazes less intent, shoulders slumped, nursing their drinks instead of pounding them.

It felt almost like everyone was catching their breath.

Considering the fact I was nursing a slight hangover of my own, I supposed I couldn't blame any of them—not the girls for being tired and worn down, or the customers for looking sad and forlorn. I could, however, blame the three people sitting across from me for dragging me out this early. Although I suppose calling them "people" would be stretching things a bit.

One of the individuals opposite me, his back pressed firmly against a red leather couch, was a Faeling—a creature born in the Fae realm, an alternate dimension of sorts which bordered ours and, occasionally, bled over. Robin Redcap, once an infamous castle-haunting baddie turned rogue spy, fiddled with his blood red ball cap, a habitual gesture that I couldn't attribute to any particular emotion. Hell, for all I knew, I brought it on; I'd never seen him fuss with it as much as he did when around me. The Faeling wore a dark blue T-shirt which read "The Hunt for Red Soxtober" in blockish red letters, spread wide across a thick, burly chest—a sentiment which admittedly won him brownie points with me.

I was born here in Boston, after all.

It was Robin who'd requested the meeting and the time, though I'd been sure to pick the venue. Ordinarily, I'd have gone with some place a little tamer, but The Seven Deadly Inn constituted familiar territory, and frankly, if there was one thing I'd learned over years spent making deals with disreputable people as a black magic arms dealer, it was to avoid the nice, relaxed locales when setting up potentially hazardous meet-and-greets.

Nobody likes it when their favorite park becomes a warzone.

So, here we were, in a strip club in the wee hours of the morning. Of course, while snagging breakfast at a strip club wasn't exactly on my to-do list, I had to admit the Inn had a few perks—even during daylight hours—that I simply couldn't get elsewhere: a decent drink selection, privacy, and enough nudity to distract my would-be clients.

What's more, it seemed that particular strategy seemed to be paying off; the other two individuals crowded beside Robin on the couch had nearly identical, utterly blank expressions on their faces, despite the fact that one was male and the other female. In fact, Hansel and his sister, Gretel, sat with their hands clasped between their knees, pointedly turned away from the stage and its promise of flesh, as if we were sitting in an office and not a lounge. Both Germans had long blonde hair, which might have passed for white in the right light, but which currently reflected the various strobes of color swimming throughout the club: red, green, purple, and back again. They each had pale blue eyes, though neither were as lovely, or captivating, as Robin's—the Redcap had grown a beard so thick and high on his cheeks that his eyes were practically all I could see of his face beneath the ball cap.

His eyes, unlike the cool gazes of his two companions, seemed to be urging me to be civil, as if he were silently worried I'd say something to piss the fairytale siblings off.

Who, me?

"So, what is it ye two want, then?" I asked, finally.

Robin sighed.

"Miss MacKenna," Gretel began, wisely deciding not to call me by my first name, Quinn, without permission, "I think we should begin by acknowledging that what my brother did to you several months ago was deplorable, and that his behavior during that time was utterly inexcusable."

I felt my eyes widen as I glanced over at Hansel, hoping to gauge his reaction. But the elder German man had already pointedly looked away. Of course, that meant he'd begun inadvertently staring at an inverted stripper, her legs spread wide on either side of the pole. His gaze quickly shifted to his shoes, his cheeks burning. I would have laughed at his expense, but honestly, I was too busy fighting the urge not to gape at his sister; of all the things I'd expected her to say, that hadn't been one of them. Thing was, a ridiculous amount of shit had happened since Hansel—Grimms' Brothers fairytale figure and one of the three attorneys who worked for the Faerie Chancery, an organization designed to both protect and control the Fae population here in Boston—and I had last spoken in his office.

Last spring, following a fresh crop of horrific murders in the Boston area, I'd been manipulated by Hansel and a few select members of the Chancery—including Robin—into finding and taking out the serial killer responsible for the deaths. To say I hadn't taken kindly to being their pawn would be an understatement. In fact, between that experience and the loss of my aunt this past summer during a cataclysmic altercation with an ancient race bent on the destruction of all things Fae, I'd pretty much written off the fair folk in their entirety; fool me once, shame on me, fool me twice, and I'll fucking end you. And yet, here was Gretel—one-third of the law office of *Hansel, Hansel, and Gretel*—calling out her brother in public for something he'd done to me months ago.

It was enough to make me suspicious.

"So I'll ask again, what d'ye want?" I asked.

"To apologize, first and foremost," Gretel replied. "It wasn't until I first considered approaching you that my brother confessed to what he'd done.

Apparently, he thought you might be reticent to help us, under the circumstances." When Hansel said nothing, Gretel nudged him. "Tell her."

"I am sorry, Miss MacKenna," Hansel said, head bowed so far down his hair trailed over the lip of his shirt collar. "I have been among the Fae a long time. I fear I have come to think as they do. To plot as they do, with little consideration for those we use to achieve our aims."

I found myself shaking my head. "We Fae don't plot, ye know."

Both lawyers frowned, wearing eerily similar, disbelieving expressions. "What do you mean 'we Fae'?" Gretel asked, incredulously.

Now it was my turn to look away. I studied the dancer's gyrations and knew, from nothing but the exposed back and curve of ass, that Heresy was on stage. True to the Inn's tradition of naming the dancers after one of the many, many Biblical sins cited in scripture, Heresy moved like a caged animal, prowling the edges of the raised dais on her knees, her dark brown skin so smooth it looked like it had been poured on. Unlike Hansel, I didn't bother looking away; I'd always enjoyed watching Heresy move, especially through a crowd—she drew more stares at just over five foot than I did at six, although my flaming red hair and bright green eyes tended to earn more lingering attention. "I meant what I said," I replied, at last. I turned back and gave the lawyers my full attention. "I'm guessin' Robin kept me little secret to himself, then."

Robin cleared his throat. "The Huntress said that if I told anyone anything about you, she'd—and I quote—'shove my hat down my throat and sew my mouth shut'."

That made me smile. The Huntress, an infamous warrior woman named Scathach, was essentially my twisted rendition of a Faerie godmother. Of course, the fact that she was training me three days a week to fight and kill using my newfound abilities—not to mention the fact that she apparently went around threatening to maim people on my behalf—should go to show exactly what kind of Faerie godmother I needed in my life.

Basically, the only reason I'd wear glass slippers was so I could turn them into shivs.

"Aye, that sounds like her," I said.

Robin grinned and nodded, his gruff voice carrying a little over the sound of Heresy's set. "I wasn't planning on telling anyone anyway."

"Is that so?" Hansel asked, eyes narrowed.

4

Robin's grin faded. "I don't work for you anymore, Hansel. For anyone. What I keep from you is my business."

"Went freelance, is that it?" I asked, curiosity getting the better of me. Trouble was, as long as I'd known Robin, he'd been a spy—albeit a spy whose loyalties I'd never entirely sorted out. But the fact remained that, while he may have kept information from Hansel and Gretel, I still wasn't entirely sure I could trust him.

"Sort of," Robin replied, staring down the elderly German man. "I applied to become an Adjudicator."

I raised my eyebrows at that. As far as I knew, the Adjudicators—of which there were only two—were Faelings responsible for governing the Faerie Chancery and its various factions. Last I'd spoken with Robin, he'd been pretty dissatisfied with that system, even going so far as to contemplate rebellion. Which meant either something significant had changed, or he had.

"That application is still pending," Hansel growled.

"That's enough," Gretel interjected. "We didn't come here to bicker like children."

"We should not have come here at all," Hansel muttered.

"How about ye tell me why ye came here, and we go from there?" I asked, ignoring Hansel's jibe. I settled back in my chair and turned my full attention to Gretel. I knew I could always pull Robin aside later and force him to tell me what was really going on, but for now it seemed like—if I wanted to get the hell out of here before the sun went down—Gretel was my girl. Woman. Whatever.

"Members of the Chancery are being taken," Gretel replied.

"Taken," Hansel scoffed. "They're being hunted."

I leaned forward, interlacing my fingers. "What d'ye mean, hunted?"

"We've had members go *missing*," Robin clarified.

"Which is why we were hoping you'd help us, Miss MacKenna," Gretel added.

I studied the faces of the German siblings and their Faeling companion, trying to decide which angle they were playing. I'd been right about what I said earlier: the Fae didn't plot. They bargained. Plotting was something unique to the human race, most of whom preferred to get as much as they could for as little as possible. Usually I didn't mind that distinction, but lately I'd come to realize that the Fae way of doing business was—while barbaric at times—at least transparent. You get what you pay for, more or less.

And yet, something told me not to discount or dismiss these two. Maybe it was the sincerity in Gretel's voice, or the barely contained anxiety in Hansel's face. Or maybe it was the fact that—despite Robin's role in what transpired months ago—I still wanted the burly bastard at my back in a scrap. I sighed. Either way, I'd dragged my sorry ass out of bed to a strip club in Bay Village in the wee hours of the morning—the least I could do was hear them out. "Alright," I said, "how about we start with the obvious question. Why me?"

"Because, we have no one else," Gretel replied. Hansel made to interrupt, looking alarmed, but his sister held up a hand. "No, we either tell her everything, or we may as well not have bothered coming at all."

"Well, that's a refreshin' change of pace," I said, smirking.

"What is?" she asked.

"Bein' told everythin'. You'd be surprised how rare that is, especially comin' from the Chancery."

"I promise this is not a trap, Miss MacKenna. Our members are being taken, perhaps even hunted, as my brother says. An alarming number have gone missing, and there's at least one dead, as far as we can tell."

"At least one?" I asked, cocking an eyebrow.

All three exchanged pained looks, their differences momentarily forgotten beneath the weight of shared knowledge. A burden heavy enough to bind them together, even for just a moment. Which probably meant I really didn't want to know.

Damn it.

CHAPTER 2

*I*t turned out I was right.

As if there were any doubt.

"We have reason to believe one of our abducted members was killed, which means it's possible others have been similarly dispatched. And, while the evidence is scarce, we suspect there was a ritual performed at the residence," Gretel said, her syntax changing ever so slightly, reverting to the anesthetized language employed by lawyers everywhere. I had a moment to wonder if perhaps that was why legalese had developed in the first place: anything to keep a safe distance from the brutality of what people are capable of. To turn words like "murder" into something softer, something less unpleasant, like "homicide" or "rape" into "sexual assault"—as if the words themselves held the potential for trauma. Gretel shook herself, her eyes haunted by a memory, as if she could still see the crime scene in her mind. "A sacrificial ritual," she added.

I shuddered. Despite my background working with notoriously dangerous individuals, not to mention Freaks—people and creatures who lived on the fringes of society, known and mentioned in various mythologies and lore—I'd never become exceptionally acclimated to gory murder scenes. I mean, don't get me wrong, I'd killed quite a few people myself over the last couple years, so I wasn't exactly deterred by violence. But as far as I was concerned, they'd all deserved it; I hadn't lost more than a few minutes sleep over any of them. And yet, I had a feeling that whatever had disturbed Gretel to this degree—an immortal who'd once been enslaved by a blind witch who lured and ate children—would likely give me a nightmare or two.

"And ye haven't gone to the police?" I asked.

"Why would we?" Hansel replied, looking amused. "The mortal police would obviously have no idea what to make of the situation. *Scheisse*, we couldn't even discuss the potential victims without them trying to have us committed. What do they know of trolls? Of goblins? Of elves?"

I started to suggest calling in the FBI—specifically a few Federal agents I trusted who specialized in hunting down monsters—but knew it wouldn't fly even before I said it; Leo and his team worked on cold cases, cases other cops and FBI agents could only shake their heads at, which meant calling them in this early, in a professional capacity, would be nearly impossible. Besides, in this instance, Hansel was right: when it came to the Fae, seeing was most definitely believing. Even Leo and his squad might have a tough time tracking down elusive fairytale creatures.

Which begged the next question.

"And yet ye t'ink I can help ye? Why?" I asked.

"Robin suggested we find someone who could track the killers," Gretel said.

"To be fair, the Huntress was who I meant," Robin replied, sounding nonplussed.

"Yes, but she has not gotten back to us, and we are running out of time. We could at least all agree that you, Miss MacKenna, have a reputation for finding things others can't," Gretel explained. "We have ten missing Fae as of this morning, and no leads to speak of. In fact, had we known your...status had changed—"

"Ye mean me bein' part Fae?" I interjected.

"What do you mean, 'part Fae'?" Hansel asked, eyes wide.

I sighed, but otherwise ignored the man, hoping to let Gretel finish her thought instead. The truth was I had no desire to get into my genetic break-down at the moment, assuming I even had the answers Hansel was looking for—which I didn't. "Go on," I insisted.

"Had we known *that*," Gretel said, waving a hand magnanimously, "we might have come to you sooner. As of now, we don't know what the missing individuals have in common, except that they are all Fae and at least tangentially connected to the Chancery. Simply put, I would have reached out to warn you, if nothing else."

I grunted. "I can take care of meself, but I appreciate the thought."

"Of course. But, regardless, it is my belief that we need an outsider to look into this. My brothers and I are all experts in our respective fields, but none of us have been able to find a pattern here. And, what's worse, the threat of our reprisal is not enough to keep the Chancery members safe, which means there is nothing to stop this from continuing. Honestly, if you can't help us, or won't, then I am not sure what we will do."

I frowned. "What about the Adjudicators? Morgause and Sir Bredbed-dle? Can't they be called in to figure this out? Or at least to protect the rest?" I asked, referring to the two arbiters of justice I'd met when I last visited the Chancery's underground speakeasy. As figures from Arthurian legend, both the enchantress and the Green Knight had been remarkably powerful, not to mention a little frightening.

Again, the three exchanged glances.

"They haven't come back yet," Robin replied, filling the silence at last.

I gaped at him. "They haven't?" Last I'd heard, the two Adjudicators had been headed to Fae to sort out the circumstances behind the return of Morgause's son, Mordred, from the dead. "But that was months ago," I said.

"Yes," Robin replied.

"D'ye know where they've gone?"

"No. And we lost contact with them around the time you got back from Moscow."

I frowned, marveling at the suspicious timing; my friends had lost contact with another individual who'd gone to Fae around that time, and still hadn't heard from him. Of course, Nate Temple—billionaire philan-thropist and closet wizard—was notoriously prone to running off and doing his own thing. Maybe it was mere coincidence. Maybe. "Wait, Robin...why d'ye put in your application?" I asked, an idea forming.

Robin fussed with his hat again. "I think you know why."

"Because ye don't t'ink they're comin' back," I supplied.

"They will return," Hansel said, as if willing it to be true. But there was something else beneath that. An uncertainty. The kind of doubt that worms its way into your every thought and action. The kind that makes you blind to the truth.

"Perhaps," Gretel replied, sharing a look with Robin above her brother's head. At that moment, I knew she and Robin had come to the same conclusion; the Adjudicators might, or might not, be coming back, but without them to cajole and defend the Fae population, the Chancery was bound to deteriorate. What they needed to survive was leadership and continuity—regardless of the form it took. Bureaucracy at its best. Or worst, depending how you looked at it. "Either way," she continued, "we're left to make the best of what we've been given."

"So, you're left with no choice but to pull from the bottom of the barrel, is that it?" I asked, smirking.

Robin coughed out a laugh. "Is that referring to me? Or you?"

"Both?" I suggested.

"I don't know what you are talking about," Gretel replied, speaking over our laughter.

"Nevermind," I said, waving that away. "Why don't ye tell me more about the missin' Fae?"

"Does that mean you'll help us?" Gretel asked, hopeful.

I shrugged. "Sounds like it's in me best interest, all t'ings considered. I'm not interested in bein' hunted down or snatched away in the wee hours of the night. So, aye, I'm all ears."

Hansel grunted. "We should send her, instead."

"I don't know—" Gretel began.

"It *would* be easier," Robin interrupted.

Gretel sighed. "It would be *quicker*, perhaps. But not easier."

"What the hell are ye lot on about?" I asked.

"The crime scene," Robin explained.

"What about it?"

"Hansel suggested we leave it intact, just in case you said yes. Thought it would be best." Robin grinned at the expression on my face, hands up in surrender. "Don't kill the messenger."

I rolled my eyes. "Fine, I'll go," I said. All three watched as I slid my jacket off the arm of my chair, each with a different expression. Hansel seemed surprised. Gretel pleased. Only Robin had the balls to look smug. Redcap bastard. "I only have one question before we go," I added.

"Which is?" Gretel asked.

"Do we have time for me to eat somethin', first? I'm starvin'."

"You have time," Hansel said, "but I would not eat anything unless you think it will taste as good coming back up as it did going down."

I snorted indelicately, but then saw the other two nodding sagely as though Hansel had said something particularly philosophical. Which meant he wasn't simply trying to be a dick, for a change. Awesome. "Fine. I'll just get a coffee to go, then."

If I was going to be horrified, the least I could do was make sure I was caffeinated.

It's the little things.

CHAPTER 3

*W*e took Robin's car—a well-kept, older model Jeep with a surprisingly roomy interior. The two Germans opted not to join us, citing other business, though I suspected they were merely avoiding the crime scene. Gretel had shaken my hand, thanking me for my help, her grip strong and firm. Meanwhile her brother had phoned their driver, referring to the Seven Deadly Inn as—I kid you not—"one of those grind-houses in the Village," as if there were a slew of rakish titty bars tucked away among the neighborhood's cluster of quaint, cozy rowhouses. Frankly, I was glad to see them go; no matter how forthcoming his sister had been, Hansel was about one smart ass comment away from having his name added to the list of the missing.

"How far?" I asked Robin once we were on the road, nursing the coffee I'd picked up on our way out, keeping it nestled between my hands, using it as a secondary source of warmth. October had initially kicked off with a fierce warm front, leaving the entire coast with a sense of unending summer; for a while there, everywhere I went I spotted folks lounging in shorts and sandals, their shoulders bare and sun-kissed. But now, with November on its way, anyone bold enough to walk the city did so bundled in winter jackets, their breath fogging up the air, huddled against the biting wind. Of course, I'd encouraged Robin to turn on the heat the instant he turned the engine over, but the Jeep was a drafty thing and left me desperately wishing I'd worn something heavier than my light leather jacket.

"To the house?" Robin asked. He shrugged. "About thirty minutes. It's in Hyde Park."

I scrunched into myself a bit and took another sip of coffee, letting silence fill the cab until, at last, the heat funneling through the vents over-came the cool fall air creeping in through the tiny gaps in the vehicle's otherwise sturdy frame. I sighed in relief, no longer having to fight the occasional shiver. "So, how've ye been?" I asked.

Robin grunted. "Well enough."

"Just well enough?"

"Things have been tough," Robin replied, shrugging.

"How so?" I prompted, unwilling to let Robin off that easy.

The Redcap sighed. "It's been a long few months, that's all. I'm sure you remember I used to think the way the Chancery was run was oppressive, right? Well, I've begun to realize there are worse alternatives."

"What, like the missin' folk?"

"No, though that is definitely part of the problem. What I'm talking about is more of an overall issue. Before Morgause and Sir Bred left, I was sure our system was broken. That it was antiquated and unfair. But now?" He flicked those intense blue eyes at me, then back to the road. "Now I'm thinking the Fae aren't meant to have that kind of freedom, Quinn. I'm thinking we simply don't know what to do with it."

I frowned. "Why, did somethin' happen?"

Robin scoffed. "What *didn't* happen, more like. I feel like I've been putting out fires for months. Without the Adjudicators to keep them in line, the less restrained Chancery members have been acting out. Jeopardizing the rest of us."

"When Mom and Dad are away, the kids will play, huh?" I smirked. "What'd they do, raise taxes on a few local bridges? Huff and puff and blow a house down? Spoil some milk?"

"You're not half as funny as you think you are, you know."

I chuckled. "It's not that I'm disagreein' with ye, I'm just sayin' it's not unheard of. People go a bit wild when they know there won't be conse-quences. And the Fae are wilder than most people."

"You think? How about you?" Robin asked. "Feeling wilder?"

The sudden shift in topic surprised me, and it took me long enough to recover that Robin started humming the "Jeopardy" theme song under his breath like an asshat. I pushed him a little. "Shut up, I'm t'inkin' about it."

The trouble was, I *had* been feeling wilder lately. Ever since I'd made an impromptu trip to the Fae realm and encountered my biological aunts— Macha and Badb, two of the three goddesses who represented the combined might of *the* Morrigan—I seemed to have gained not only super-human abilities, but also a wicked lack of inhibitions and a rather active subconscious. Now that I'd had time to process my trip to Fae, to dissect the whole experience, I realized embracing my wild side had felt eerily like being brownout drunk on a caffeinated mixed drink, the uppers and downers too intermingled to distinguish from one another, the world speeding by in a blur of light and sound. The result was a version of myself who'd basically been reduced to a hormone-driven teenager on a weekend bender—a woman so convinced of her own brilliance, of her own immortality, that she was willing to take on the whole fucking world.

Consequences be damned.

Fortunately, I'd had plenty of experience with lowered inhibitions, which meant I knew how to control my impulses better than most—and they say drinking is bad for you. Except, now that I knew my wild side was there, I could sense that inner voice knocking about in the back of my skull, urging me to give in to my baser impulses, waiting for the right moment to take me over completely.

Talk about peer pressure.

"Let's just say it's been a rough few months for me, as well," I said, at last.

"Yeah, the Huntress told me about what happened in Moscow. Did you really free a goddess?" Robin asked, changing the topic once more.

"Aye, that happened," I replied, frowning. Granted, it had been a combined effort between myself and Othello—a close friend who'd helped rescue a few of my other companions from the clutches of an immortal madman over the summer. I shivered, recalling for a moment the unbelievably cold, barren environment we'd found ourselves in at the time—not to mention the mind-bending reality of staring into the giant eye of a goddess whose physical body stood taller than a mountain.

But I'd only told Scathach that little tidbit after she'd cornered me during a training session a month ago, which meant she and Robin must have spoken recently. "What's the deal with ye and the Huntress, anyway?" I asked suspiciously, wondering why the Huntress was running around telling Robin my secrets. Well, maybe not secrets, per se. But still. "I didn't realize ye two were that close," I added.

"We weren't. Aren't. But she's asked me to keep an eye on you, when she's not around. So, she tells me things, keeps me updated. Usually that means potential threats to watch out for and what not. Besides, I think she likes talking about you. You should hear her." The Redcap lifted his chin a bit and did his best impression of Scathach's voice, "Quinn is as stubborn as any I've trained, but with more raw talent than anyone since Cú Chulainn. One day, she may even surpass him." His voice raised another octave. "Basically, I love her with all my heart. She's the prettiest, most dangerous, sexiest—"

I punched him in the arm not attached to the wheel. "She did *not* say I was the sexiest anythin', ye liar."

"I was editorializing," Robin hissed, jerking his arm to his side, away from me.

"Is that a fancy way of sayin' ye were makin' shit up?" I asked.

"Exaggerating, maybe. She does care for you, I think, in her own way. It's hard to watch over anyone for years and years without giving a shit about their well-being. Besides, you two are a lot alike. In temperament, anyway." Robin used one knee to steer and rubbed at his arm, briefly, as if to take away the sting. "Moody bitches, the both of you," he muttered.

"Maybe. Although I'm pretty sure she would've stabbed ye, instead," I said. "Hell, she still might if I tell her ye called her a bitch."

"You wouldn't," Robin said, eyes wide with sudden panic, staring at me.

"Eyes on the road," I commanded. "Won't do us any good to die before we make it to this crime scene of yours."

"Right," he replied, gripping the wheel firmly in both hands. "About that, are you sure you want in on this?"

"Worried Scathach will string ye up if ye get me killed?" I teased.

Robin's face turned serious. "She isn't the only one of us who cares about you, Quinn. If I could have kept you out of this, I would have. I've got a bad feeling that whatever has been taking our members isn't planning on stopping anytime soon. If anything, I think it's going to get worse."

I turned away to study the horizon, marveling at the slate grey sky that had moved in along with the cold front. The air had felt heavy for days now, as if at any given moment the downpour would begin in earnest, drowning us all in a deluge of rain. The thought reminded me of the day Dez had died;

it'd been raining then, too. "I'm not plannin' on leavin' ye to do this alone, Robin." I turned back to look at the burly man. "That's not what friends do."

Robin looked surprised. "Are we friends?"

"Not if ye don't stop tryin' to keep me out of harm's way for me own safety, no. But otherwise, aye." I reached out and squeezed his beefy shoulder, letting him feel the tensile strength in my fingers—so much more than there had been only a few months before. "Call me sexy again, though, and I may have to beat the livin' shit out of ye, friends or no."

The Redcap snorted, but his smile was genuine, white teeth flashing beneath all that beard hair. "Noted. No more compliments for Quinn."

"I love compliments," I said, settling back into my seat. "But only if I've earned 'em. Bein' called sexy is somethin' I reserve for men who've seen me naked."

"Fair enough. Speaking of, how's Detective Jimmy Collins these days?" Robin asked, referring to my former lover as if his existence—not to mention our relationship—were common knowledge.

"How the hell d'ye know about that?" I asked.

"Potential threats, remember?" Robin quipped. "So how about it? Any juicy updates?" The Redcap actually waggled his eyebrows.

I shook my head. Last I'd spoken with Jimmy, he'd enrolled in the FBI's new agent training course, planning to join up with Leo and his team in the Special Investigations Cold Case Office, AKA the Sicko Squad, located in the Bureau's Salt Lake City branch. While we hadn't exactly rekindled our brief affair, I was glad to report things had at least been fairly cordial, lately. Even a little flirtatious. But between the distance and the trajectory our lives were taking, I was beginning to doubt it would ever be more than that. Which was alright; honestly, it was simply nice to have ended at least one relationship without either of us needing a fucking ambulance.

Not that any of that shit was Robin's business.

"We're not that good of friends, yet, Robin," I snapped.

He laughed so hard at that his shoulders shook but said nothing else.

Smart Redcap.

CHAPTER 4

*T*he house, as Robin had referred to it, was actually one of those decrepit shacks you occasionally find smack dab in the middle of a well-to-do neighborhood, obscured behind trees that have grown too large and grass that has grown too long. My guess was the landholder, whoever it was, had owned the lot long enough to defy city ordinance and ignore all those pesky laws that force homeowners to mow and shit— leaving this nice stretch of suburbia with one hell of an eyesore. Of course, that didn't mean the hovel had no function; as we stepped through the knee-high grass, I could see at least a half dozen beer bottles strewn about, as well as the discarded remnants of fast food wrappers and water-logged pizza boxes. Considering the evidence, I was willing to bet this shack, in all its creepy, ruined glory, was the local hangout for rebellious teenagers and high school burnouts alike. Hell, I'd have put money on the probability that the local cops had a shit detail that included stopping in to check this place out—whatever it took to keep the lot free of riffraff and junkies.

Then again, maybe they weren't needed, after all; as we got closer, I felt something. Something sinister. A vibe, maybe. Whatever it was, it made my skin crawl. I suddenly wanted nothing more than to turn the fuck around and go back the way we'd come. "Ye feel that?" I asked, eyeing Robin side-long as we stomped inexorably forward.

The Redcap nodded and held out his arm, letting me see the goose flesh that had prickled on his own skin, the thick, dark hairs standing straight up like that of a threatened animal. "It's this place. Whatever they did here."

"They?"

"You'll see."

I grabbed at his arm, latching my hand around his wrist. "Tell me what I'm in for, Robin."

"You didn't seem to care, before," he said, looking surprised.

"Aye, but that was when I thought findin' out would only make it worse. Like lookin' down before ye jump out of an airplane. But that was before we pulled up to fuckin' Amityville," I said, waving absentmindedly at the abandoned house, close enough now that I could see how much of a ramshackle mess it really was: the windows had been shattered, then boarded up. A pink slip of paper had been taped to the door, standing in stark relief against the brittle, weather-worn wood. From here, I could see it was a one-story, which meant that whatever had happened would be contained to one floor, at least—probably visible the moment we walked in.

If we walked in.

"It really won't make sense if I simply tell you what's in there," Robin said. "Or I would have done that and saved us both the trouble of coming. Besides, what if you catch something I missed? That we all missed? You've seen some occult shit doing what you do, I know you have."

I sighed. That was true, although perhaps not as true as Gretel and Robin wanted it to be; just because I'd seen "some occult shit" didn't mean I could place any of it. My expertise was in locating rare items, technically, but that was more networking than research. Over the years, I'd learned it was far easier to pick the brains of experts than it was to become one. So, I'd capitalized on a lot of those experts owing me favors and paying in information, which meant the best I could likely do was take a look and—depending on what I found—start asking around.

Of course, that meant I'd have to go inside.

"I hate ye right now, Robin, I hope ye know that."

Robin grunted in acknowledgment. "Come on, let's get this over with."

I followed the Redcap, trailing directly behind like a shadow, marveling at the rampant overgrowth as we went, momentarily taken in by its untamed aesthetic. In a way, the lot had its own sort of wild, undomesticated beauty—nothing like the clean, sharp look of a freshly mowed yard.

The abandoned lot was a place only casually touched by humankind, which made it more vibrant somehow. Less artificial.

"Ready?" Robin asked, reaching for the knob. I started to make a joke about always being ready, but, before I could, he turned the knob and thrust open the door—apparently, that had been a rhetorical question. After a moment, the barrel-chested Faeling stepped through and held the door open for me, beckoning with one meaty hand. The fact that he had to do it at all meant I was probably stalling. Damn it.

I sighed and slid past him, stepping into what I could only assume had been a living room; moth-eaten chairs were perched beneath the broken window, their upholstery so faded I couldn't tell if they'd once been decorated by tiny flowers or tiny skulls. A slew of metal folding chairs were stacked up in a corner, rust-stained and covered in cobwebs. More bottles and cans were scattered about, smothered in dust. From the state of the room, it looked as though no one had used this place in quite a while. Of course, I figured that was unlikely, given the fact that I was here to look at a crime scene of some kind.

"When does the show start?" I asked.

Robin jerked his head towards the narrow hallway that connected to the living room. "The grand finale is behind the second door on the left. The master bedroom."

Something about the way he said that bothered me. The master bedroom. Meaning there was probably more than one in this fairly small place. Had something been done in the other room? "If that's the grand finale, then what else is there?" I asked, warily.

"If you want a prelude, go into the kitchen, first. Then look behind the first door you see down the hall. Not sure you'll want to keep going after that, but that's the order that will probably make the most sense."

"You're a terrible tour guide, ye know that?"

"I've seen the whole show, remember?" Robin's blue eyes flashed with something cold and unhappy. "The sooner you get to snooping, the sooner we can go."

I sighed. "Fine, kitchen it is," I said, trying not to think about the fact that the kitchen is where you keep all the knives.

Happy thoughts, Quinn.

Happy fucking thoughts.

CHAPTER 5

The kitchen was surprisingly tidy, especially for a rundown shack no one seemed to give a shit about. It was almost as if someone had cared for it recently—clearing out the spiderwebs and dust, polishing the countertops, cleaning out the sink. Of course, it stood to reason that the same person who'd done all that work had contributed to the current mess: six bowls lined the kitchen counter, though two had been haphazardly overturned, their contents spilled out and down the cabinets to form congealed puddles on the tile floor.

I sidestepped the goop to study the upright bowls. Each was made of a different material: wood, metal, plastic, porcelain, glass, and stone. The two overturned bowls were plastic and wood, respectively, which probably explained why they appeared otherwise undamaged. The others primarily held various herbs—elderberry and licorice root I recognized, but that was it. I'd have to ask Robin about the rest once this was all said and done. Fortunately—or perhaps unfortunately—the two liquids that had poured out from beneath the bowls were easier to identify. The first had likely been lavender-infused water; I could tell from the smell and what little liquid remained in the partially overturned bowl.

The second was blood.

I'd have loved to say that I had to lean in, to smell that copper penny aroma to be sure, but I didn't; I knew what dried blood looked like. What I couldn't decide was whether or not it had been taken by force. There was something about the amount, maybe, or perhaps simply the state of the container; I'd seen a man's throat slit to fill a wooden bowl, once, and it had filled the bowl and then some, splashing all over the surface, leaving flecks behind. This bowl was clean, worn smooth where hands had slid over its wooden surface time and time again.

I took another long look around the kitchen, trying to see what else I might have missed. In the end, I found only one other clue: the flat edge of a boot print along the corner of one of the puddles. An unbelievably massive boot print. I pulled out my phone and took pictures of it all, determined to figure out what the other herbs were, and just how big a person's foot would have to be to make that mark. Ordinarily I'd have said male right off the bat, but after seeing Skadi's broad, naked back blot out the sky a couple months back, I wasn't taking anything for granted.

Yay, equality?

"Everything alright?" Robin called.

"Aye, just wrappin' up in the kitchen. Are ye sure ye don't want to join me for the next room?" I teased, working my way around the kitchen towards the doorway which led to the hall, careful not to step in any other icky shit which might have ended up on the floor; cleaning crap off leather boots can prove as difficult as getting it out of jackets—more so if you take the treads into account.

"Thanks, but no," he replied.

"Chickenshit," I muttered. Of course, I wasn't exactly in the mood to march into the next room, either. I was beginning to see why Gretel had called it a ritual, but so far—excluding the blood in the kitchen—I hadn't seen enough to suggest it was one of the sacrificial varieties. Which meant things were probably going to get a lot worse before they got better. I took a deep breath and made a beeline for the first door in sight, willing myself to simply open the damn thing and get it over with, exactly how I'd talk myself into diving into a frigid pool on a hot summer day. In fact, I had my hand wrapped around the knob and the door halfway open before Robin called out, "Shit! Not that one!"

But it was too late.

CHAPTER 6

I briefly considered shutting the door but knew there was no point; even from the doorway, I could easily see everything there was to be seen. The curtains—ragged and a shade of yellow that might have once been white—had been pulled wide, exposing a window that was still intact but smeared and grimy. Dull blue light shone through the glass, leaving the room itself lit, but muted as if it were dusk instead of a little past noon. Ordinarily, the dimness might have been nice—perfect for napping— but today it wasn't. Today, all I wanted was for someone to pull those curtains completely closed, to shut out all that light and leave the room pitch black for good. Because, with the curtains spread and the afternoon light wafting in, I could see the rest of the room.

The bedsheets were a crumpled mess, stained brown with dried blood, stuck together in a matted pile that defied gravity, like hair gelled into clumps and left stiff. The mattress had soaked up the rest of the blood like a sponge, leaving the top half dark and the bottom half cream-colored like a two-toned Rothko painting. I began taking in other things without wanting to, no longer processing the information, simply filing it all away for later in case any of it might be useful. Like the fact that there were no pillows. Or that the walls were covered in various spatter patterns—great big arcs in some places, but only a few drops in others. Or that the floor beneath the bed was remarkably clean, as though someone had mopped it. I shook my head and tried not to breathe too deeply, noting with relief that the smell—an earthy, metallic odor—had been made less terrible by the fact that it was cold out, which meant at least I wouldn't have to deal with flies or the rancid stench of death.

Once I was able to breathe again, to think, I asked myself the only question I could ask after staring at all that grisly shit: where was the body? I stepped into the room, just one step, and that's when I felt it. I glanced up towards the ceiling, my eyes drawn by something I couldn't describe. A sensation, maybe. Or a premonition, like déjà vu, as if I'd already done this before—as if I'd stood in this awful room, the bed just slightly off center, one curtain drawn further than the other, in a dream. Or a nightmare.

But there was nothing to see except a dusty ceiling fan, the sockets for the lightbulbs gaping empty. And yet...and yet there was something. I reached out a hand towards that ceiling and felt it—power. Magic. Energy. Lifeforce. Whatever you wanted to call it, I could sense it gliding over my skin, like cobwebs, invisible and yet unmistakably there.

And then, suddenly, it wasn't.

"Shit, Quinn, I'm sorry," Robin said. I jumped, startled, and reached for the Kahr PM9 in my shoulder holster out of habit, but the look on Robin's face stopped me before I could pull it out and aim; he'd folded his arms over his chest, the guilt visible, somehow, beneath all that facial hair. Usually I'd have given him shit just because I could, even knowing he hadn't meant to scare me or send me into this room first, but—after what I'd seen—I didn't much feel like teasing.

"Well, someone died in here," I said as I eased my hand off the butt of my pistol, my voice sounding calm even to my own ears. I realized I was a little shocky, my nerves a little fried. I wasn't sure what it said about me, but—at that moment—I think I'd have rather been out shooting people who deserved it than standing in a room where someone had been butchered. I couldn't think of a better word. If they'd been alive, I might have said tortured. But I was hoping whoever all that blood belonged to hadn't been —for my sake as much as theirs.

"Yeah," Robin replied.

"And the other room is less awful, ye said?" I asked.

"Depends." He held up a hand. "It isn't as grisly. But I don't know if it's less awful. Come on, I'll go in with you."

"Lead the way," I said, resigned to see things through to the end. I stepped back into the hallway and shut the door firmly behind me. The Redcap brushed past me, and in the process I felt the faintest sensation—almost like a breath of wind caressing my arms. Nothing like what I'd sensed in the room, but Robin seemed to feel it, too, rubbing his arm like I'd shocked him. "What the hell was that?"

I shook my head. "I have no fuckin' idea." I considered reaching out to touch the Redcap directly, to find out what had caused that odd sensation, but decided against it. Between what I'd sensed in the room a minute ago and the general heebie-jeebies this house gave off at all times, I wasn't eager to find out what that would do, or feel like; I preferred normal, everyday reactions to normal, everyday occurrences. Like getting cold when it was cold out. Hot when it was hot. Maybe even the occasional gut-clench when I saw someone I wanted to makeout with for no reason. You know, ordinary shit.

The kind that *isn't* prime material for an exorcism diary.

Was that too much to ask for?

"We'll figure it out later," I said, finally. "Right now, I just want to get this over with and get the fuck out of here."

Robin seemed a little suspicious but didn't prod. "Alright, follow me."

I did as he asked and almost immediately spotted the door Robin had meant for me to try; it was visible from the other side of the kitchen doorway, closer towards the end of the house than the entrance. He opened it and stepped inside, letting me decide if I was ready for yet another horror. I wasn't. But I also wasn't about to walk out without seeing the last room; I was already going to have nightmares, so why bother balking now?

This room was similarly lit to its predecessor, but considerably smaller and remarkably unfurnished in comparison to the master bedroom. If anything, it looked more like what you'd expect of an office, the window mounted lower and facing south. Of course, it was immediately obvious that the room had been used for other reasons, and recently: thick iron manacles hung from the ceiling, suspended in mid-air by thick chains. Another pair lay unhinged on the floor, attached to the base of the nearest wall. I shuddered, realizing why Robin had insisted I enter this room, first. "So, whatever, whoever, left all that blood behind was kept here?" I asked.

"That was our guess," Robin said, pointing to the chains. "And those are why we figured it was one of our members, before you ask. Not many people use pure iron anything anymore, after all."

Now that he mentioned it, I could practically smell the iron in the room. It wasn't just the chains. It was almost as if the whole room had once held iron tools; my skin tingled, reacting to the peculiar odor the way some people react to certain soaps or to sunlight. If we didn't walk out soon, I knew I'd end up with hives. "How d'ye find this place?" I asked, holding one hand over my face as if to ward it off. "What tipped ye off, I mean?"

"A cop came by two nights ago. Probably thought he was chasing off some horny teenagers, or something. We think he spooked whoever was here, which is why they left everything behind in such a hurry."

"And how is it ye lot found out about that?"

"We have connections in mortal law enforcement. Members who keep an eye out for weird shit. Sometimes it's connected to us, sometimes it isn't. But with all the missing Fae, we've been paying more attention than usual. Which is why, when Gretel got the heads up, we sent someone in to check it out. Didn't take long for us to figure out this wasn't a normal killer, or a normal victim. These chains, those herbs in the kitchen, not to mention the fucked up vibe this place gives off...so, yeah, then we took the crime scene over."

"Took it over how?"

"A little glamour, mostly. We reached out to a few Members who can make memories fuzzy. It's something we've been doing for a long time. Ever since mortals first started to tell stories of us. How else do you think we keep all the shit our kind gets up to out of the papers?"

"As if people even read the papers, anymore," I muttered, not sure what else to say. The Faerie Chancery had been stepping in, taking over crime scenes, for what? Decades, if not centuries, or even millennia? Which meant they'd been using glamour—a type of illusion magic the Fae could wield—to hoodwink the human race for most of its existence. It wasn't a comforting thought. But I suppose I couldn't blame them; humans had a tendency to kill harmless creatures who presented absolutely no threat to them, so I could only imagine what they'd have done to the Fae. At best? They'd have ended up on the endangered species list right alongside the whales, leopards, and lemurs. At worst? Well, let's just say they'd have something else besides tails and scales in common with the dinosaurs.

Robin shrugged. "Either way, this is what we're left with."

"What did the cop say he saw? Anythin'?"

"He claimed there was more than one person in the house. That two left by the back door. It was dark then, though, and the cop didn't see much. There's no electricity here, obviously."

"So how could they see?" I asked.

"Who?"

"The ones who did this. I mean, without electricity, how were they able to move around?"

Robin looked puzzled. "Hadn't thought about it. Candles, maybe?"

I nodded. "Maybe, but I didn't see any. Which means they must have taken them before they left. Seems like an odd t'ing to take with ye if you're runnin' from the police, especially if it means leavin' behind the bowls and the bloody sheets. Besides, why run? If it was just one uniform, why not stay and fight?"

"We asked ourselves the same thing. That, and the obvious question: why wasn't there a body found?"

I cursed. "I honestly hoped ye lot had moved it," I admitted. Granted, a huge part of me had been glad not to find a body in that room to go with all that blood, but I *had* anticipated seeing a body, eventually. Something to help me figure out who or what had done this.

"Nope. We haven't touched anything. The scene is almost exactly how the cop found it, if only a little less...fresh."

I shook my head. "This doesn't make any sense."

Robin nodded. "I know. Let's go back outside. The iron in here is giving me a rash."

I cursed a second time, realizing it was doing exactly what I'd hoped it wouldn't: a slight rash was spreading up my arms, leaving them red and splotchy. Ordinarily, I could walk around largely unaffected by the city's ever-present iron—though I'd had to Fae-proof my apartment more than once since my time in Fae had effectively popped the anti-magic bubble I'd had since birth. But Robin was right: there was no way one of us could stand to be in this room for very long without suffering. Which meant that —if one of the Chancery members had been held here—he or she would have likely been in a great deal of discomfort, even pain. "Aye, let's go," I said, praying we'd find out what the hell had happened here.

Because payback was a bigger bitch than I was.

And I intended to let her fuck shit up.

*O*nce outside, the rash faded, as did the skin-prickling sensation that had enveloped us the moment we got too close to the shack and its gruesome interior. In fact, now that we were further away, I felt almost giddy. Euphoric. Hell, if I hadn't been so cold, I felt like I could have glibly skipped all the way back to Robin's ride, humming the chimney sweep jingle from *Mary Poppins*. "Any chance ye suddenly feel like ye could go ten rounds with Rocky Balboa?" I asked, flexing the fingers of my right hand, wondering where this sudden burst of energy had come from.

Robin cocked an eyebrow. "No, why?"

I shook my head and decided to focus on the here and now. "Nevermind. Listen, what makes ye t'ink this is connected to your missin' members, aside from the fact that ye t'ink one of the Fae is involved?"

Robin had shoved his hands in the pockets of his windbreaker, head ducked low enough that his ball cap hid his face from view. "We don't know if it is, but it seems like too much of a coincidence to rule it out. All the members were taken from their homes. We've got enough witnesses saying the same thing to put that together. But none of the witnesses actually *saw* the abductions. It's like the missing members went home and simply disappeared without a trace in an instant. No struggle, just gone."

"How d'ye know they disappeared and didn't just leave?" I asked.

"A couple of them went missing only moments before someone came to check back in on them. But even without that, we know a few had families. Lovers. A small number of members leaving, especially with no one to call them back? Maybe. But this many, in only a couple weeks? Personally— although I'll never say it to his face—I think Hansel's right. I think someone is hunting us down. I simply don't know how, or even why."

I nodded, agreeing that it seemed unlikely. I mean, the Fae were remarkably strong, occassionally vicious creatures; even the smallest of them could do some serious damage if they so chose. Hell, I'd taken a savage cut or two from fucking Tinkerbell, for fuck's sake. The odds of taking any of them against their will without a fight seemed slim, at best. And yet, here we were. "What herbs are in the kitchen?" I asked, recalling my question from earlier.

"I've got the list back at my place, but I can't remember them all."

"Get me that list."

Robin walked around to his side of the Jeep, over half his body obscured by the vehicle, fishing in his pocket for his keys. "Why? Think there's something there?"

I waited for him to unlock my side before climbing into the cab, grateful to be out of the crisp, biting wind, my feeling of euphoria fading incrementally. "Maybe. Herbs like that might mean t'ings to certain Freaks. If ye get it to me today, I can run it by my date."

Robin paused, key in the ignition. "Did you say date?"

"Aye, that I did," I said. Ordinarily, I'd have simply ignored Robin's disbelieving face, but I wasn't in the mood to sit in his Jeep all afternoon. "Quit lookin' at me and drive, Redcap." Robin glared at me, but turned the engine, pulled away from the curb, and together we left the creepy-ass house with all its horror behind.

Good riddance.

CHAPTER 7

The night was full of stars, constellations interrupted only by the shadows of distant trees like the bottom row of pitch black teeth gnawing on the sky. Skies like these were rare for me; I'd spent most of my life in Boston, where stars were drowned out by the hazy glow of city street lamps. My date stood with her face bathed in the light of the campfire I'd made, her body naked, the wind caressing her thick, furrowed flesh as she studied the plot of land I'd picked out with pitiless, pitted eyes.

"I don't like it," Eve, the reborn Tree of Knowledge, said. Her wooden flesh rippled as she spoke, revealing the face of a young woman, her eyes and mouth formed out of the burls of her trunk, her cheeks and brow fashioned from deep, jagged lines in the wood, a tiny knot for a nose.

I groaned and hung my head between my knees. "This is the fourth place we've tried out in as many weeks. I'm startin' to wonder if ye aren't too picky for your own good."

The relatively empty stretch of land we'd camped on lay on the fringes of a state park over an hour outside Boston's city limits, hidden away beneath the shadow of a craggy cliff along the secluded edge of a deep ravine. It had taken days to find, not to mention several hours to reach, which meant—considering I was covered in dirt and sweat from having to hike with Eve riding my spine like the world's prickliest hiking backpack—I wasn't in the best of moods, to say the least.

29

"Did you know one out of every ten children suffers from neglect?" Eve replied, as if I hadn't said anything. But I'd long ago learned that asking seemingly nonsensical questions was her way of holding a conversation—her way of expressing herself.

I threw my hands up and groaned. "I'm not tryin' to leave ye here alone forever, ye daft bush! I'm just tryin' to make sure ye can grow!"

Looking at the poor, potted plant, I knew my concerns weren't unwarranted; in the last few months she'd grown so large that, had I not come back from Fae able to deadlift trucks, I'd never have been able to pick her up let alone trek up across a state park with her in tow. In fact, she'd grown so tall that lately the tips of her extended limbs brushed up inadvertently against the walls and ceiling of my apartment, gouging into the wood and paint; these days my living room looked like it belonged to an epileptic Edward Scissorhands.

"Quinn, if you leave me here, I'll have no one to talk to," Eve said.

"I thought ye didn't like talkin' anyway," I said, trying to turn it into a joke.

Eve shrugged, her leaves rustling with the effort, their golden shimmer almost breathtaking to behold. "To you, maybe. But to everyone else? Who knows?"

I frowned at her. "That was really mean."

"It was meant to be a joke," she said.

"Was it?"

Her limbs dipped a little. "I don't know. I'm sorry. I simply don't want to end up alone in the middle of nowhere, Quinn. I don't know if I could take it."

I didn't bother stating the obvious. That—unless she wanted to draw attention to herself—Eve had to spend the rest of her days in the middle of nowhere; as a gilded tree with the gift of gab, she wasn't exactly inconspicuous. If anyone ever found her, the best we could hope for was that she'd become a tourist attraction, an oddity that drew the same people who hunted after Carhenge or Bubblegum Alley. At worst, she'd end up stolen away by some shady arm of the government and dissected. "Ye and I both know why it has to be this way," I said at last, sounding as tired as I felt.

"Does it?" Eve asked. "I'm not so sure."

"Whatever it is ye want to say, say it," I urged. "The sooner ye do, the sooner we can get the hell out of here and head home." I stirred the embers of the fire I'd built, sending sparks soaring into the air amidst plumes of chalky white smoke.

"Take me to Fae," Eve said, her voice laden with anticipation. Despite their anatomical differences, her expression reminded me a lot of what you might see in the face of a child asking for an overdue allowance, or a teenager begging for their first car—her barely restrained hope intermingled with the potential dread of being told no.

"Wait, ye want me to what?" I asked.

"You heard me, Quinn. Please."

I glanced away and tossed the stick I'd been using to stoke the fire onto the pile of burning wood, watching as it wobbled precariously and finally fell, one end among the flames, the other outside the circle of stones I'd used to keep the campfire from spreading. All the while, I weighed the consequences of what she was asking, knowing without a doubt that this wasn't an idle request or some sort of joke; Eve's sense of humor was typically as dry as she was. "Before I decide, can ye at least tell me why ye want to go to Fae?" I asked.

"It's simple," she replied, her response so immediate I knew she'd anticipated this conversation, that she'd planned her arguments well in advance. "In the Fae realm, my existence would not be considered so remarkably strange. From what I know about the realm itself, I wouldn't even be a novelty, there."

I shook my head, unconvinced. "That may be true. But what if they recognize ye for what ye are? What's to stop 'em from demandin' your help or offerin' ye a trade? Ye don't know 'em like I do. The Fae are dangerous, Eve. They're manipulative and self-servin' creatures who won't hesitate to use ye if they get the chance."

"You think I don't know what they're like?" Eve asked, branches twitching, eyes narrowed to thin slits. "Believe me, I know. Probably better than you do. I've only been living with one for as long as I can remember," she spat.

I opened my mouth, closed it, and turned away. It turned out my night vision was shot after staring into the flames for so long, and yet I continued to stare out into the dark rather than face Eve's accusation. Was I dangerous? Manipulative? Had I tried to use her for my own gain? Of course, the answer was yes to all three. But the real question—the unspoken question which kept me turned away from the light—was whether or not I regretted what I'd done.

If only I had the right answer.

"There *is* more to you than that," Eve said softly, her tone surprisingly gentle, as if she could sense the conflicting emotions within me. "I have known you long enough to know that—though you often take as if it is your right—you also give." Eve sighed. "Look, I know I'm a burden to you, but I—"

"No," I interrupted. "You've never been a burden, Eve. Not once. Hell, without ye, without your help, I'd never have found out the truth." Of course, what I didn't say aloud was what the truth had cost me. That—without Eve's intercession—Dez might still be alive, my powers unawakened, my questions unanswered.

"The truth," Eve said, her voice bitter. "Sometimes I wonder if that's why I was created in the first place. To offer knowledge, only to see it lead to pain and suffering. Is that what the truth is, you think? Was I designed to be an evil thing?"

I wasn't sure what to say to that. Despite my Catholic upbringing, I'd never really concerned myself with humanity's fall from grace or the many theological questions it raised; I'd been too busy fighting with the nuns over skirt lengths and skipping class to give a shit about something as abstract as original sin. It all struck me as a bunch of allegorical bullshit—a way to keep people from making up their own minds about the world. But maybe she had a point. "I'm probably not the right person to ask," I replied honestly, turning back to face my companion. "But if I've learned anythin' from me time in this world, it's that everythin' comes with a price tag. Love, sex, money, all of it. Everythin' we are and do is a transaction. Why should knowledge be any different?" I asked, studying her forlorn face, her sagging branches. I sighed. "Ye really want to go to Fae?"

"Yes, I do," she said, perking up slightly.

"Then I'll take ye," I said. "I can't tell ye when, exactly, but as soon as I can manage it, we'll go."

"Why not now?" she asked eagerly. I could tell she was excited, but also wary—like a kid whose parents promise that trip to Disneyland but can't say *when* they'll be going; even children learn pretty quickly how to sift through the bullshit adults tell them.

And Eve was no child.

"Because right now I'm tryin' to stop Chancery members from bein' hunted and potentially killed," I explained. "Speakin' of which," I said, drawing out the list Robin had sent me earlier in the day, "any chance ye could help me? The sooner I wrap this up, the sooner we go," I added.

"So we are clear, once you're done, you swear on your power you'll take me to Fae with you?" she asked.

I started to respond in the affirmative, but hesitated. It was true I was overdue for a trip to Fae. I'd promised Peter Pan I'd come back to see him and the Lost People, not to mention the fact that I had some unfinished business to take care of there. But if I was being honest with myself, I wasn't sure I was ready yet; the last time I'd gone, I'd been completely overwhelmed by my wild side and nearly died at least a half dozen times. As such, the odds of surviving another trip weren't exactly in my favor. Still, what I'd said before was true: I owed Eve. I owed her a shot at having a life outside my living room, at talking to someone other than a grouchy bitch like me, at carving out a life for herself—good or bad. "I swear on me power that once I'm done, I'll take ye to Fae."

The instant I said it, I felt something tug at my heart, making me gasp. But the sensation fled as quickly as it had come, leaving me with little but an accelerated pulse and a premonition of what might happen if I failed to follow through on my promise. Meanwhile, Eve's leaves brightened incrementally, like a dimmer switch being turned up. "Then, yes, I'd be glad to help," she replied. "What is it you want to know?"

I read off the list of herbs, including the lavender water and the blood, which had turned out to be pig's blood, according to lab reports Robin had acquired. I briefly filled her in on what all I'd seen in the cabin, sticking to the barest description possible; I really didn't want to dwell on shit like that in the middle of the night, in the dark, in a location so far removed from civilization. ""D'ye have any idea what all this might be used for?" I asked.

Eve's limbs swayed as she shook her head from one side to the other. "The items you listed may be used for dozens of purposes, depending on the intent. I can think of over nine-thousand possibilities which could fit the setting you described. But all are circumstantial, at best. You would be better off consulting with a witch."

"A witch?" I asked, trying to keep the surprise out of my voice, but failing. It wasn't so much that Eve had recommended one—honestly, her suggestion made total sense; witches knew all sorts of things about herbs and how to use them. It was simply that the last person to mention a witch to me had been my mother's ghost, during a dream in which she claimed I'd soon meet someone capable of telling me more about the power I had inside me, not to mention who my father was. It'd been months since then, but somehow, I doubted this was a coincidence.

I touched the watch on my wrist out of habit, running my thumb along the silver sundial, and realized it had moved again; something it hadn't done since I'd last used my power to make time stand still during a firefight in Moscow. The watch itself had been a gift from two very talented, likely immortal, leather workers who—it seemed—had a knack for giving the right presents to the right people. And yet I still had no idea how it worked. It sure as shit didn't tell the right time of day; I knew that much.

"There are several stores in Boston known to traffic in rare herbs," I realized Eve was saying, "but only one name comes up with consistently positive reviews. Would you like me to give you the address?"

I smirked. "Ye know, you'd have made one hell of a secretary in another life."

Eve folded her lower limbs in on herself just below her mouth, almost as if she were crossing her arms over her chest. "I was the Tree of Knowledge in the Garden of Eden in my past life. I was not, and will never be, anyone's secretary."

I held up my hands in surrender. "Alright, alright, don't get your leaves in a bramble," I said, grinning. "So, what d'ye say we get the hell out of here, while ye give me that address?"

CHAPTER 8

*T*he address Eve gave me was on Newbury Street, a popular Boston shopping destination which, thankfully, wasn't terribly far from my apartment. Considering how long it had taken us to get there, not to mention that I'd been forced to take a quick shower and change, I'd needed the extra time. Unfortunately, despite the hour, the street remained packed with pedestrians—mostly individuals snagging a late snack or tossing back a few before calling it a night—which meant I had to wade through the linked arms of couples unwilling to unclasp their hands and old buddies leaning drunkenly into one another as I searched for the herbal store. Fortunately, Newbury's sidewalks had been built to accommodate the extra traffic, and I was able to find the shop—a glass storefront in the basement of one of those 19th century row houses—without having to threaten anyone to make way or die.

I was beginning to think tonight might be my lucky night.

Sure, it might have seemed silly to think so, but between avoiding the foot traffic and the fact that the little boutique remained open so late, I could at least admit I was on a roll. After all, most of the stores on Newbury Street closed well before midnight, content to lock up and avoid the witching hour. Of course those shops typically sold clothes or accessories; the likelihood that Wortcunning Corner—which lacked both the meticulously crafted window displays of a designer store as well as the pretentious ambience of a jeweler—fit that particular bill seemed awfully slim.

In fact, now that I'd gotten a closer look, the shop's exterior struck me as remarkably dissimilar from what I'd come to expect of Newbury's uniformly glitzy storefronts. If anything, Wortcunning Corner seemed designed to ward away customers; their sign was a drab thing, hung over the door like an afterthought, the glass of their windows grungy and almost impossible to see through. Oddly enough, when I went down the small flight of stairs to peer through those windows, I realized the store was lit by candlelight, not electricity. I wrapped my hand around the doorknob, wondering who in their right minds would use candles these days, especially in the basement of a rowhouse. "Fuckin' firetrap," I muttered. But, when the knob turned under my hand, I went in against my better judgment.

In my experience, you can read any given room using a variety of senses —sights, sounds, and smells being the most prevalent. But I've also found that being observant isn't enough; it's what you do with what you've observed that tells you what you need to know. It's noting the coats lined neatly up on the hooks by the door and knowing to take off one's shoes without being asked. It's smelling the faint musky odor of dog and being prepared when a mongrel comes howling towards you with great, loping strides. It's hearing a gun cock in a distant room and identifying cover should you need to draw your own.

The very first thing I noticed about Wortcunning Corner was the smell.

The shop reeked of pumpkin. Not pumpkin spice—that cinnamon-coated swill Starbucks sells by the bucketload—but actual pumpkin. The earthy, cut-flower odor you get when you carve out the entrails of that plump orange gourd. It was a smell that encouraged nostalgia, that reminded me of Halloweens spent in my dining room, hands slick with juice and seeds, tracing patterns Dez had helped me draw with the tip of a knife.

It was the smell of a place that was cared for. Loved, perhaps.

"Can I help you?" a woman asked, drawing my attention towards a wall lined with shelves, each holding glass jars of various sizes and shapes. The woman, a tanned beauty with long, curly hair, dressed in blue jeans and a sweater, swiftly restocked one such jar and turned to face me, hands clasped in front the way so many saleswomen do when they want to appear non-threatening.

"Aye, I'm lookin' for someone who can help me identify some herbs," I said. Almost instantly after saying it out loud, I realized how vague and ridiculous that sounded. "Someone who knows rituals," I added, hoping that would narrow things down somewhat.

The woman's eyes narrowed, but her smile remained fixed in place. "Hold on, I'll get the owner." She left through a backdoor, leaving me with little to do but peruse the shelves. The glass jars shimmered beneath candle-light, hard to see into, although I found each meticulously labeled, their contents scrawled out in silver Sharpie across black electrical tape: Devil's Claw, Fennel Seed, Meadowsweet. I was so engrossed that I'd made it halfway down one aisle before I felt someone behind me.

I turned to find a man standing in the doorway, watching me. The first impression I got was size; he was tall, taller than me by a few inches at least, with shoulders that practically burst the seams of his flannel button-down and thighs which made his jeans look painted on. The second impression I got was the utter masculinity—the sheer handsomeness—of his face, soft-ened only somewhat by the waves of his shoulder-length hair and the twin, nearly invisible dimples that rode his stubbled cheeks when he was smiling, like now.

"My sister says you wish to talk about a potential ritual," he said, step-ping forward into the light, staring at me with mismatched eyes. One blue, the other brown. Still, now that he'd mentioned it, I could clearly see the resemblance—he had the same dark hair as his sister, the same tanned skin, not to mention the slightest trill of a Spanish accent, barely audible in those rolling r's. But it was those eyes I couldn't stop staring at, their imperfection almost glaring in contrast with that otherwise flawless face.

In the end, it took me longer than I'd like to admit to respond, and—even then—all I could manage was a breathless, "Aye, that's what I'm here for."

Those dimples deepened as his smile grew wider. "Perfect. Please, tell me how I can help." He gestured as he moved, putting the counter between us before leaning forward to rest his bare forearms against the countertop. The moment he did, however, a silver pendant spilled out from beneath his collar, dangling in mid-air. It was a triple moon symbol—twin crescents facing in either direction, flush against the circle which sat between them. A symbol meant to represent the triple goddess. A symbol worn by only one sect of Freaks, as far as I was aware.

"You're a witch," I blurted out in surprise.

The smile dimmed, then vanished as he straightened. "I am sorry, but I do not think I can help you, after all. Please leave, we are closing soon."

I held up my hands, waving them. "Sorry, I know it's none of me business what ye are. Ye surprised me, that's all." I didn't bother mentioning the fact that the last few of his kind I'd met had been skinwalkers—witches who'd sacrificed their familiars for the ability to shapeshift. Or that, until I'd met them, I'd always assumed witches were women.

Sexist, I know, but you live and learn, right?

"What is it you want?" he asked, those two-toned eyes dancing with suspicion.

I took a deep breath and let it out slowly, trying my best not to rise to the challenge in his voice. "Let's start over," I said. I took a few steps forward and held out my hand. "Me name is Quinn MacKenna. What's yours?"

He studied the hand, then reached out to clasp it. "Maximiliano Velez. Call me Max," he said, wrapping his large hand around my own. In that instant, a brush of something—like what I'd felt between Robin and I earlier, but more intense, somehow—slid up my arm, sending a shiver down my spine. I clutched at his hand by accident and felt his own grip tighten in response. Our eyes met, but this time it wasn't suspicion I found lurking there, it was curiosity.

I quickly let go and stepped back, rubbing my hand against my jeans like I was eight years old again and afraid of contracting cooties. "Pleasure to meet ye, Max."

He drew his own hand back, kneading his palm as though it had come away sticky. "And you, although I believe I have you at a disadvantage, Señorita MacKenna."

I cocked an eyebrow at that.

"Your reputation precedes you," Max explained. "Tell me, what brings a dealer of antiquities such as yourself to my humble store?"

I frowned but knew better than to lie about who I was, or even to feign surprise; it wasn't like there were that many Quinn MacKenna's matching my description out there. Besides, just because I'd never heard the name Maximiliano Velez didn't mean he hadn't heard of me; it's not like I was in the classified ads or anything ridiculous like that, but it would be fair to say my name got passed around often in certain circles. "Listen, this is strictly personal, I swear," I assured him. "I'm here on me own business, no one else's."

Max smiled and held his hands out wide, his shirt gaping open at the neck to reveal a smooth expanse of chiseled chest, the triple moon symbol resting in the hollow of his throat. "Then please, let us talk business. What is it you would like to try? How about biotin? It is very good for your hair and nails. Ginger? Chamomile? Maca?" He finished by folding his arms over his chest, clearly suspicious despite my assurances—as far as I could tell, he'd listed nothing but herbs and supplements used to treat weight loss, promote better sleep, and increase someone's sex drive.

I fished out my list and began to read the ingredients—all but the pig's blood, because I wasn't sure how he'd react to that and didn't want to give him another excuse to ask me to leave. By the time I looked up, Max's face was serious, almost harsh without those dimples to offset his square jaw and broad, sweeping cheekbones. He stepped around the counter, which put him much closer than I'd have liked, and held out his hand for my phone.

"May I take a look?" he asked.

I passed it over, watching as he flicked his eyes over the screen, the soft blue glow playing across his face, highlighting his single blue eye. I shook my head, chasing away the urge to reach out and run my fingers over his thick brows, to let them rest over the bowed curve of his lips. They looked soft, yet firm, the kind of lips that could press against yours hard enough to bruise, but still be tender enough that you'd let them slide across your throat. Lower, even.

I shook my head, chasing the thought away.

Jesus H. Christ, I needed to get a grip.

I clenched my fists, knowing even as I did it that a little pep talk wasn't going to be enough; it'd been a little under a year since Jimmy and I had last hooked up, and I hadn't had the time or inclination to do anything since. Sure, there had been a couple potentials—namely a certain vampire from New Orleans and an immortal apple-picker—but both had flaws I couldn't overlook. Surprisingly, Alucard's flaw hadn't been that he was a blood-sucker—though at first that had been a big deterrent—but that his loyalty was to Nate Temple, a wizard from St. Louis I kept butting heads with. Johnny Appleseed's flaw had been easier to point out: I simply hadn't been able to determine how much of my attraction to him had been real and how much of it metaphysical. In any case, I'd refrained from sleeping with either of them.

Which apparently meant, so long as I stood in the presence of a hunky, attractive man, I was screwed.

Figuratively speaking.

"Well, what d'ye t'ink?" I asked, reaching for my phone.

He passed it back. "I think that is a very in-depth list for someone on personal business," he replied. Something in his voice made me look up at him, and I realized he was angry, his distrust from earlier evident in his downturned lips and clenched jaw.

"If I show ye a picture of how they were ordered, and contained, could ye tell me what ritual they might have been used for?" I asked, choosing to plow ahead anyway.

He cocked an eyebrow but nodded, his anger leaking away somewhat, replaced by confusion. I fiddled with the screen before handing him the phone once more—the shack's kitchen counter displayed, including all six bowls and their varied contents. From the angle of the photo I'd taken, you couldn't make out much else about the room, which made me less concerned about sharing it with a relative stranger. Max stared at each bowl for a few seconds, then pointed to the one I knew he'd find the most compelling. "What was in this one?" he asked.

"Pig's blood."

A hiss came from the other side of the doorway, and I realized Max's sister had been leaning against the wall, eavesdropping on our conversation. She stepped into the light, her pleasant, servile expression a thing of the past. "Why would they do that?" she asked, directing the question to her brother.

Max shook his head. "Señorita MacKenna, please, meet my sister, Camila."

"Why, Max?" she reiterated, ignoring me completely.

The big man sighed and handed me the phone back. "I'm afraid we cannot help you, Señorita. Please, I must ask you to leave."

"Why? What is it ye two know?" I asked, suspiciously, my gaze oscillating between Max and his sister. "Tell me, please." When neither answered, I flicked my finger across my screen, revealing one of the pictures of the blood-soaked room I'd taken before Robin and I had left the shack. I held it up for them to see. "Tell me, or this may happen again."

Camila took one look and stepped back, a hand to her mouth, eyes wide. Max merely studied the photo, his expression sad, but not surprised— almost as if he'd expected to see a bed covered in blood and thicker liquids. I lowered the phone, slowly, letting them revel in the horror of whatever had been done to leave that much blood behind. I expected Max to say something, to ask me to leave again, maybe, but it was Camila who spoke, first.

"You have to tell her, Max," she urged.

Max folded his arms over his chest once more but refused to meet his sister's eyes. Instead he stared up at the ceiling, as if imploring a higher power to intervene on his behalf. "If I do, he will come for us, Camila. You know he will."

"So, we leave," his sister replied, shrugging. She said something in Spanish I didn't catch, but which seemed to irritate Max.

"I am tired of running," he snarled, flexing his arms and chest in frustration, as if he could contain all the violence within himself if he simply held tight enough. Then, so suddenly it almost made me jump, the tension flowed out of him in one long, drawn-out sigh. "But you are right, as usual. Whatever they have done this time, it cannot be allowed to continue."

"Is someone goin' to fill me in on what's goin' on?" I asked, cocking an eyebrow. The two turned to me, each unhappy in their own way. I slid my phone into my back pocket and adjusted my jacket, brushing my fingertips over the slight bulge of my pistol for reassurance. "Never hurts to ask."

"Let's go upstairs," Max said. "I need a drink if we are going to keep talking about this."

"Whiskey?" I asked, hopeful.

Max raised an eyebrow. "I was thinking a beer. But we have that, too, if you would prefer."

I smirked. "What can I say? It's been a long day."

"I have a feeling it's about to get longer," Camila said, before disappearing through the doorway once more.

"Is she always so optimistic?" I asked, keeping my voice low so she wouldn't hear me. Max stared down at me with his mismatched eyes, shook his head, and followed his sister without another word, those kissable lips turned down into a fierce scowl.

Huh. Maybe that shit was genetic.

CHAPTER 9

*M*ax and Camila's upstairs flat was a cozy, two bed, two bath joined by a communal living space and a small but functional kitchen which seemed overwhelmed by the sheer volume of assorted cookware. Pots, pans, cutting boards, strainers, even a damn rolling pin lay strewn about—as if at any moment Suzy Homemaker might burst in to bake us a fucking souffle. Now, before you start defending your God-given right to bear Teflon, keep in mind I have nothing against people who religiously cook their own meals—I simply don't understand them. Especially my fellow city dwellers. I mean, why waste all that time preparing dinner when you live in a town chock full of restaurants and bars that deliver damn near 24/7? Of course, I wasn't about to say any of that to Max or Camila; even I knew better than to criticize their questionable lifestyle choices while sitting at their dining room table. Instead I led with, "Lovely place ye got here." Then, as a follow-up, "So, about that drink?"

"I'll get them," Camila said, angling towards the kitchen with a proprietary air. "Max can start explaining, in the meantime. He enjoys that, don't you, Maximiliano?"

Her brother merely shook his head, a smile tugging at his lips. "She teases me because I talk too much," he explained. "But this once, perhaps, I think I should let the guest go first."

"Alright," I replied, "and what is it you'd like to know?"

"For starters, what are you?" Max held up a hand to ward off whatever I was about to say. "A woman, yes, that I can plainly see." His smile flickered to life once more, though it seemed to have considerably more heat to it now that we were sitting only a few feet across from each other, our knees almost touching. "But what else?"

"Why d'ye care?"

"I care because I felt you. I felt your power when we touched, which is no small thing. And then, of course, there is the fact you knew what I am. Though not what flavor of magic I practice, clearly, or you would have used a different word."

I pointed to the necklace around his throat. "Your charm is what clued me in on the whole witch t'ing. As far as I know, only witches wear 'em."

He raised his eyebrows. "And just how much *do* you know about witches? Or witchcraft?"

"Not much," I admitted. "Less than I thought, apparently. This is the first time anyone has mentioned flavors of magic, before."

Max settled back, clasping his hands together, studying me. "'I guess I will be the one explaining, after all. First, there are many flavors, many classifications, especially depending on which tradition a witch is brought up in. In some parts of this and other countries, you will meet voodoo witch doctors. In others, Native American shamans. My sister and I descend from a different philosophy. Camila is a bruja, and I am a brujo. We inherited our magic from our *abuela*, our grandmother."

"How come I've never heard any of this before?" I asked.

He shrugged those massive shoulders. "Witches do not generally advertise. We prefer our place in the shadows. Avoiding persecution has become a way of life for us."

"'Regard not them that have familiar spirits,'" I quoted, citing a passage from the King James Bible I'd memorized to piss off Dez; she always hated it when I quoted "that abominable Protestant bastardization." Personally, I didn't have anything against the King James version, except that it sure made a lot of shit sound more ominous than it had to. Take the second half of that passage, for example, "neither seek after wizards, to be defiled by them." Of course, it wasn't terrible advice; I could think of a certain white-haired ex-Vatican vixen who might benefit from it.

Maybe I'd send Callie Penrose a highlighted version for Christmas.

"Leviticus," Max said, drawing me back to the moment at hand. "I am

43

impressed, but *si*, this is how we are treated." Max hunched his shoulders a bit and stared off into space over my shoulder, lost in his own, private thoughts. Meanwhile, I took the opportunity to study the man while his sister finished preparing the drinks. Not the way a woman admiring a handsome man might, but as a businesswoman evaluating a potential asset —someone I could choose to trust, or keep things from, depending on what he could offer in return.

Before I could decide one way or the other, however, Camila brought our drinks over on a tray and placed them in the center of the table. Max snatched up one of the beers and twisted the top off, tossing the bottle back with an easy familiarity I recognized and appreciated. Camila did the same, though she took her time about it. Which left the whiskey and the rocks glass for me. I poured two fingers full and took a bracing sip. "Alright, so let's say all that is a given," I said, licking my lips. "What flavor of witch d'ye believe did what I showed ye?"

Camila made to respond, but Max held up a finger. "She still has not told us what she is," Max cautioned. "I would rather know if we can trust her before we start revealing things about ourselves that could get us in trouble. If she wants answers from us, she will have to offer some of her own."

"I swear I didn't come to bother either of ye. All I wanted was to find someone who knows more than I do about these t'ings," I replied, choosing not to take offense to Max's sudden skepticism. "But the truth is I can't tell ye what I am, because I don't know yet, meself. It's complicated."

"Try us," Max insisted.

I sighed. "Well, if I had to put money on it, I'd say I'm one of the Fae. But I may be human as well, at least on me da's side. Haven't exactly gotten a solid answer on that one, yet."

The shop owner and his sister simply stared at me, expressions disbelieving. I half-expected Max to react first, but it was Camila who scooted away from me, holding her hand up in a warding gesture, fingers curled to form an odd symbol. "The Fae are not...they are not welcome here," she stammered. "How did you get past our wards? Max, how did she get past our wards?" Camila began to mutter hysterically in Spanish, still scooting back, one inch at a time, the legs of her chair squealing as they slid across the tile floor. Meanwhile, Max had yet to react at all except to further scrutinize yours truly. It wasn't a sexual look, but it wasn't completely devoid of heat, either—as if he couldn't quite decide what he wanted from me.

I didn't like it.

"The wards are designed only to warn us, Camila. Not to keep the Fae out," Max replied soothingly. "Besides, I believe her. Whatever she is, she did not feel Fae when we touched."

"Listen," I interrupted, turning so I could face them both, "I don't know what your problem is with the Fae, and I don't rightly care. Lord knows I have enough issues with 'em, meself. But I'm tryin' to track down a killer who's targetin' Faelin's in this city. Faelin's with families and friends and such," I added. "Ye know, people who'll miss 'em."

"Wait, are you saying the blood on that bed belonged to one of the Fae?" Max asked.

"Max, I want her gone!" Camila demanded, her voice shrill and panicked.

"Camila, don't be so hasty, we—"

"Get her out! Out!" she screamed, rising so fast her chair clattered to the floor. She continued to hold that hand out towards me, her fingers bent as she backed up to press herself against the living room window, eyes so wide I could see the white all the way around.

Max looked at me with an apology ready, but I was already polishing off my glass of whiskey and rising up out of my own chair. "Don't ye worry, I'm leavin' and won't be back to bother ye, I swear," I said, waving them both off, sounding surprisingly calm. Truth was, not too long ago, I might have pulled my gun and threatened them, demanding they tell me everything they knew. But in the last year or so I'd learned the hard way that—contrary to popular opinion—the threat of violence doesn't always work as an inter-rogation method. Sure, some folks are willing to sell out their own mothers the second they see a gun. But I've found most simply clam up and freeze, too scared to think, let alone talk. And of course there are others—mainly people like me—who see a gun and lash out without thinking, consequences be damned.

Basically, I had no way of knowing which reaction I'd get from either of the Velez's, which meant there was little point in threatening them. At best, they'd spill their guts, and I'd be left with two new enemies to contend with. At worst, they'd turn me into a toad and sell my carcass to the nearest high school biology lab. So, rather than escalate the situation, I made for the door, making a mental note as I went to ask around about Camila; maybe

Robin would have some insight into what the Fae had done to terrorize an otherwise sane, capable woman.

"I will walk you out," Max offered, angling for the door.

"No, I do not want you—" Camila began.

"Don't bother," I interjected. "I know the way."

"I need to make sure the shop is locked up and double-check our wards, Camila," Max said placatingly. "Trust me, she cannot harm us here."

I briefly considered drawing my gun and proving him wrong just because I could but managed to quell the urge; if he wanted to play peace-keeper, I wasn't going to stand in his way. Of course, that didn't mean I was going to wait around while they made up their minds. "T'anks for the drink, Camila," I said, ducking through the doorway with Max hot on my heels, ignoring his sister's startled gasp.

Once downstairs, however, a mere five feet from the door, Max grabbed my arm and whirled me around. I'd been half-expecting it, which is why I had my gun out and pointed at his stomach before he could so much as take another breath. But it turned out his focus was on the ceiling, not me or my gun. "Shh," he cautioned, pressing a finger to his lips. After a few creaks passed—Camila moving about upstairs I assumed—he looked down at me. "She is scared. Worried. I am sorry for that."

"Let go of me arm," I growled.

He did, but stayed close, seemingly unconcerned about the gun barrel shoved up against his body, which was unfortunate; it was a firm body. It would be a shame to ruin it. The instant I thought that, I could feel heat creeping up my cheeks, and took a step back. Fortunately, a few of the candles had dwindled or died since we went upstairs, and I doubted he could see my face clearly enough to know what I'd been thinking. "What d'ye want?" I asked.

"I need to talk to the witnesses if you want me to help you," Max whispered, his faint accent and the dim, romantic lighting making the words more intimate than they had any right to be.

"What witnesses?"

"The families and friends you mentioned. Whoever might have seen or heard something."

"Someone has already talked to 'em," I replied. "They didn't have anythin' worth sayin.'"

Max smiled and shook his head, close enough that I felt his hair brush across my cheek. "I believe they were being asked the wrong questions. I would ask them instead what they felt. Focus on sensations."

"Sensations like what?" I asked, baffled.

"Like nausea. Or terror. Or lust. Look, whoever or whatever is taking your Fae brothers and sisters is using some sort of spell. Those herbs, the ones you showed me, can be used for many things, but every spell a witch casts colors their soul. Some spells are so black, so unnatural, they taint the soul, until one day the caster is no longer even human. But some are the exact opposite, cast by witches whose essences are so pure they become worshipped as pagan saints. Most, I've found, are somewhere in between. But your witnesses will know what they felt, if they think back to it, even if they remember nothing else. If your witnesses can tell me how they felt, what they sensed, I can tell you what spell might counteract it. Maybe even the aspect of the witch who cast it."

"And just what aspect of witch are ye?" I asked, suspiciously.

He took a step back, raising his hands in surrender. "I told you. I am a brujo. But I am also a man. Not an evil man, but certainly not a pure one, either." He flashed me a knowing smile that fled almost as quickly as it came. "Still, if nothing else, I am a man who would prefer not to have the deaths of others on his conscience, be they Fae or human."

Camila's voice echoed down the stairwell before I could respond. "Max, is she gone?"

Max jerked his chin towards the door. "You should go," he hissed.

"What about the witnesses?" I asked, thrusting my gun back into my shoulder rig as I edged towards the door.

Max was already shaking his head. "I can't leave Camila alone right now."

"What about tomorrow mornin'?"

"Too soon. She'd be suspicious. You will have to question them in my place," he replied. "Ask them what they felt. Remember, focus on what they sensed. See if anything strikes you as particularly odd."

"Ye know this would be a lot easier if you'd tell me what your sister has against the Fae," I hissed, wrapping my hand around the door handle.

"Max!" Camila called again, more panicked this time.

"Later," Max said, shooing me out with his hands.

"Whatever," I replied. "How will I reach ye once I've talked to the witnesses?"

"Check your phone, I put my number in it while you were looking elsewhere. Now go!" He flashed me a wink, then headed for the stairs. "*Si*, she is gone, Camila!" he called. "I am locking up now."

I stepped outside and let the door shut behind me as quietly as I could, taking slow, measured breaths before joining the street's diminished but still present traffic. I retrieved my phone and scrolled down through the contact list but didn't see Max's name. For a moment, I thought he must have lied to me, but then I scrolled back up and found an unfamiliar contact under Hombre de Tus Sueños.

Literal translation: Man of Your Dreams.

Cocky little shit.

CHAPTER 10

*T*he next morning, I met the handful of witnesses who'd been in the area when the Chancery members were taken, all of whom turned out to be a hodgepodge collection of storybook creatures I'd heard of but never actually seen. The first was a hideously disfigured, mud-covered Ballybog who worked for the sanitation department, followed by a bright-eyed selkie who moonlighted as a diving instructor, a pooka loan shark, and a web-footed kelpie who claimed to be affiliated with the United States Coast Guard.

Lucky they'd repealed "Don't Ask, Don't Tell," I guess.

Uncomfortable with the idea of moseying on down to the Chancery's underground speakeasy to conduct the interviews, especially after my last visit—a social call during which I and the rest of the bar patrons had very narrowly escaped death and potential dismemberment—I'd opted to commandeer my friend Christoff's pop-up bar for the occasion. It wasn't exactly neutral territory, but Christoff had a reputation for being a good host even among the Fae. Besides, it was still a bar; hard to turn down an invitation that came with the promise of inebriation.

Fortunately, Christoff hadn't been hard to convince; his bar's grand re-opening was set a few days from now, but until then was basically aban-doned. We'd finished all the renovations and whatnot weeks ago, leaving behind a Monster Movie bar theme that was so over-the-top it was absurdly comical. In fact, as far as I knew, all that was left to do before the bar opened was to finish stocking the booze and test out the themed cocktails. Though, for some reason, Christoff had seemed reticent to let me help with that.

Stingy bastard.

As it was, I'd decided to stand behind the bar and interview the witnesses one at a time, so their individual responses didn't influence each other; all it would take was for one of the lot to start raving about having felt sick to their stomach the day of the disappearance to have them all whining and moaning about a half-remembered belly ache. Of course, this particular approach meant that, while I conducted the interviews, Robin had to keep an eye on the others, doing his best to keep them occupied—not that he minded. I got a sense the Redcap was simply glad to be doing something other than sitting on his hands, waiting for someone else to go missing.

Before the witnesses had arrived, I'd told Robin all about my trip to Wortcunning Corner and my interactions with Max and Camila. Sadly, he'd been as clueless as I was as to why Camila had flipped out, except to remind me that witches are longer-lived than most mortals, which meant her response might have been based on a grudge carried over a span of years, even decades. Personally, I didn't buy it; Camila's reaction had been too raw, too knee-jerk, to be attributed to a decades-old grievance. Very few people get that worked up that fast over something they've been stewing over for years. Grumpy ass old men, maybe, bitching about how their neighbors never cut the grass. But to go into hysterics at the mere mention of a name? The only people I knew who did that were those who'd been hurt—hurt bad enough and often enough that they routinely saw threats where there were none.

People like me.

"Are you even listening to me?" a male voice, surprisingly refined, brought me back to the situation at hand.

"Aye, sorry. Please, go on. Alby, was it?"

The pooka, face covered in coarse black fur, ran his hands over the lapels of his expensive suit jacket and nodded—an action only slightly impeded by his ludicrous bunny rabbit ears, which had a tendency to flop onto his face when he wasn't paying attention. "Quite. As I was saying, I didn't see a thing."

"Well, not to be insensitive, but is it possible ye heard somethin'?" I asked, staring pointedly at those ears.

Alby's mouth pursed and one of the ears twitched. "No."

"How about a feelin', then?"

"A what?"

I propped myself up, hands pressed flat against the bar top. "Tell me what ye do remember. From your point of view. Try and recall exactly how ye felt. A play-by-play, if ye will."

"Listen, Miss MacKenna, I have a business to run, as I'm sure you can understand. I don't have time to—"

"Ye are welcome to go at any time, Alby," I interjected, offering a smile that I knew didn't reach my eyes before raising a finger in warning. "T'ing is, right now you're treatin' this like it isn't your problem. And perhaps you're right. Maybe whoever or whatever is doin' this will keep huntin' down your neighbors, leavin' ye to live your life, free as ye like. Or maybe it won't. Maybe you're next. But no matter what happens to ye personally, I can promise ye this: if ye don't do what ye can to help your own people, that *business* of yours is goin' to dry up. And fast."

"Is that a threat?" Alby hissed, ears perked straight up now, his freakishly long fingers gripping his dress slacks so hard I knew they'd be a wrinkled mess by the time he stood up.

"Can't do business if ye don't have clients," I replied, spreading my own hands wide to emphasize the fact that *I* wasn't the threat, that in fact we were on the same side. "All I'm sayin'."

Alby raised his chin, doing his best to look down his muzzle at me. But of course, after a brief staredown, he broke first. He glanced away and fiddled with his tie, his button-nose twitching. "It was late. I was in the office, going over the books in the back room. Ennis usually hangs around until I told him to go home, but some nights—like that night—I'd forget, and he'd sit out there all night waiting for me to send him home." Ennis—I recalled from Robin's brief description of the missing Fae—was an ogre and one of Alby's leg-breakers, an enforcer who made sure Alby's loans got repaid, with interest. "Listen, I know Ennis isn't the brightest wisp in the bog, but I made sure to get him a ground-floor apartment close by. Walking distance, so he doesn't get lost. It never even occurred to me to check on the big lug once I realized he hadn't waited around for me. Honestly, I didn't even think about it, really think about it, until the next day when he didn't show up for work."

"Any chance ye noticed somethin' odd that night? Maybe on your way out the door?"

"Like what?"

I shrugged. "Anythin' out of the ordinary."

Alby's nose twitched again. "I remember it was cold."

I cocked an eyebrow, declining to comment on the obvious because I could tell from Alby's expression that he'd recalled something, something he'd forgotten; his eyes were unfocused as if he was replaying a memory in his head. "What is it?" I asked.

"The cold. It was odd, because this was back at the beginning of the month, before the weather turned. I remember I left the office thinking I'd need to wear a jacket the next day, but then I hadn't needed it at all. In fact, the only reason I was reminded of it now was because I had to double-back to put my jacket away the next morning, which made me late for a meeting." Alby's yellow eyes met mine, and they were puzzled. "What could that mean? That it was cold?"

I shook my head. "I have no idea. But don't say anythin' to the others. I want to see if they felt the same t'ing, or not."

"Can't take my word for it, is that it?" Alby said. The pooka let out a deep breath and slid off his barstool, standing nearly as tall as me in his three-piece suit. Taller, if you included the ears. He seemed to gather himself in pieces, drawing his shoulders back before adjusting the cuffs of his shirt-sleeves. In a matter of seconds, the loan shark was unnaturally calm and self-assured once more, his momentary confusion and discomfort discarded like a half-smoked cigarette pitched out of a moving car. "Catch this thing, won't you, Miss MacKenna?" Alby said, fussing with his tie. "It's screwing with my money. Oh, and if you see Ennis, please do tell him to get his ass back to work."

"Aye, I'm sure that'll be the first t'ing out of me mouth," I replied, sarcastically.

Alby finished with his tie and left, marching right past the others and out the door. Robin cocked an eyebrow at me, but all I could do was shrug. In my experience, when shit goes sideways, most people turn into carica-tures of themselves. Some get hysterical, others freeze, and a few step up. But not everyone reacts that way. Occasionally there are those who simply go right on living, oblivious to the world around them, content in their ignorance. My best guess? Alby the pooka was an entitled asshole, and not even the threat of being abducted or losing out on business was going to fix that particular personality flaw.

"Alright, send over the next one," I called with a small wave as I scoured the bar in search of my friendly neighborhood bartender, hoping he'd take pity on me and bring me a cocktail—one of the themed ones, if I was lucky. At least now I understood why those poor private investigators always seem to have a glass in hand in the movies.

One witness down, and I already needed a drink.

CHAPTER 11

*B*y the time I'd polished off the Godzilla—a sake-based monstrosity as big and green as its namesake—I'd independently verified that two of the remaining three witnesses had recalled it being unusually cold during the supposed time of the abduction. Enough, at least, to suggest a pattern of some kind. As the last witness headed for the door, Robin joined me at the bar, and I filled him in on what I'd discovered. "Does that mean anything to you?" Robin asked. "It being cold out?"

"Not at all," I replied.

"Then why are you grinning?"

"Because, this means I have to call the man of me dreams."

Robin arced an eyebrow. "Come again?"

I didn't bother explaining. Instead, I took out my phone, found Max's contact information, and hit send. As I waited for the call to connect, I wondered how he'd sound over the phone. Would that Spanish accent be thicker? Would his voice be as deep, as masculine, as I remembered? Fortunately, I didn't have long to find out; he answered on the third ring. "Max? It's Quinn MacKenna." I waited for a response, half-expecting the man to make some crack about me not being able to resist calling him, or something equally suave. But he didn't.

Instead, he screamed.

The sound of glass shattering buzzed in my ear, though it was a distant sound, as if Max were watching an action movie on TV. An explosion came next, much louder this time, much closer. More screams, almost too faint to make out, though I could tell it wasn't Max screaming anymore. The voice was definitely a woman's. Camila's? Suddenly I could hear the woman better, as if she'd come closer. It was Camila, and she was screaming her brother's name, shouting words in Spanish until the phone crashed against something solid. The sudden thump was so loud it forced me to move the phone from my ear. "Max!" I yelled. "Max are ye there?!"

More thumps, but no answers.

"Max, tell me where ye are! Can ye hear me?!"

Robin faced me, his eyes wide, mouth open. "What's happening?"

"I don't know." I cursed, pressed the phone to one ear, and pinned my hand to the other, trying to catch anything that was being said. Any clue as to where they were, or what was happening.

But the line went dead.

I stared down at my phone for a moment, then leapt over the bar with one hand, clearing it so easily in my hurry that I nearly landed on a table five feet away. I skidded to a halt and spun around, realizing I didn't have time to wait for an Uber or to hail a Taxi. "Robin, I need ye to drive me!"

"Where?" he asked, fetching his jacket from the barstool.

"Wortcunnin' Corner," I replied, taking a blind stab at Max and Camila's location; it was the only possibility I could think of. If they weren't there, then there was probably nothing I could do, but I would worry about that later. "I'll give ye directions on the way. Now hurry!"

The Redcap didn't need telling twice.

Which was good, because I was already out the door.

CHAPTER 12

*W*hen we turned onto Newbury Street, it was obvious the cops were already on site—their flashing lights visible through the gaps in traffic. By the time we'd parked, I'd already spotted several uniforms herding a growing crowd of pedestrians away from the immediate area surrounding Wortcunning Corner. Unfortunately for them, it appeared that corralling the masses was proving even more difficult than usual—unsurprising considering it basically meant creating a roadblock in the midst of retail rush hour. After all, no self-respecting shopper would let a crime scene derail their march from one boutique to another without at least seeing what the fuss was about, much as no driver ever seems capable of cruising past a wreck without slowing down for a good, long look at the damage.

Once I'd gotten closer, however, I realized the comparison to a wreck was too close for comfort: the grimy windows had been shattered, blown outward onto the sidewalk as if from an explosion within. The sign had fallen to the ground, shattered into pieces. Scorch marks blackened the brick facade in thick blotches, like the ashen fingerprints of a giant. The door had clearly been kicked in, the wood splintered where the lock had given way. All in all, the once underwhelming storefront was almost unrecognizable in the aftermath of whatever had gone down here, the difference so great I could hardly believe I was looking at the same shop.

I took a moment to bob and weave, craning my neck to see beyond the crowd of onlookers, but—once I was sure there wasn't any more I could learn from back here—I carved a path through the bystanders to find whoever was in charge. My best guess was a plainclothes detective, or a fire marshal, or maybe someone from the ATF; it looked enough like a bomb had gone off to earn their attention. Finally, after forcing my way to the front of the crowd, I spotted someone standing within the police barricade, though it definitely wasn't who I'd expected—or even wanted—to find.

"Maria! Maria, over here!" I called, waving.

Detective Maria Machado was a short, Hispanic woman with an attitude problem who, as far as I knew, loathed my guts. In fact, she'd threatened to put me in jail so often over the last few years it had practically become a running joke—not the humorous kind, mind you. More like the sad, cosmic kind. Still, as Jimmy's former partner, at least I knew her well enough to suspect I could tempt her to tell me what had happened so long as I was prepared for a little grilling.

"Jesus, what the fuck are you doing here, MacKenna?" Maria asked the instant she saw me, practically snarling,

Ok, maybe a lot of grilling.

I waved her over. "I'll tell ye, but ye have to come here," I hissed. I actually watched Maria swallow her response, noting the crowd of potential witnesses. She jerked her head, indicating we meet where the crowd was thinnest. I did what she asked, skirting the edges of the rabble as though I was trying to resume my seat in a darkened movie theater, mumbling apologies as I went.

"Alright," Maria said, once I'd arrived. "What do you want? In case you hadn't noticed, I'm a little busy."

"I didn't realize this was in your jurisdiction," I said, raising an eyebrow.

"It isn't. The owners are family friends. Now answer my fucking question before I arrest you for interfering with an investigation."

See? At this point, I was pretty sure she couldn't help herself. Still, the outburst surprised me; if she thought I was interfering now, she was about to get well and truly pissed. "I know Max and Camila," I said, hoping that would get her attention.

It did.

"What was that?" she asked, taking a step forward, cocking her head to the side as if she'd misheard me.

"I was on the phone with Max while this was happenin'," I explained. "I came as soon as I could."

Maria stepped all the way into me this time, invading the hell out of my personal space in the process, and grabbed my jacket with both hands. "Why is it whenever shit goes down in this town, and I mean the absolutely batshit crazy shit, you're always the one in the middle of it, MacKenna?"

I took hold of her wrists, as gently as I could. "Just lucky, I guess. Now, let me go, Detective."

"Make me," Maria said, jerking on my jacket, her eyes practically seething with hate.

I considered crushing her wrists, or at least putting enough pressure on those brittle bones to show her that—if it came down to arm wrestling—I'd win. But, in the end, I decided to handle it like any reasonable adult woman would. "Talked to Jimmy, lately?" I asked as cattily as I could manage.

Maria immediately let go and stepped back, the expression on her face so pitiful I opened my mouth to apologize. But the words never left my mouth, because that's when she slapped me—striking so fast and so hard I actually tasted blood. I blinked away tears of surprise, then turned back to face the detective, probing my swollen lip with my tongue. Maria, meanwhile, cradled her limp, likely broken hand. "Ye know," I said, "I'm not really the turn the other cheek type. But I t'ink ye ended up with the raw end of that deal, so I'll let it go this once."

Maria simply stared up at me, mouth hanging open, eyes wide with shock. Then, when the shock finally wore off, came the pain. She pressed her mangled hand to her chest, grinding her teeth so as not to cry out. It almost made me feel bad to see how much damage had been caused by my remarkably durable, inhuman flesh.

Almost.

"Detective Machado, what the hell is going on here?" a man asked, coming up from behind Maria. He wasn't quite my height but made up for it in bulk; the epaulets of his uniform were forced to stretch almost impossibly far to meet the seams at his sleeves, which were covered in chevrons. He had the face and build of a bulldog, jowls tugging at the corners of his mouth, eyes beady, barrel-chested and bow-legged.

"This bitch," Maria said through clenched teeth, "broke my hand."

"Actually, Sergeant," a nearby uniform said, "I saw the whole thing. Detective Machado grabbed that woman first, then slapped her. Hard."

Machado glared at her fellow cop, but the younger officer wasn't backing down. Instead he gave her a flat stare, as if daring her to contradict him. I began to wonder if Maria had pissed off more people than just me, lately; cops usually went out of their way to protect their own, in my experience. At that precise moment, a few industrious pedestrians actually started corroborating what the uniform had said, yelling and pointing fingers from behind the barricade. By the time they started calling for Maria's blood, I realized I'd become the center of attention.

Not good.

I raised a hand. "I don't want to press charges!" I called. Then, in a much softer voice, I addressed the Sergeant. "Listen, the only reason I'm here is because I believe I was the last person to have contact with the owners of this shop. Detective Machado here was takin' me statement, but when I insulted the owner, the Detective took it personally. I didn't realize they were close. It's as much me fault as it is hers." I caught Maria's gaze and held it, willing her to stick to that story and let the cards fall where they may, for both our sakes.

"Did you say you were the last to talk to the..." the Sergeant checked his notebook, "Velez's?"

I nodded. "Aye, that's what I said. I called, and the owner—Max—picked up in the middle of whatever happened here."

"Machado, go see the EMTs, get that hand checked out," the Sergeant said, dismissively, his eyes never leaving mine. Which meant he didn't see the hateful glare Maria directed at his back. "Now, please," he continued, "Ms...?"

"MacKenna," I offered.

"MacKenna," he said, nodding. "Come with me."

I ducked under the outstretched arms of the officer who'd come to my defense, found Robin in the crowd, and gave him a subtle thumbs up, letting him know everything was alright. The Redcap surreptitiously tipped his hat to me as the Sergeant, whose last name I learned was Stone—yes, Sergeant Stone—escorted me to the top of the stairs that led down to the storefront, though no farther. From that vantage point, I could see that the shop's interior looked even worse than its exterior: the glass jars had all been busted, their contents blown around the room, the shelves ripped free from the walls. Only the counter stood intact, though it bore some of the same scorch marks as the brick outside.

"So, what did you hear when you called?" Sergeant Stone asked, pen poised above his notebook.

"Not much. Max answered, but I don't t'ink he had his phone in his hand. More like in his pocket. I heard screams. Camila's, I t'ink. Explosions. But it was all muffled." I shook my head, wishing I had more to offer. "D'ye have any idea who might have done this?"

"We're looking into several possibilities," Stone replied.

Meaning they had absolutely no idea.

"Was it a bomb?" I asked.

His eyes narrowed. "We have someone looking into that."

Translation? He knew but wouldn't tell me.

"Is there anythin' ye *can* tell me? Are Max and Camila in there? Were there any witnesses? Anythin'?"

"Your friends weren't found inside, no. In fact, until you came along, we had no reason to suspect they were here when this happened. We haven't been here long, ourselves."

"But that means you'll have people lookin' for 'em, right? Now that ye know they were here?"

He gave me a long, considering look before responding. "Show me the call you made."

I sighed, yanked my phone out of my coat pocket, and showed him. "I'm not lyin' to ye, Sergeant."

He studied the phone, then nodded. "I'll have my people start canvassing as soon as we're done here."

I raised an eyebrow. "What else d'ye need from me?"

"How do you know the Velez's?" he asked, and I could sense suspicion lurking beneath that seemingly innocuous question.

"What's that got to do with anythin'?"

"Just answer the question."

I narrowed my eyes. "Am I under arrest?"

"Should you be?"

"I'll take that as a no. In which case, I don't have to answer any of your questions. In fact, now that I've told ye everythin' I know, I t'ink I'll be on me way." I turned to leave, but the man grabbed my arm before I got more than a couple feet away. Unfortunately for the brutish Sergeant Stone, I've never been inclined to let anyone touch me, especially not a man accusing me of—well, whatever it was he was accusing me of; I jerked my arm free, tearing it loose so forcefully I took him along for the ride. Off-balanced, Stone collapsed to one knee with a grunt, clearly surprised to find me looming over him, one hand cocked back in case he needed to be put down a second time. "No one puts their hands on me without permission," I snarled. "D'ye understand me?"

Stone got back to his feet, wincing with the effort. By the time he was upright, however, his face was mottled with anger. "Expect to have a police detail following you around for the next few days, Ms. MacKenna. For your protection." He said the last sarcastically, through clenched teeth, and we both knew exactly what he was actually saying. He didn't trust me. Hell, after less than a couple minutes of conversation, I was fairly sure he didn't even *like* me.

I'd have loved to say it was a personal best, but it wasn't.

We all have our talents.

"If ye t'ink your men are good enough to keep tabs on me," I said, "then be me guest. But keep in mind, I have plenty of eye witnesses back there who saw your detective slap me, not to mention ye grabbin' me arm just now. If ye t'ink I'm bad, then ye clearly haven't met me lawyer. By the time he's done suing your department, ye won't have a fuckin' badge, let alone all those fancy stripes."

Stone's expression grew sour. "That'll be all, Ms. MacKenna."

"Go fuck yourself, Sergeant," I said and stomped off, too pissed to care which direction I went so long as it was away from Stone and his veiled threats. Of course, I regretted mouthing off almost the minute I stepped away. When you got right down to it, Stone was just doing his job. Honestly, I'd have been suspicious of me, too, had I been in his shoes. A witness who shows up only a few minutes after the cops claiming to have vital information pertaining to the victims?

Yeah, definitely fishy.

The only reason I'd gotten so defensive, I realized, was because I hadn't been prepared to explain the nature of my relationship with Max and his sister. Hell, if I'd have told him the truth—that I had asked for their help solving kidnappings and a possible murder before Camila had effectively kicked me out of their shop—I'd have ended up answering questions at the nearest precinct until dawn. And if I'd lied—claimed I was a frequent customer or even Max's girlfriend, perhaps—then I'd have run the risk of being exposed down the line.

Lose-lose.

"What the hell happened back there?" Robin whispered, meeting me in the middle of the street as I hustled towards the Jeep.

"I'll tell ye on the way back, for now just drive," I snapped. "Please," I added, realizing how bitchy I sounded. "We need to get out of here, fast."

Frankly, no matter what I'd threatened to do to him personally, I was willing to bet Stone would put a tail on me as soon as possible; he struck me as the tenacious type. If so, our best bet was to leave Newbury Street before the traffic cleared out. Fortunately, Robin took me at my word and started the car without complaint, not even pausing long enough to ask me why we were in a rush. In fact, it was a full five minutes later before anything was said.

Ironically, when someone finally did speak, the voice belonged to neither of us.

"I think I know who came after your people," Camila said, from the backseat, her voice hoarse. "Because they came after us, too."

CHAPTER 13

The shock of discovering a stowaway in his backseat surprised Robin enough that he accidentally drifted into the other lane, which meant the revelation was simultaneously accompanied by a series of curses, car horns, and close calls. Camila cried out in pain as she was flung about in the backseat, and I glanced behind to find her covered in first-degree burns, one of her eyebrows singed off, her hair matted with dried blood. Bruises were beginning to blossom over one cheek and down her arms. She wore a stained blouse and torn jeans, but no shoes—her feet bare and bloody. Probably from the glass. I knew then that it wouldn't be long before Stone found evidence to support my kidnapping theory; forensics likely wouldn't overlook bloody footprints.

"Jesus, Camila, what the fuck happened to ye?" I asked once Robin got the Jeep under control.

"I told you," she said, her voice tight with pain. "They came for us."

Before I could ask who the hell "they" were, however, the tell-tale whirr of sirens had us all looking through the rear-view window. "Fuck," I cursed, spotting the unmarked police car closing in on us from behind, weaving through traffic like a maniac. Had Stone really had enough time to put a tail on us before we left? Or were we simply that unbelievably unlucky? Either way, I wasn't looking forward to whatever was going to happen next.

"I take it ye don't want to be found and taken to the nearest hospital?" I asked Camila, who shook her head vehemently. "Of course not," I muttered. "That'd be too easy."

"So, what do I do?" Robin asked.

I considered the question for half a heartbeat. "Wait, are ye any good at glamour?" I asked, an idea forming.

"Not really," Robin admitted. "Little things, if I concentrate. A teacup into a coffee mug type shit."

"How about a human bein' under a blanket to a bunch of nothin' under a blanket?" I asked, drawing out a dusty sheet piled on the floor of the backseat.

"Maybe?"

"You cannot let him use his Fae magic on me," Camila said, voice breathy with fear. "Please, you can't."

"Listen," I snarled, "ye have two choices. Either we let the nice officer take your crazy ass to the hospital where ye belong, or ye shut up, stay put, and let us *Faelin's* try and keep ye safe. Now which is it goin' to be?"

Camila clamped her mouth shut, tears brimming.

"Alright then," I said. I turned to Robin. "Pull over and let me do the talkin'. Concentrate on makin' her look like anythin' but a damn body."

"Your plans really suck, you know that?"

"Do it," I hissed, tossing the sheet over Camila as gently as I could. She winced but stayed low and kept silent as Robin pulled over. The Redcap rolled down the window and put both hands on the steering wheel, trying to look as harmless as possible and only mildly succeeding. Guys Robin's size tend to set off alarm bells no matter who you are, and all his Red Sox gear would only make him seem more like a threat; Sox fans rarely made it into the news for acts of charity. Don't believe me? Try wearing a Yankees jersey around town during playoff season—twenty bucks says the jersey doesn't make it.

But of course, it turned out it wasn't Robin's window the cop wanted rolled down.

It was mine.

"Get out with your hands in the air!" Maria yelled, gun drawn one-handed, aiming at me through the glass.

"Is that Maria?" Camila asked, poking her head out from beneath the sheet. I would have told her to get back down, but I didn't want to give Maria an excuse to shoot me. Instead, I stayed perfectly still.

"Now!" Maria yelled.

I raised both hands as slowly as I could, but ultimately it wasn't me who nearly got her head blown off. In the end, it was Camila who kicked open the backdoor and leapt out of the Jeep, shouting, "Maria!" as loud as her strangled voice was able and headed straight for the woman holding a loaded firearm.

For a brief second, I panicked, thinking Maria might shoot her by accident, but—at the last possible instant—the detective pointed her gun skyward. Camila, apparently oblivious to the danger, drew Maria into a bone-crushing hug. "Oh Maria! It's awful, they took Max!" Camila cried.

The battered woman started speaking in Spanish far too fast for me— with my rudimentary grasp of the language—to comprehend. I debated lowering my hands now that the gun wasn't pointed at me but decided against it; I was fairly certain Maria's steel bullets wouldn't kill me, but I wasn't eager to find out for sure. Besides, do you have any idea how hard it is to clean a leather jacket soaked in blood?

Let's just say I'd spent a small fortune on tips alone at my local dry cleaners.

"Is it true?" Maria asked, staring into the eyes of her friend.

Camila nodded. "*Si, es cierto.*"

Maria disengaged from the hug long enough to put her gun away. I noticed a few cars slowing to a crawl as they passed us, clearly intrigued by our little drama. Of course, none stopped to see what was actually happening, or to offer assistance. Fucking useless bystanders. "I didn't realize..." Maria trailed off. "MacKenna, I owe you an apology."

"Does that mean I can put me hands down, now?" I asked.

Maria nodded, which was a relief; my shoulders were starting to cramp up.

"We have to get him back, Maria," Camila urged.

"Can I make a suggestion?" Robin chimed in, leaning over the dash to make sure we could all hear him. "Can we maybe take this conversation elsewhere? I'm feeling a little exposed over here, seeing as how I'm the one who got pulled over. Besides, I think Camila over there could use some medical attention."

Maria searched Camila's injured face and nodded. "I'll take you to the hospital."

"No!" Camila said, shaking her head. "No hospitals. Please. You know I cannot go there."

"Damnit. You're right," Maria said, looking suddenly very tired. "I forgot. How about my place? We could go there?"

I frowned, wondering why Maria wasn't insisting on taking Camila to the nearest emergency room. Granted, I wouldn't have pressed the issue, either, but then I thought hospitals were over-sanitized slaughterhouses. Maria, on the other hand, was a cop. I'd seen her bend the rules before, sure, but that had been to keep Jimmy—her partner—out of the line of fire. Camila was a civilian. An injured woman who needed treatment and probably a police detail, depending on who had come after them. So why had Maria agreed? And why had Camila balked at the idea of being admitted? Between the woman's aversion to both hospitals and the Fae, I was seriously starting to regret having ever gone to Max's shop in the first place.

Christ, what if Eve really was cursed?

"No, I don't think that would be a good idea," Camila said at last. Her panicked expression had faded considerably, and—despite the damage—she looked the same as she had last night, her hands clasped once again. "Besides, I need to talk to this one," she said, tilting her head towards me. "It is important."

Maria pursed her lips, but—shockingly—didn't argue. Instead, she turned to me. "Would you be willing to come with us?"

"To your place?" I asked, cocking an eyebrow. "After ye assaulted me in public and then drew a gun on me in broad daylight? Ye must be out of your fuckin' mind."

"I said I was sorry."

"Aye, well, I never said I forgave ye," I replied. "Besides, I have a better idea. Camila, go on and hop back in the Jeep, though mind those feet. Maria, ye can follow us, instead."

"Follow you where?" Maria asked as Camila clambered back into the Jeep, leaving behind dainty, bloody footprints on the concrete sidewalk that made me want to wince.

"Somewhere safe," I replied. "Ye sure you're alright to drive?" I asked, jerking my chin towards the detective's injured hand.

"It's just a sprain," she insisted, eyes hardening.

I shrugged. "Suit yourself."

"Where to?" Robin asked as I hopped in the passenger seat and slammed my door shut.

"Where else?" I said, with a sigh. "Let's go back to the bar. At least there we can find some booze."

"Always the pragmatist," Robin quipped.

I let that comment stand, though—as we prepared to head back to my favorite bar with a burn victim and a cop who'd threatened me with violence twice in under an hour, and all that merely because I wanted to find out what the hell had happened to a hunky guy I'd met only the night before—I wasn't feeling all that pragmatic.

But hey, booze.

CHAPTER 14

*M*aria gave Christoff's bar the long, lingering look it deserved, eyes roving over the cardboard cutouts and paper mâché recreations of some of Hollywood's most famous monsters, including my personal favorite: a version of The Creature from the Black Lagoon rising from the floor as though from a lake, its arms extended, clawed fingers hoping to drag down any unwary passersby. Christoff had rigged it so if you stepped too close it would wail, just loud enough to make you jump and potentially—if you were the easily frightened type—wet yourself.

"Charming place," Maria said, voice dripping with sarcasm.

"Ye don't have to be here," I said, matter-of-factly.

"And you do?" Maria asked.

"Can I get you ladies something to drink?" Christoff interjected, his Russian accent thick and cloying, and yet somehow warm and sincere. "And maybe a First Aid Kit for the young lady?" he suggested, eyeing Camila.

"I'll get the kit," Robin said, pushing away from the table we'd commandeered.

"Ye don't want to hear this?" I asked.

Robin waved that off. "You can fill me in later."

"I'll take a *cerveza*," Camila said. "*Gracias.*"

"I don't need anything," Maria said, though I noticed her voice was laced with pain; she'd kept her hand below the table, where the others couldn't see it.

Christoff nodded. "You're welcome. Be right back."

"Ye aren't goin' to take me order?" I asked. "What kind of bartender are ye?"

"You know where the liquor is," Christoff said, dryly.

I scowled at the Russian man's back but made no move to get up. Instead, I turned to Camila. "So, ye said 'they' came for ye. Who would 'they' be?"

"The Salem Witches," Camila said, refusing to meet my eyes, her voice small and timid.

"Come again?" I asked.

"They don't like to be called that, but in many ways it's who they are, who they've been since this country was first settled. The Salem Witches. The Coven of Ipswich."

I held up a hand. "Ye can't mean *the* Salem witches, can ye? As in the Salem Witch Trials witches?"

Camila shook her head. "That was all a show they put on for the locals. Regulars were getting too close to their secrets, so they pitted the citizens against each other. But there *were* witches in Salem. Real ones. Witches who crossed the ocean among the first pilgrims, hoping to escape the lingering effects of the Inquisition. And they've been here ever since, though you'll find most come from the shores of Ipswich, not Salem."

"What the hell are you talking about Camila?" Maria hissed, her voice so low you'd have thought we were in a library. "Are you in shock? Because you're not making any sense."

Camila sighed. "Maria, you know what Maximiliano and I are. You've always known. Your own mother was a practitioner, and yet you refuse to believe in our world. Ever since you were a girl, you teased us for our beliefs." She turned hard eyes to the woman. "But Max and I aren't the only ones with the Gift, are we?"

Maria looked as though she'd been slapped but said nothing. Instead, the color drained from her face and she practically flopped back in her chair, looking faint. She tugged at her sleeve and set her injured hand on the table as gingerly as she could manage, hissing through her teeth in the process. It looked bad; two of her knuckles had swollen to the size of walnuts, while the skin itself was a mottled mess of color ranging from green to purple. "Fine, I admit it," she said. "My hand hurts."

"Christoff!" I yelled.

"I already told you, get your own!" The Russian called back from the kitchen.

"Don't ye worry about me! But get somethin' for Maria while you're back there. Somethin' strong. And tell that good for nothin' Redcap to hurry the hell up with the First Aid Kit. We've got two injured now!"

"What happened to her hand?" Camila asked, suddenly concerned.

"She slapped me. Hard," I added, giving Maria the look she deserved.

"You slapped one of the Fae?!" Camila asked, covering her mouth with her hand in surprise.

"One of the what?" Maria asked, brows furrowed, the glazed look in her eyes fading a tad now that she had something besides the pain to focus on.

"She doesn't know?" Camila asked me, frowning.

"Ye want to explain it to her? Be me guest." I crossed my legs and leaned back into my chair, rocking slightly. "But after that wee dispute ye had about witches, I can hardly wait to see how you'll explain what I am."

Camila's frown turned into a scowl, made uglier by the burns and bruises marring her face. Fortunately, Robin seemed to have found the First Aid Kit; he knelt beside the two women and began pulling out various supplies, including two pill bottles worth of pain relievers. I left him to it, rising to go make myself the drink Christoff had teased me about. By the time I was finished, the bartender had dropped off Camila's beer, as well as a shot for Maria, and had ambled over to me. "What mess have you gotten into now?" Christoff asked.

"That woman's brother," I said, flicking my eyes to Camila, "got himself taken by witches. Salem witches, apparently. *The* Salem witches."

That earned a raised eyebrow. "And now you will what? Save him?"

I scoffed. "Since when do I go savin' people I hardly know?"

Christoff chuckled. "You believe you are too practical for this?"

"Aye, what of it?" I asked, defensively.

"Nothing, except I think you lie to yourself. I would put money on you confronting those witches in the next twenty-four hours." Christoff raised a hand in a placating gesture. "Not a lot of money, but enough."

I frowned. "I mean I was plannin' on goin' after the witches, but not to save Max. I need to find out who's kidnappin' the Chancery members, and this is the first real lead we've had. I go to a reputable store hoping to find out more about a crime scene, and the witches kidnap the one person who'd offered to help? It's too big a coincidence to ignore."

"Ah, yes. You must instead save the Chancery members you hardly know. *Now* it all makes sense." Christoff winked, but walked away before I could tell him off, humming some jaunty tune under his breath.

I shook my head. Was Christoff right? Why *had* I signed on to help Gretel in the first place? It wasn't like I owed her or her organization anything. Hell, after getting rid of their murderous problem child, they probably owed me. And yet I hadn't asked for anything in return—which wasn't like me. Was it simply because they were Fae? My kind, technically? Or was it something else? Had I gone soft, determined to play the hero?

My eyes wandered as I considered the answer, eventually settling on Camila's face and the marks she bore; she winced as Robin ran an ointment over one of the burns. In that instant, I could remember treating my own burns after fleeing a building on fire—the agony of every waking moment as I waited for them to heal. And then there were the bruises from the hand that had gripped my ankle—bruises which had taken days to fade, though not nearly as long as it had taken my knee to recover, to bear my weight without giving out.

I flexed that knee out of habit, expecting to feel the sharp, sudden burst of agonizing pain just below my kneecap that accompanied the exaggerated movement. And yet...there was none. Not even the slightest twinge remained. When had that happened? I thought back to my last several months of training with Scathach and realized practically none of my aches and pains bothered me anymore. Courtesy of my transformation, perhaps? If so, I honestly wasn't sure how I felt about it.

As much as I disliked pain, I hated the thought of forgetting more.

And with that, I suddenly knew I hadn't gone soft. Not really. People like me didn't go soft; we held onto our pain, our scars, too mangled to believe in childish, make-believe shit like heroes or villains. Hell, I'd learned years and years ago that no one was ever coming to save you, especially not from yourself. But maybe that's what this was about—the real reason I'd agreed to work pro bono for a change: I considered the missing Chancery members to be victims. And victims deserved someone like me. Not to rescue them. Not to save them. But to avenge them.

Because that...that I could do.

"Where would they have taken your brother?" I asked Camila, sliding back into my chair with a drink in hand.

She shook her head, still unwilling to meet my eyes. "I don't know. The Coven is who we feared might come for us after talking to you. Once we saw the ritual, we thought it might be them. All that blood..."

"What the hell is she talking about? What ritual?" Maria asked, leaning forward, forcing Robin to move with her; he was winding tape around her hand and wrist to keep it from moving too much. I was actually surprised she'd let him help her but didn't bother poking at it. Instead I spun until the detective and I were looking directly at each other.

"Listen, Maria," I began, "from here on out there's goin' to be a lot ye won't understand, or even believe. I plan to go after Max, and I'll try me best to get him back, but I can't afford to explain everythin' I say, or to hold your hand." I cringed at the expression, doing my best not to look at the taped monstrosity on the table. "Ye know what I mean."

"Your saying I'd be, what, holding you back?" Maria asked, her voice unnaturally low—her bad cop voice, from what I recalled.

"Aye, that's exactly what I'm sayin'."

Maria grunted and slammed her good hand onto the table. I think the reaction surprised us all, but I quickly realized it was more than that. Robin, who'd been closest to her, fell back to the floor, clutching his chest. Camila, too, looked pained as she collapsed into her seat. It took a moment longer, however, for me to feel it—little more than the faintest skin-prickling sensation. Then it rode me, a wave of power that made my arms spasm and my pulse race.

It wasn't magic. Not like what I'd felt wizards use—a binding of the elements manifesting itself in tendrils of flame and ice. It was more like potential. An aura of power, perhaps, which crashed against me like the tide. It had no structure. No intent. The power was just suddenly there, pulsing outward from Maria in waves.

After what seemed like an eternity, Maria finally lifted her hand from the table, and the power dissipated. The diminutive detective fell back into her chair, breathing so hard I thought she might faint. But she didn't. Instead, she spoke between gasps, "Tell. Me. Everything."

So I did.

Because I wasn't about to argue with the witch.

CHAPTER 15

I passed Maria the bottle of water she'd requested, retrieved the gas pump, and latched it back in place, ignoring the prompt that materialized on screen as I got behind the wheel, confident the message would disappear momentarily. Sadly, no receipt was necessary; this trip sure as shit wasn't for pleasure—especially not with Maria tagging along— but it definitely wasn't for business either. Which meant no tax write-offs for Quinn.

"What are you planning to do once we get there?" Maria asked as I pulled us out of the gas station in the rental car I'd procured that afternoon —a necessary precaution seeing as how Stone had promised to keep tabs on me and Maria had repeatedly refused to let me drive her unmarked car. By "there" Maria meant Salem; after talking things over with Camila, it'd seemed the most likely destination aside from Ipswich, a coastal town another hour north and too damn cold to contemplate visiting at the moment. Robin had offered to tag along, but I'd asked him to report in to the Germans, instead—though in private I'd urged him to keep an eye on Camila. Frankly, I'd have been happy to make this trip alone, but Maria hadn't offered to tag along so much as told me she was coming. Still, she was a decent detective, when she wasn't acting like a total bitch; maybe she'd be useful.

Or maybe I'd have to tie her to a tree and leave her to rot.

The day was full of possibilities.

"Figured I'd do what I did with Max and Camila," I replied. "Reach out to some of the resident occultists, see who stands out. Camila said the witches like Salem because they can hide in plain sight. Maybe we'll get lucky and find one of 'em playin' shopkeeper." I shrugged. "Unless ye have a better idea."

"Not really. All this magic shit is beyond me."

I cocked an eyebrow at that. "Really? After the show ye put on in Christoff's bar, ye could've fooled me."

Color rose in Maria's tanned cheeks. "That sort of just happened."

I grunted. "That kind of power doesn't come from nowhere, ye know."

Maria stared at her bandaged hand, face sullen. "No. It comes with a price."

"What's that supposed to mean?"

"I don't want to talk about it. We aren't friends. I don't even like you. So, drop it and drive."

I merged onto the highway that took us from Boston to Salem—a fifteen-mile drive that took almost an hour with the usual traffic and even longer on the weekends. "Ye know, I piss off a lot of people," I began, "but I'm pretty sure ye had a problem with me from the beginnin'. What was it about that set ye off? Was it me and Jimmy?"

Maria sniffed. "Please. Jimmy's a grown man. He can do what—who—he wants."

"Then what?"

"I just had a bad feeling about you, that's all." Maria looked out the window, face turned from me. "I get those, sometimes. My mother liked to call it a gift. She cast spells and brewed potions, sold her services under the table. Until one day a client came in accusing her of swindling him, spouting some bullshit about his ex-wife. Wouldn't have mattered much, except he had a gun." Maria made a sound low in her throat. "Magic. What a crock of shit."

We drove in silence for a while after that before I ventured another question.

"Alright, so ye sensed somethin' was off about me. Fair enough. But what about after that?"

"After that?" Maria scoffed, swiveling around to stare at me. "Haven't you realized yet that you're the common denominator when everything goes to hell? It's like you're a magnet for the worst shit imaginable. Hell, we can't even explain to the top brass because no one would ever believe us. Do you know how many times we had to lie to cover for you? Jimmy especially. For Christ's sakes, he had to join the FBI thanks to you!"

"Excuse me?"

"Oh please, don't pretend like you don't know what's happened to him. He won't talk to me about it, but I've seen what he becomes. What he turns into. He's not even the same person, now. Ever since he got out of that hospital. After helping you." Maria practically spat the last, glaring at me from the passenger seat.

I shook my head, unsure what to say in my defense. It was true, Jimmy *had* become a monster after coming to my rescue. But since then he'd embraced that side of himself and seemed more at peace now than he had when we first met. And sure, I'd given him the nudge towards a role with the Bureau, but that's all it had been—a nudge.

"I t'ink you're wrong about Jimmy," I said, at last. "But I can't really argue with the rest, except to say that it wasn't me intention to drag ye lot into any of this." I made a vague gesture towards the horizon. "But just so ye know, me world—the world your superiors refuse to believe in—has always been there. Freaks die left and right every day and no one on your side even notices. Were-animals kill each other in battles of succession. Vampires slaughter humans on the fringes of society. For fuck's sake, why d'ye t'ink we're even here? Why am I the one lookin' for missin' fairytale creatures?" Now it was my turn to glare at Maria. "Maybe if the Regulars stopped shovin' their fuckin' heads in the sand, I wouldn't have to keep solvin' other people's problems."

I turned back to the road, tirade complete, exhausted and fed up. I was tired. Tired of having to explain myself to the ignorant asshats who refused to accept the world as it actually was, instead of how they wanted it to be. Tired of having to lie to protect everything and everyone I cared about. Tired of having to collect favors on the off-chance that it all went sideways. Don't get me wrong, so much of what I did for a living hinged on operating under the radar and exploiting that ignorance, but—at that precise moment —I felt I'd have given it all up if I could simply send someone reliable after Max and the missing Fae, someone who wouldn't let me down.

As if you'd ever let that happen, a voice inside my head whispered. Not some disembodied, supernatural voice. Just my pesky subconscious, calling me out on my bullshit. I sighed, knowing deep down that it was right; I'd spent most of my adult life buying into the "if you want something done right, do it yourself" philosophy. Frankly, I wasn't sure I even had it in me to step aside and let someone else handle the situation. Any situation.

Control freak, anyone?

"So, what?" Maria asked, breaking the silence. "Am I supposed to give you a fucking cookie?"

"Honestly, I'd settle for ye bein' less of a bitch," I replied.

That shut her up.

Which was good, because I was done talking, and we were almost there.

CHAPTER 16

*E*xcept that was as far as we got.

Little more than a couple miles out, the car—a nearly new, luxurious Cadillac XTS—shuddered. The interior lights began to flicker on and off, and the radio—which I'd left untouched lest I risk Maria complaining about my taste in music among other things—began blaring heavy metal grunge one second, followed by Bible thumping rhetoric the next. Then the power steering gave out, forcing me to yank at the wheel to keep from drifting into the other lane.

"What the hell is going on?" Maria yelled.

I didn't bother explaining that I had no idea; I was too busy trying to pull over to the side of the road without getting us killed. Fortunately, we'd left the main highway behind, and traffic was lighter headed directly into town, which meant I was able to pull onto the shoulder before the car died altogether. And it did indeed die; the instant I made it past the rumble strips the vehicle gave one final jerk before the twangy country ballad on the radio cut off and we were left in complete silence. I jiggled the key, pressed the gas pedal to the floor, and even tried cycling through the different gears, but nothing was working. Which made no fucking sense.

"Any chance that magic show ye put on earlier can fix a busted car?" I asked, mostly to keep from screaming in frustration.

"No." Maria leaned forward and pressed her good hand to the dash. "But it could have done this."

"What?"

"My mother used to charge for crap like this. Hexes, she called them. I remember one time, she caught me watching TV when I was supposed to be doing chores, and suddenly the TV wouldn't work. It stayed like that for a week. White noise, static. After that, I always did my chores."

"Can ye, I don't know, counter it somehow?" I asked.

Maria shook her head before I'd even finished the question. "She never taught me how it worked. Besides, for all I know, you rented a piece of shit car."

"Very constructive," I quipped. I pulled out my phone, hoping to call the rental company and see what they could do for me. But my phone wasn't working. It, too, was dead. "You've got to be fuckin' kiddin' me," I hissed.

"What now?" Maria asked. She caught sight of my phone, drew hers out, then cursed. "If Stone tries to get hold of me, and I don't pick up, I'm going to be in deep shit."

"Well, that's too bad. Of course, maybe our phones are pieces of shit, too," I said, mockingly, showcasing the luxury vehicle and our fairly new phones as if that were even possible.

"So, what now?" Maria asked, mouth pursed.

"I guess we walk."

Maria gave me a flat look. "I don't think so." She got out and worked her way around the car to stand on the edge of the road, toeing the white line. I joined her, wondering if she was going to try hoisting her thumb out to bum a ride from someone. Instead, she raised her badge. "Someone will stop," she asserted.

Yeah, I thought, because people love getting pulled over by the police and having their vehicle requisitioned. But I didn't say anything; Maria was probably right. We just had to wait for some do-gooder with a hard on for law and order, or maybe another cop, to spot us, and we'd be set. We could always come back for the poor Cadillac.

But no one stopped. In fact, after watching the eyes of several passing drivers, I realized they weren't even looking at us. Not avoiding us, either. They simply weren't noticing the two women perched on the side of the road, clearly in need of help; we might as well have been invisible. I nudged Maria. "Is it possible to hex people? To make it so no one sees 'em?" I asked.

Maria cursed, but put her badge away. "I have no idea." She slid a hand over the butt of her gun, as if considering a more violent alternative, but eventually turned on her heel and started marching down the road in the direction we'd been going.

Guess we were walking, after all.

I trailed the older woman, sliding my hands into the pockets of my jacket, and let the brisk walk take away some of the chill. At this rate, it would probably take an hour to reach Salem, give or take. By then, I figured, the sun would be setting, giving us maybe a couple hours before most of the shops closed down for the night. Truthfully, the delay sucked—especially since it meant someone, or something, seemed dead set against us reaching Salem—but it could have been worse.

Of course, the instant I thought that, I knew I shouldn't have.

CHAPTER 17

*M*aria broke off first, headed directly for the nearby woods, wobbling precariously in her sensible, but ultimately impractical, heels. We'd walked for maybe ten minutes, me trailing, a grass-covered slope on our right, the occasional car buzzing by on our left. No one had stopped for us, but by my estimation we weren't terribly far from Salem's city limits. What the hell had gotten into Maria? I called out and jogged after her as fast as my own boots would let me, but she hadn't even slowed; she'd trudged into the tree line and promptly disappeared.

"What the hell!" I shouted.

But, the instant I reached the spot where she'd suddenly peeled off, I understood what had drawn her away from the road; it was there, calling me, tugging at me like the tide, drawing me forward in one long rush. Power. An immense power, like nothing I'd ever felt before, so alluring I was already among the trees before I stopped to wonder what I was experiencing, the road a good thirty feet back. I froze. How had I lost that much time? I didn't even remember stepping into the grass. I pressed myself against the nearest tree and stared off into the woods, hoping to find the source of this strange, seductive energy. But instead, I spotted Maria moving between the trees, her dark blue pantsuit barely distinguishable in the twilight gloom that seemed to be getting deeper and deeper. She no longer walked awkwardly, which probably meant she'd kicked off her shoes.

"Maria!" I called. I let go of the tree, thinking to chase after her and drag her back.

But that's when it pulled again.

I ended up on my knees in the dirt, breathing labored, my hair hanging in limp tendrils against my sweaty back. Time had passed; it was a few degrees colder out, the sky darker. The road was nowhere in sight, and I couldn't tell which direction I'd come from. Trees—their leaves that peculiar shade of burnt orange which fades to brown as darkness settles—were all I could make out. My hands hurt. In the dim light that remained I noticed tiny scratches all along them, though a few were deeper and bled a little. My coat bore similar marks, the leather scoured here and there, but still intact—probably all that had saved my arms from getting cut up. I got to my feet, hoping to find Maria, but refusing to take another step. Whatever was pulling us, compelling us to wander aimlessly through the forest, was powerful. Strong enough to take our minds along for the ride. Which meant I sure as shit didn't want to meet it.

Of course, what I wanted didn't seem to matter. The power drew me in again, this time with such force it felt like someone had shoved a hand into my lower back and thrust with everything they had. The shock of it stole my breath away, which is all that stopped me from screaming.

I came to in darkness.

This time, I found myself wrapped around yet another tree, hugging it so hard my biceps were threatening to cramp up. I was bathed in sweat, breath ragged, chest tight. The sun had set completely, leaving the air frigid, the woods unbelievably dark. All except for a pinprick of light in the distance. A fire, big enough to be seen from a distance, its light emerging between the trees like it would through the iron grates of a glowing furnace.

I used the tree to right myself, brushing at the dirt on my hands and knees, wincing at the cuts on my palms. My cheek hurt, and I knew without touching it that I'd sliced it open on something. When I stood, I could feel my ankles throbbing and the blisters on my feet; my boots were more fashionable than functional.

Still, I chose to limp forward.

Not because I was drawn to that distant fire, though the promise of warmth alone might have been enough to get me moving again, but because I could sense somehow that *this* was my intended destination. That somewhere among those flames was the power I'd fought against. Just as I sensed that maybe, just maybe, if I only stopped fighting it, I wouldn't be sucked back under.

But, even with my newfound determination to play along, it was slow going. Everything ached or burned. Honestly, I hadn't felt this shitty since my last training session with Scathach, when she'd tossed my bag—including the latest cell phone Othello had gifted me—into a gorge and told me to fetch it, climbing equipment not included. *That* had been a grueling ass day, but even then, I'd had the prospect of a nice, hot bath to look forward to. I seriously doubted I was going to find a great big tub out here in the wilderness.

Of course, it turned out I was wrong about that.

The man-sized cauldron—yes, I said cauldron—sat perched between two massive wooden pillars, beneath a bonfire that stood as tall as I was. Granted, I'd never actually seen a cauldron in person, but I knew instinctively what I was looking at; ironically, while *Hocus Pocus* had prepared me for many of life's challenges—the loss of a beloved pet, how effective salt is in a pinch, the repercussions for stealing candy—I'd never have guessed its greatest gift would be providing me with the proper name for a great cast iron bowl.

Fortunately, once I'd made peace with that, I was able to focus on the clearing itself, which turned out to be natural rather than man-made. Staggered cliffs surrounded the dell on three sides like an amphitheater, the stone interrupted only occasionally by industrious, scraggly trees which poked out at odd intervals, limbs clawing out from between the crags like fingers from the grave. And, from the edge of the valley where I stood hidden within the shadow of a tree, I realized there were people moving beneath that firelight.

A few dark figures stood on every cliff, cloaked and hooded, staring down at the valley's inhabitants: a dozen or so women in white dresses so thin I could see the shape of their bodies beneath, spinning in slow circles beneath the light of the moon. Two more cloaked individuals held Maria on her knees not far from the fire itself, although she seemed uninterested in struggling. If anything, she seemed captivated by the rising flames and the twirling women.

I drew my gun, wondering what in the hell I was going to do, when I saw a new silhouette—this one dressed in a red cloak, the hood wider and less imposing—emerge above the cauldron, stepping out onto the lip of a cliff's edge that must have led directly to the top of the bonfire. It was an eerie sight from my vantage point; it appeared almost as if the newcomer were floating in mid-air.

"The other has come," the woman said in a voice loud enough to carry, catching an odd echo that sent her words reverberating around the valley. That voice, a sultry, husky thing, sent shivers up my spine. When she spoke, the women in white ended their slow twirls, spinning as one to face the woods with such calculated precision it made my skin crawl. Their expressions were neutral. Bland. Empty.

"Come out, child," the woman called.

I felt the power press against my back, trying to thrust me forward into the light, but I fought it. I thrust my nails into the wood of the tree I hid behind and gritted my teeth, digging my poor, aching heels into the soil.

"Such willpower," the woman said. "But perhaps for the sake of one's companion?" She snapped her fingers, and one of the cloaked figures holding Maria produced a blade, pressing it against the detective's unprotected throat. I cursed inwardly.

"Perhaps not." She raised her hand to snap again, her pale hand and wrist hovering just outside that crimson robe.

"Stop!" I yelled. I stepped out into the light, gun pointed at the woman standing over the cauldron. The shot caller. The one who'd drawn us here. "Let her go or I'll shoot!" That pale hand lowered, but the knife at Maria's throat remained. Before I could yell out another warning, the woman reached up and slid her hands back, drawing the red hood away from her face.

And what I saw left me breathless.

CHAPTER 18

*A*lthough many people fail to recognize it, we're surrounded by beauty every day. A stunning smile. A graceful slope of cheek. A full-throated laugh. These small, bright treasures are not something we necessarily take for granted, but they don't always move us. In fact, more often than not, people shy from it. They catch a glimpse of something lovely, realize they're staring, and look away rather than risk embarrassment. This woman's beauty, on the other hand, was not the kind you could look away from.

Hers was the sort that captivated you with its stark contrasts, its flawlessness. It was there in the cast of her almond-shaped eyes, the curve of her cheekbones, the pout of her mouth. It was there in the way she held herself, one shoulder tilted up, her head cocked just so, as if listening to a sound only she could hear, the graceful line of her pale neck bright against the spill of her raven black hair.

I felt the pull again, only gentler this time. Not a shove from behind, but a caress across my face. I started to lower my gun, certain I didn't want to shoot this woman. She hadn't done anything to me, after all. And yet, the instant I thought *that*, I knew it wasn't my thought; if I simply waited for everyone to hurt me *before* I drew on them, I'd be dead already. I raised the gun and sighted. "Knock that shit off," I growled.

The woman smirked. "I am doing nothing. It is your own reaction to my power, to the power gathered here, which has drawn you. Just as it drew this one." She pointed at Maria. "Her power resonates with ours. Yours, however..." she trailed off, studying me.

"Well, if it wasn't ye, then why not let us walk out of here and pretend this never happened?" I asked, more concerned about our immediate safety than with anything she had to say.

"If that is what you wish, please feel free to go. You are, of course, welcome to stay. To share in the power. As long as you do not interfere with the ritual."

"Ritual?" I lowered the gun, though I didn't holster it; holding a shooting stance too long would only tire my arms out, and I wasn't sure yet what was even going on. Questions first, death and mayhem later. And who says you can't teach an old dog new tricks?

The raven-haired woman flashed a smile and waved imperiously, signaling for the women in the white dresses to resume their gyrations, their breath fuming in the night air, wrapping around their heads and throats like tendrils of fog. The two cloaked figures holding Maria stepped away, the blade disappearing in the process, and approached the base of the cliff behind the fire, lost momentarily from sight.

I considered going to Maria's side, but decided against it; from where I stood, I had the better vantage point and could shoot anyone in the valley—always a plus. Of course, it might have been simpler to drag Maria to her feet, slap her until she regained her senses, and get the fuck out of here. Except part of me wanted to stay, wanted to know what had dragged Maria and me into the dark woods against our will.

I regretted that desire almost immediately; the two cloaked figures appeared once more at the woman's side, a man strung between them. Even before they dragged him completely into the light, I recognized that exceptionally masculine face, partially hidden behind his mane of long, dark hair. Maximiliano. Except his face didn't have that same quiet intensity as it had the night before. Much like his sister's, it had taken a beating: blood had dried on one side of his face, caked along his skin. From where I stood, I couldn't make out the bruises, but I knew they'd be there. Of course, his face looked practically untouched compared to his bare upper body, which was a mass of discolored flesh and more dried blood. Two jagged slashes crossed that once finely sculpted chest from collarbone to just above his nipples.

"What have ye done to him?" I whispered.

The raven-haired woman reached out, winding her finger in Max's hair. "This one swore he had nothing to tell us, that he knew nothing. I asked him if he'd cross his heart," she said, sliding one fingernail along the unmarked flesh, along the edges of his wound, "and hope to die. And yet, he continued to lie to us." She removed that finger, pressed it to her lips, and spoke so softly I almost didn't hear her over the crackle of the fire. "X marks the spot," she murmured.

One of her cloaked flunkies drew that knife and raised it as if preparing to sink it deep into Max's heart. I saw the big man's eyes flick to the naked blade, not afraid, but tired. So tired.

I fired before I could even think about it.

Everyone froze, including the one with the knife. I held my gun pointed skyward. "The next bullet goes into ye, if ye even t'ink about puttin' that knife any closer to him," I growled, glaring at the blade-holder.

"I did warn you not to interrupt," the raven-haired woman said, the weight of her displeasure palpable. She waved a hand, and the dancing women froze again, facing me. "I wish it hadn't come to this," she said, and for some reason, I believed her. Of course, that didn't mean I gave a shit. I stared down the nearest woman in white. "Make a move and I shoot," I warned.

"I think not," the woman said. She spat out a word, making a sound as she did so that was almost like a hum, the word itself unintelligible.

I dropped my gun with a curse, hissing through my teeth. My palm was red, not yet blistered, but it was a burn—no doubt about it. My gun lay smoking in the dirt, the metal almost white hot, though it cooled shockingly fast. "My sisters!" the raven-haired woman called, raising her hands. "Tonight, the Coven of Ipswich discovers what has happened to our own! But first," she pointed at me, then Maria, "we deal with our uninvited guests."

I had a brief moment to marvel at the sheer, freakish coincidence that we'd inadvertently stumbled upon the very witches we'd been seeking before I realized that—according to this strange woman—Maria and I were the uninvited guests.

Great. Just great.

CHAPTER 19

Fights, in my experience, are rarely the carefully orchestrated dances you see in John Woo movies, or even Zack Snyder's gritty, freewheeling panoramas with their epic voice-overs. In reality, they are haphazard, chaotic messes. In a real knock-down, drag-out fight, you're as likely to slip and bust your face as to be expertly thrown and manhandled. Hell, most people are as likely to break their own hand throwing a punch as they are to get knocked out taking one. Naturally, experience helps—especially when you're up against amateurs—but no matter how well you're trained, no matter how many times you've delivered a finishing blow or fended off a bigger, stronger opponent, no fight is guaranteed to go down precisely how you predict it will.

Honestly, you'd have a better shot winning the lottery.

Which is why, as the women stalked towards me, I knew my odds of walking away unscathed were pretty damn slim; getting jumped by a mob, even one made up of barefoot women in sheer dresses, was sure to be a messy, ugly affair. But that's the thing about my life: it had rarely dealt me the best hand, but it didn't seem to give two shits if I played by the rules.

Which was good.

Because I had an ace up my sleeve.

I broke into a run, except to call it "running" would be like saying an Olympic sprinter "jogged" across a finish line; I moved with inhuman speed, cutting the distance between myself and the women in half between one breath in the next. By the time I was among them, they'd managed only to raise their hands up in a universally defensive stance, protecting their faces, too surprised to do much else.

But I wasn't aiming for faces.

I brought down the first woman with a savage kick to her knee from the side. She shrieked and fell to the ground, low enough that my elbow took her in the back of her head. She crumpled, her scream of pain cut short by the blow. The next woman had stopped shielding herself and turned to face me, which meant my front kick connected with her gut and not her hip, as I'd intended. She flew back into two others with enough force to send them all sprawling into the dirt. Four down. I spun, searching for my next opponent, but it was too late.

Because, despite all my training, I was still far too used to fighting people. Regular, average, ordinary people. But these women weren't ordinary. They were witches. Witches who very likely had never planned on fighting me at all.

You see, it turned out this was the only true drawback of my enhanced speed and strength—my obliviousness. In the superhero flicks, the world simply slows down for the would-be hero, as if their brains could somehow process things faster, allowing them to dodge bullets and fists with ease, even make minute adjustments to inanimate objects. But that wasn't what it was like at all; I moved fast, hit hard, and had almost no time to recalibrate. Since going to Fae, my body reacted far faster than my brain. Which, sadly, meant I occasionally failed to think things through before taking action.

Like now.

I found the remaining women encircling me, their hands raised as one, not defensively this time, but palms up, arms stiff and straight. They were chanting, harmonizing in an eerie, sing-song language that raised the hairs on my arms. I tried to move, to shoulder check the nearest of them, but managed only to drift forward in slow motion, almost as if I were underwater—the spell they cast keeping me from gaining any kind of momentum.

Still, I ground my teeth and inched towards the nearest witch. She was young, younger than the others, and I could tell she was surprised to find me able to move at all beneath the weight of their magic; the whites of her eyes showed as I closed in, and gravity began to reassert itself as she gaped, her chants forgotten. I grinned and took a full step, driving my heel into the ground, the pain of my poor, blistered feet a thing of the past.

Adrenaline was a wonderful thing.

Just one, I figured. Take out just one of these witches, and I'd be able to lash out at the others, to break free from this cage and end this. But in the end, it didn't matter; I'd forgotten about the witches I'd knocked to the ground. They joined the circle, chanting at a slightly higher pitch, their dresses soiled, faces tight with anger. Suddenly, the sensation doubled, making it truly impossible to move. I felt lighter than air. Ephemeral, as if I'd shed my skin. Which is why I could only watch as one of the cloaked flunkies approached the bonfire with Maria in tow.

"End this," the raven-haired woman said.

The voice from beneath that hood was male and barely audible, but I caught his firm resolve as he raised Maria's chin, a blade of polished ivory positioned over her throat. "We will feed you to the flames, but not alive, as so many of our kind have been condemned. Know that your sacrifice serves a purpose. May the Triple Goddess embrace you, sister."

"Stop!" I wanted to scream, but couldn't. I couldn't feel my lips. My tongue. All I could do was strain with everything I had to free myself, to save that slack-faced detective, to save the wounded, tortured Max. To protect everyone I'd put in harm's way. Because that was the truth; if I hadn't called out to Maria when I first saw her, if I hadn't sought out Max and his sister to find my answers, if I hadn't begun poking around into those disappearances to prove I cared, none of us would even be here. Which meant that, yet again, I was to blame for the shitstorm that had descended upon us.

At that precise moment, I felt something alien respond to my anger, to my frustration. I could feel it graze my floating consciousness—all the power gathered here, the same power which had practically dragged me kicking and screaming into this valley. And it could sense what I wanted. It knew how I felt. That alien power reached out to me, neither a shove nor a caress, but an embrace that made my own power dance like ants over my skin, almost the way it felt to have goosebumps break out all over one's body.

But it was more than that.

It was like my pores had all opened up at once. Or like I'd shoved a fork into a light socket. Or like I was the fork. Or maybe the outlet. Basically, the sensation was indescribable. But what I *could* describe was the immediate effect: I could feel my body. Which meant I could move. I flung out my arm, screaming, the burgeoning power within me seeking a way out. It soon found the power inside me, the kernel of invisible something that I accessed whenever I truly lost control. The two powers mingled, and the world froze.

Froze, and then time began to wheel backwards.

It began slowly, at first; Maria and her cloaked executioner moon-walking away from the roaring bonfire, the very flames flickering eerily in reverse. The two dirt-stained witches facing me lowered their arms crawled back under their companion and laid still. The circle around me widened as the witches backpedaled, my power returning them to their original positions. The instant I realized what was happening, I sensed I could make it go faster. That I could spin the world on its axis until the sun broke out over the horizon, the day reclaimed. I felt the power in the valley urging me on, as if it could care less what I did, so long as I did it now.

I fed on that built-up ritual energy, that magic, and channeled it into my own, letting my power spill into the air. Soon, the witches in white were dancing once more, Max and the raven-haired woman no longer in sight, Maria on the edge of the clearing, drawn by the very force I'd channeled. In the back of my head, a voice whispered, insisting I could do more. That I could go back further. How far back, it wondered? Could I use it to rewrite history, to save everyone, even those I'd already lost? But, before I could answer that question, the power fled, chased away by some other force.

"Enough!"

The raven-haired woman marched towards me, weaving through her scantily clad companions, moving so gracefully, so beautifully, she seemed unreal. Or perhaps surreal—like a dream come alive. Time reasserted itself, and the witches in white skittered away, surprised to find me standing in their midst. Several of the cloaked figures drew blades, though each seemed to be made of a different material. I felt for my gun, hoping to find it returned to its holster, but it wasn't there. In fact, I couldn't see it anywhere. Damnit.

Fortunately, I wasn't the only person armed with a gun in the valley.

Unfortunately, that meant my only backup was Detective Maria Machado.

"Hands up and drop the weapons," Maria shouted from the edges of the forest. "And Quinn, what in the actual *fuck* is going on?"

Everyone turned to look except the raven-haired woman, who simply laughed. It was a joyous, sensual sound—the euphoric burst of laughter that comes trickling out of a partially closed bedroom door a moment after the moans die away. She held up her hands. "Do as she says and put away your weapons," she declared. "It seems we will not be conducting our ritual, after all." Murmurs of discord whispered through the ranks, but the blades disappeared. "Now, you two," she looked from me to Maria, "please be so kind as to join me." She smiled, turned, and headed for the cliffs. "We have much to discuss."

"Ye must be out of your ever-lovin' mind!" I snapped. "Ye may not remember it, but ye just tried to have us killed for the sake of your precious ritual. Not to mention what ye did to poor Max."

"What's that about Max?" Maria yelled.

"Later!" I hissed.

Maria started to say something in response, but I was too busy staring after the raven-haired woman, who merely glanced back at me over her shoulder from a couple dozen feet away. "Oh, I remember," she replied. "I have seen your little parlor trick before, after all. Spinning yourself back through time using all the magic we worked so hard to cultivate, very clever. But then your father always thought he was quite clever, too. Constantly popping up where he wasn't invited and pretending like he knew everything you were going to say before you said it."

"I'm sorry, me what?" I asked, slack-jawed.

She turned all the way, then, and stared at me with one perfect eyebrow arched high, half her face obscured in shadow. "You don't know," she said, turning it into a statement.

"Know what?" I asked, breathlessly. "Who the hell are ye?"

She looked away, those shadows crawling further across her face, her expression lost to the darkness. "My name is Morgan. I was a...friend of your father's."

I took an inadvertent step forward. "Who? Who was he?"

Morgan cocked her head, revealing a sad, solemn expression. "Come with me, Merlin's daughter. We have a great deal to talk about, I think."

CHAPTER 20

I found myself standing outside the mouth of a cave tucked away in the furthest recesses of the ridge, where we had all gathered at Morgan's request. I was surrounded by a host of unfamiliar faces, many of which bore unhappy, even irate, expressions; the once shrouded figures had removed their hoods, while the women in white had been given cloaks of their own lest they catch cold and die. At my request, they'd given one to Maria and me, as well. The bulky robes weren't particularly fashionable, but I needed the extra layer of warmth; I hadn't exactly come prepared to go traipsing about in the cold. Besides, between hiking haphazardly through the woods, throwing down with a bunch of witches, and being a living conduit for an absurd amount of ritual energy, I was starting to feel a little like a tattered dishrag.

Oh, and let's not forget about the added shock of finding out my father was supposedly Merlin.

As in, *the* Merlin—preternatural prophet, King Arthur's greatest advisor, and arguably the most powerful wizard ever to have walked the earth.

"Everyone, please return to your homes," Morgan was saying, facing the coven. "I will call on you all, soon."

"But what about Pearl? And Dolores?" one of the witches asked. It was the young, frightened woman from before, except now she sounded defiant. Angry, even. "Without the ritual, how will we find them?"

Morgan raised a hand, silencing the crowd before the discontent could spread "The ritual was a means to an end. Its purpose was to help us find our missing members. The power we gathered called to these strangers," she dipped her head towards the two of us. "The magic even allowed one of them to use her power rather than allow unnecessary bloodshed. As such, we should assume that the magic served its intended function, and that these strangers will find Pearl and Dolores for us."

"Fat fuckin' chance," I muttered under my breath.

Maria elbowed me. Hard.

"What was that for?" I asked, rubbing my side.

"Stop trying to get us killed," she hissed.

I scowled at her but said nothing. One, because she likely wouldn't believe that I'd saved both our lives only a half hour before. And two, because she was probably right. It was best to play along, for now; we could always pick a fight later.

By the time I returned my attention to Morgan and her coven, I found their ire had mostly dissipated. In fact, most appeared mollified by Morgan's explanation, as if it was all very logical that the ritual magic conveniently plucked the two of us up out of nowhere to come and save the day. Personally, I didn't buy it; I'd felt the magic coursing through me, and not once had I felt any sort of conscious intent. If anything, I'd sensed a remarkable amount of pliancy, as if the magic would have done what-ever I wanted of it—even if that meant tearing a hole in the fabric of time.

Which, now that I was thinking about it, bothered me quite a bit. I felt like all I had were questions. Like, what was this power of mine? How did it work? Would I really have been able to turn back time indefinitely? And, most importantly, with enough juice, how far back could I go?

What if I could literally undo all my mistakes?

What would I give to make that happen?

"But if what you're saying is true, then why shouldn't we stay, and hear for ourselves what is to be done for our sisters?" the young woman chal-lenged, interrupting my troubled thoughts. She spun to look into the faces of her companions as if willing them to agree with her.

This time, however, it wasn't Morgan who answered. "Serena, you forget your place," a man said, placing one dainty hand on the woman's shoulder. I recognized the voice; it belonged to the cloaked flunkie who'd held the knife to Maria's throat. He was a dark-skinned Middle Eastern man with heavy-lidded eyes.

"Why am I the only one who seems to care what happens to them?" Serena asked, shrugging off the man's hand, glaring at her fellow witches. Most met her gaze evenly, their expressions neutral, jaded—as if they'd seen it all before. None looked away.

"Enough," Morgan said. "Serena, stop acting like a petulant child."

"But High Priestess, I—"

Morgan hissed, and the coven as a whole took a collective step back, leaving Serena to stand alone before the High Priestess—whatever that meant. "Have I not sworn to bring your friends back?" Morgan asked, her voice so soft it was almost a whisper. Power played in the air, pulsing off the raven-haired witch in waves that I could feel from a dozen feet away. It wasn't quite as intense as what Maria had done earlier that day, but it was close. And yet, somehow it bothered me a hell of a lot more. Just a taste, and I knew this was the barest brush of Morgan's true power—as if she were merely flexing all that latent metaphysical energy for Serena's benefit.

"Yes, High Priestess," Serena mumbled.

"Then is it me you doubt?"

Serena shook her head so fast her hair flung about her shoulders. "No, High Priestess. I..." she sobbed, covering her face with her hands. "I'm just worried about them. That's all. I'm...I'm sorry," she said, the sobs coming faster now. "I thought we'd finally get some answers."

Morgan's power disappeared in a rush that left us all shivering. She nodded and reached out with both arms. "Come, little one," she said, and Serena stepped into that embrace. "It's alright," Morgan reassured her, patting the back of Serena's head like you might a child. "We will find them, I promise."

Serena nodded, her response muffled against Morgan's cloak. The remaining coven members began to disperse, winding their way back down the cliff face using the dwindling light of the bonfire to see by, retracing their steps down the same crooked path we'd taken to get up onto the ridge. "Bertrand," Morgan called to the petite, dark-skinned man, "please, see to our guests and collect the sacrifice. I will be along shortly."

Bertrand nodded and waved to the two of us. "Come with me."

"He can't be serious," Maria said, staring at the cave with a dubious expression. I shrugged and started to follow after Bertrand, but Maria held out a hand to stop me. "This is a bad idea."

I sighed. "Listen, I appreciate your concern for me well-bein', but I t'ink Max is in there," I said, sidestepping her outstretched arm. "Which means I'm goin' in whether I have a guide or not."

"Wait, Max is what?"

"Ye heard the High Priestess mention a sacrifice, right?" I asked. I jerked my chin towards the cave entrance. "Well, Max was their sacrifice. And me guess is this is where they were keepin' him hostage."

While Maria was processing that, I headed after Bertrand, who hadn't stopped to wait for us before heading into the mouth of the cavern. But Maria snatched at the folds of my cloak with her uninjured hand before I could get very far. I glanced back, realizing Maria bore almost no signs of being dragged through the forest against her will—none of the scratches I'd collected, nor the matted, leaf-strewn hair. If anything, she looked the same as she had before heading into the woods. Hell, even her shoes had survived; she must have walked with them in hand, though somehow her feet hadn't suffered in the exchange. Which made me wonder, If I hadn't fought against the pull of that alien power, would I have ended up similarly unharmed?

Oh well, wasn't like I could turn back—oh, wait.

"What is it ye want, now?" I asked, shaking off that thought.

"Why do I have the feeling you know a hell of a lot more about what's going on than I do?" she asked.

"Because I do," I replied, drawing the robe out of her hand.

Of course, that wasn't going to help me much; the only reason I knew more than Maria did was because she knew jack shit, whereas I at least had the faintest inkling of what was going on. Maybe. Hopefully. Really all I knew for sure was that, somewhere in that cave, I might find some answers to questions I'd been asking my whole Goddamn life.

Oh, and Max. Couldn't forget about Max.

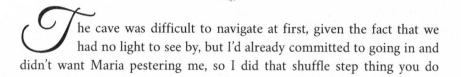

*T*he cave was difficult to navigate at first, given the fact that we had no light to see by, but I'd already committed to going in and didn't want Maria pestering me, so I did that shuffle step thing you do whenever it's too dark to see. Which is why, when Bertrand hit the light switch mounted on the wall ahead of us, I looked remarkably ridiculous; I stood like a surfer, arms held out to either side, my stance wide, as if I were coasting along the tunnel of an epic wave.

"This way," Bertrand said, taking off down a corridor that branched off from the entrance. I sighed and followed, noting the oddly decorative sconces strung between thick wires that ran along the cave walls. After the primitive cauldron display, I had to admit I was surprised; modern electricity didn't jive with the creepy, cloak-wearing coven I'd met thus far. But if the 21st century motif bothered Bertrand at all, he didn't show it.

In fact, he seemed hardly interested in us at all; he led us to a massive chamber without so much as a word. The ceiling high above our heads dripped with toothy stalactites, chairs of various sizes and shapes circling what appeared to be an altar carved in the stone. "Choose," Bertrand said, holding out his hand towards the chairs. "But choose wisely." Then, before either of us could reply, he turned on his heel and left.

"D'ye t'ink he quoted *Raiders of the Lost Ark* on purpose?" I asked.

"What?"

I glanced over my shoulder at Maria. "Ye know, Indiana Jones."

"Never saw it."

"Well, now I know we'll never be friends."

"Took you long enough," she quipped, brushing past me towards the chairs. She studied them, ignoring my frown, and finally settled into a sturdy, upright number that looked like it could have been used as a stress-inducing torture device, its back so rigidly straight that it should have been impossibly uncomfortable.

"And which will you choose?" Morgan asked, appearing behind me like a wraith.

"Jesus Christ!" I said, pressing a hand to my harried heart.

"My apologies," she said. "I didn't mean to scare you."

I simply glared at the woman. "Ye don't scare me," I insisted, as if saying it aloud would make it true. Trouble was, she did scare me. The power I'd felt from her earlier had set my teeth on edge—reminiscent of what I'd felt when in the presence of a minor god, as opposed to a witch. Lately—and while I would always bet on myself in a straight fight—I was beginning to realize that without my anti-magic cage to even the playing field, I was way out of my league. Which meant, if I wanted to survive, I was going to have to learn how to use the magic I'd been given, and fast.

"Don't be silly," Morgan replied, dismissively. She approached the altar, giving me a wide berth in the process, her smile placating. Once before it, she showcased the chairs once more. "Choose."

"Is this some sort of test?" I asked.

"Testing my patience, maybe," Maria muttered.

"Of sorts," Morgan replied, ignoring the detective.

I took a long look at the various options, eyes flicking from one chair to the next. The circle had everything—a plush leather Chesterfield, a freshly stained adirondack, a two-toned plastic beach chair, a worn recliner, a wobbly director's chair, a paisley-patterned armchair, a hand-carved rocking chair, even a barstool. I eyed all of those and more, lingering on a few, but mostly wondering what this test was all about. Finally, I spoke. "I'll stand."

Morgan laughed that bedroom laugh of hers. "Interesting choice."

"But she didn't choose," Maria observed.

"Even refusing to sit tells me something about her," Morgan replied. "We are each of us drawn towards the familiar, or the preferred. You, for example." Morgan tipped her head towards Maria. "You chose the Brewster. It is an unforgiving piece of furniture, endurable only to those who have immaculate posture. It is also gaudy, in its own way. I take it you are used to suffering discomfort for the price of pageantry. Between that and your repressed magical aura, I'd say...Catholic?" Morgan chuckled at the reaction that earned, waving off Maria's attempt at a reply. "A guess, nothing more."

"So, what is it ye learned about me?" I asked, partly out of curiosity, but also because I could sense Maria's sudden discomfort. Ordinarily, I'd have let her dangle, but she had a bad habit of threatening to arrest or shoot anyone who made her uncomfortable.

Speaking from experience.

"I learned that you refuse to play by the rules. You were drawn to the barstool, out of familiarity, I expect. Also, the captain's chair," she noted, indicating a beautifully carved piece of furniture smothered in black leather. "It is an ambitious choice. But instead you chose to stand, in spite of the fact that to do so is the least comfortable option. My guess is that you are a stubborn creature. Willful. Arrogant, perhaps."

"Aye, well, ye missed a few identifiers, but otherwise spot on," I replied, tipping an imaginary hat.

Morgan's smile widened. "I aim to please. Now, I believe we had business to discuss."

"About that, I—" I began.

Morgan held up a hand. "Please, give me a moment. I'd prefer to save us all some time." She reached into the folds of her robe, and, for an instant, I felt a prickling urge to defend myself from whatever she was about to do. Maria tensed as well, her own hand settling on the butt of her gun. But all Morgan withdrew from her robe was a brown leather pouch, tied up at one end with ribbon. If she noticed our sudden relief, she had the grace not to say anything. In fact, she hardly seemed to take note of us at all; she unwound the ribbon and deposited the contents of the pouch into one hand. "Long ago," she said as she slid her fingers over the items in her hand, "there were those of us who practiced the art of divination. For many practitioners, it is an imprecise method. They turn their tarot cards or read their tea leaves and make bold guesses about the future, merely speculating. But their focus is always very narrow. A question with only one correct answer."

Morgan closed her hand into a fist and cast it over the altar as if she were throwing dice. But what spilled across that stone table wasn't dice. They were bones. Tiny bones like those you might find in your fingers or toes. And eye teeth, their points worn down with age. Some were braided with string, others painted in odd, orbital patterns. Morgan studied the result, probing here and there with one thin finger. "I see. You've come looking for more than merely the brujo. You've come seeking my sister's wards, as well the one who took them. How interesting."

"What the hell is she talking about?" Maria asked.

I shrugged.

"Are you not tracking missing Fae?" Morgan asked, pausing to look up at us.

I frowned. "We are, but how d'ye know..." I drifted off. Her sister's wards. Her sister. "You're Morgan," I said, incredulous.

"I believe we've been over this," she replied.

"Morgan *le Fay*," I added, for emphasis.

Morgan's smile dimmed. "I always hated that nickname."

"Who the hell is Morgan le Fay?" Maria asked.

"She's..." I struggled to answer Maria's question. Not because I couldn't, but because the answer was so complicated. How was I supposed to explain that Morgan le Fay was a figure as infamous, not to mention as controversial, as any ever mentioned in literature? That—as Morgause's sister—she was also reputedly related to King Arthur. That, according to legend, Morgan le Fay was an enchantress who may have apprenticed under Merlin or Morgause, or both, depending on which story you believed.

"That's not important," Morgan replied. "What matters now is that you find and save what few of your Fae charges remain while you still can."

"What about your missin' witches?" I asked, suspiciously. "And what about what ye said about me da? If ye t'ink I'm goin' to leave here before findin' out everythin' ye know, you're in for a surprise."

Morgan smirked. "Your father would have chosen to stand, too, you know. But no, Merlin's daughter, I expect I will have to answer your questions, if only to save you from yourself. But, before I do, I believe you should ask some of your friend." She waved, and I realized Bertrand stood behind us, one of Max's arms draped over his shoulders, straining to support the much bigger man. Max looked better than he had on the edge of the cliff, but then his chest wounds were covered by a ragged black t-shirt which hid the blood, leaving only his injured face to mourn.

Still, it was enough.

"What did you do to him?!" Maria screamed, rising from her seat, hand going for her gun.

Morgan barked a command in an unfamiliar language. Maria froze, and I don't mean she simply stopped moving, I mean she literally froze, her body covered in a thin veil of frost. "I will release your friend once she has calmed down," Morgan said, turning to me.

I shrugged. "We aren't friends."

Morgan cocked an eyebrow. "Oh?"

"High Priestess?" Bertrand interjected, sounding pained.

"Set him down in the recliner," Morgan replied. "After that, you may leave. Thank you, Bertrand."

"Of course, High Priestess."

Once Max was settled, Bertrand did as directed, leaving Morgan and I staring at one another from across the room. Despite the chilly weather, Maria seemed to be thawing out a bit; a small puddle had formed at her feet. Max, meanwhile, was practically comatose. His eyes fluttered a bit, but he seemed otherwise completely unaware of his surroundings. "Why d'ye torture him?" I asked.

"I will let the brujo answer your questions," Morgan replied, walking around the altar and making her way towards a small shelf carved into the wall that I hadn't noticed before. On it stood a chalice and a series of flasks and vials. She began mixing these with practiced, precise motions. "Administer this potion. It will help heal his wounds and revive him. Once he's awake, ask your questions. I think you'll find our actions justified, if a bit...barbaric." She finished preparing the potion and walked it over to me.

"Why should I trust ye?" I asked, brows furrowed.

"Don't be ridiculous. You should never trust anyone," she said, passing me the chalice.

That actually made me smile. "Then what is it ye want?"

"After," she replied, jerking her chin towards the invalid man on the recliner before leaving the chamber, her red robe fluttering theatrically behind her. I glanced down at the cup in my hand and swirled the pale yellow liquid, wondering if she'd be bold enough to poison the man we'd come to save. Bold enough, maybe, I decided. But somehow, I sensed she had other plans for us.

"Alright, big guy, it's time to take your medicine," I said.

Here's hoping I'm right and it doesn't kill you, I added, silently.

CHAPTER 21

*M*ax's eyes, red-rimmed and bloodshot, flew open. He drew in a deep breath the way you might after almost drowning, the expansion of his lungs causing his shirt to pull taut against his broad chest. Then, he screamed. It was a blood-curdling sound, so tortured I clamped my hand over his mouth, ignoring the odd sensation of his lips and tongue —coated in the sticky contents of the liquid I'd poured down his throat— against my palm. "Hush!" I said. "It's me. It's Quinn. No one is goin' to hurt ye."

Max whimpered beneath my hand, but the screaming stopped. His eyes flicked to my face and widened with terror, then surprise. But once I was sure he wasn't going to continue screaming, I slid my hand away, rubbing my palm against the borrowed cloak. Max licked his dry, cracked lips. "How did you find me?" he asked.

I shook my head and spotted Maria in my peripheral vision; she was thawing out, but slowly, the spell Morgan had cast still in place. "No idea," I replied. "I'd like to say luck, but I'm startin' to wonder if there isn't some sort of cosmic plan in the works that keeps puttin' me in shit situations. Are ye alright?"

Max began to shake his head, then frowned. He sat up, running his hands up and down his chest. The shirt was stiff with blood, and yet Max didn't seem to be in any pain. "They cut me," he said, almost as if to himself. "But then why…"

"Their High Priestess gave me a potion that was supposed to heal ye," I explained. I raised a hand and passed it along the side of his face, fingers trailing along his brow. "Even your face is lookin' better. The burns are already gone."

"But why would she do that?" Max asked, leaning into my hand, letting it cup his cheek as if drawing some sort of security from my touch. I fought the urge to pull away, sensing that the big man needed the contact.

"She said you'd have answers for me," I explained. "Like why, for example, is it that she and her coven broke into your store and kidnapped ye in the first place?"

Max closed his eyes and brushed his face against my palm, like a cat scent marking his territory, his stubble prickling my skin. "She and her witches tracked Camila and me. They thought we had taken their sisters."

"But ye didn't take 'em," I said, turning it into a statement.

"No, I believe it was our old master. The man Camila and I used to work for. The one who took your Fae," he said. I drew my hand back, clenching it into a fist. Max opened his eyes, staring placidly at me, his expression oddly content. He looked anesthetized, lobotomized. Drugged.

"Are ye sayin' ye know who took the Fae?" I asked, shocked.

"I suspected when you read the ingredients. They are similar to what Camila and I would have used to cleanse an evil place. But when you showed us the picture of that room, I knew." He shivered, then cocked his head a little, staring at me. "You are really pretty, you know that?"

I scowled at the man, wondering just what had been in that potion. It had healed him, that much was obvious, but it also seemed to have loosened his tongue quite a bit. At least for the time being. "Were ye goin' to tell me any of this?" I asked, the first hints of anger leaking into my voice. "And what d'ye mean, 'cleanse an evil place'?"

Max smiled. "Did you not feel it? The evil? It stains the soul, what they did in that room. But it stained the room, too, I bet. The whole house, perhaps."

I shuddered, recalling the eerie sensation that had crawled up and down my skin the whole time I was in that shack. Was that what they'd been trying to do when the cop had found them? Clean up after themselves? "Ye didn't answer me first question. When were ye goin' to tell me the truth?"

"I could not," Max confessed. "The risk to us was too much. Camila wanted to help you at first, even if it meant having to run again, but once she found out what you were she wanted nothing to do with it. With any of it. And I did not blame her."

"Oh, well that's just great," I spat. "T'anks for all the help."

Max merely looked at me, too docile to appear guilty.

"Fine. So, what d'ye mean, 'run again'? Run from what?"

"Our former master."

"And who the hell is that? More importantly, what the fuck does he want with the Fae? Or the witches, for that matter?"

"I do not know what he wants," Max admitted, light returning to his eyes in tiny increments, as if he were trying to claw his way back from wherever Morgan's potion had taken his waking mind. "He never showed an interest in dealing with the Fae or covens in the past. If anything, Victor went out of his way to avoid other supernatural groups. He preferred his anonymity."

"Victor?" I asked. "That's his name?"

"*Si*, Victor."

"And ye and your sister used to work for him?" I fought the urge to grab the man by his shoulders and shake the answers out of him. The problem was I had too many questions. I hated feeling like this—so powerless and uninformed. I took a deep breath. "Why? Who is he? Tell me everythin', no more secrets, or I swear I'll hand ye back over to Morgan and her coven."

Max met my eyes without flinching, which told me all I needed to know about the lingering effects of the potion; threats meant nothing to him at the moment. Still, he answered my question. "He found us when we were still very young," Max began, "living in Miami after our *abuela* passed away. Camila was working at a club. I worked in the kitchens. We had left Boston behind us, but not our traditions. Not our magic. Somehow, Victor found us. He knew what we were and sought us out, promising to pay more money than we had ever seen. We knew it was too good to be true, but again, we were young. Young and foolish and poor." Max's eyes had glazed over with a faint horror, his hands balled into fists in his lap. "Victor was a genius. A madman. He called us his assistants. His technicians."

"What exactly did he have ye doin'?" I asked, puzzled by Max's fear.

"Very little, at first. Camila cleaned the lab. I was his driver and did any heavy lifting that needed to be done. But, as time passed, that changed. Camila started having nightmares about something she'd seen in the lab but would not talk about it. After that, I began to get suspicious about the late night trips to the Everglades we took once a week. I wanted to know what he was hiding. So, one night I offered to join him, to see for myself what he was doing. He agreed. Gave me the heavy duffle bag he always took from the trunk and told me to follow him…" Max trailed off, as if he didn't want to continue.

"What was it? What d'ye see?"

"The bag was full of body parts. Severed arms and legs." Max shivered. "But, of course, I did not know this at the time. We took a boat. It was dark, impossible to see, and yet he seemed to know exactly where he was going and how to get there. We did not speak. I lost track of how long we were out there. An hour, maybe more. I began to worry he was planning to push me overboard, to feed me to the alligators. But finally, we stalled. He had a flashlight and turned it on the water, and that's when he took the bag from me and opened it, tossing the limbs overboard. It took me a minute to realize that was what they were. Limbs. Sometimes nothing but hands and feet. And, of course, that is when I saw them."

"Saw what?" I asked, a sense of unease tightening my gut. Maybe it was the story itself, or maybe it was the way Max looked as he told it—the dread on his face building with every uttered word.

"Monsters. Creatures that looked like men but were not. They tore at the body parts with their teeth, drifting around our boat. Maybe a dozen of them, scaled, with lizard eyes and crocodile teeth. I was horrified, and I knew he could sense it. 'These are my pets,' he said. That is what he called them. His pets. I called them *monstruos*, monsters. But that only made him laugh." Max shook his head, his hair falling about his shoulders, the tension in his shoulders straining the seams of his t-shirt. "He laughed and said, 'No, those I make back at the lab. Would you like to see?' But I could tell he was not asking. That is when he told me his real name. His full name. Doctor Victor Frankenstein. And, as I watched those lizard men feast on the remains of what had once been people, I believed him."

I merely gaped at the muscled Hispanic man in front of me. Dr. Frankenstein? Seriously? Still, looking at Max's troubled face, I could tell he wasn't lying, or at least that he believed what he was saying. Honestly, a few years ago, I might have laughed in his face. But these days I knew enough supposedly fictional characters to start a band of would-be legends. Morgan le Fay. Dorian Gray. Johnny Appleseed. Hell, if I only I could carry a tune, we might have gone on tour and rocked the world's collective faces off.

"Alright, let's say I believe ye. What happened then? What does any of this have to do with why he's here, and what he's done with the Fae and witches?" I asked, prompting him to finish his spiel; assuming Morgan was right, we really didn't have a whole lot of time to waste gabbing the night away.

"After that, I wanted to leave," Max continued. "Camila, too. But we were also scared, and that is when we met Ygor, a Fae who worked for Victor. He was the one who bound us to his master. He used magic we'd never seen before to do it. Fairytale magic. After that, Victor used our knowledge, our abilities, to perform more experiments. He liked to say he was a pioneer, bridging the gaps between magic and science."

"But ye managed to get away?"

"Si. In the end, it took us six years to figure out how to break the hold Ygor had put on us, and even then, they were able to track us. Last time, Ygor caught Camila, alone. He tortured her." Max met my gaze and held it, his two-toned eyes imploring me to understand how much that had pained him, and I knew in that moment that the effects of the potion were no more. "Once she escaped, we decided to come back home, to Boston. We had heard there was power here, power enough to ward away Victor and his minions. But now I am beginning to think I was wrong, that maybe we drew him here. That we are to blame." Max hung his head.

"Ye t'ink he's stealin' away Faelin's and witches to get to ye?" I asked, cocking an eyebrow.

"No. That is not his way. If he wanted to come for us, he'd have done it quietly. Whatever he is doing now, there is some other reason behind it. He has only evaded notice this long because he stays in the shadows. Nothing about this, other than the disappearances themselves, is subtle. He has the Faerie Chancery out looking for him, and now the Coven of Ipswich. It is unlike him to be so...reckless."

"How do we find him?" I asked, at last.

"I do not know."

"Would ye tell me if ye did?" I asked.

Max looked up at me, the sincerity on his face making him appear much younger, despite the stubble playing over that long, thick jawline. "I would. I am sorry for not telling you the truth. Trust is not something that comes easily to me, anymore."

"I know the feelin'," I quipped, then sighed. "So, it's back to the drawin' board, then."

"Not necessarily," Morgan chimed in, stepping into the chamber as if on cue. "I believe I can find this Doctor Frankenstein, if that is what you wish."

I turned to face the High Priestess, wondering how long she'd been listening, but decided it didn't much matter; if we wanted to find the missing Fae, I'd be willing to take whatever help I could get—depending on the price. "What is it ye want in exchange?" I asked.

"That's simple. When you rescue your Fae friends, make sure you find Pearl and Dolores," Morgan replied, holding out her hands as if that were the obvious course of action. "As High Priestess, it's my job to make sure everyone in our ranks is safe and accounted for. If, as I suspect, they have been taken against their will to replace this man," Morgan pointed at Max, who actually flinched, "and his sister, I would like to see them returned."

"What about me answers? The ones ye promised me?" I asked, eyes narrowed.

"They'll be here when you get back. Consider this an act of good faith. You save my people. I help you save yours. Then we can have our little chat, and I can tell you all about that power of yours." She glanced pointedly at my wrist and the sundial attached to it with an arched eyebrow. "Though it seems someone has already tried to do so. Wherever did you get that, by the way?" Something flashed behind her eyes. Envy, I think.

"Ye know if ye double-cross me, I'm goin' to come for ye," I threatened, shielding my watch from view with one hand, unwilling to share its origins with a complete stranger who'd tried to have me killed in an alternate reality.

"Of course," she replied, smirking.

"Then tell us what ye know, unfreeze Maria, and we'll be on our way," I said, pausing long enough to draw Max to his feet, hefting the heavy son of a bitch with ease. He seemed surprised, then wary, as if I'd tricked him somehow by being so much stronger than I looked.

Boys.

"The brujo stays," Morgan interjected.

"Wait, what? Why?" I asked.

"Insurance, to ensure you return with my people as well as your own."

I frowned. "But I need him. He knows who we're goin' up against. What we're up against. If ye want me to find your witches, he has to come."

"Then the woman who is not your friend stays," Morgan replied with a shrug, as if it made little difference. I glanced over Max's shoulder at Maria, who was likely only a few minutes away from regaining use of her extremities. Max turned, noting Maria for the first time, and gasped.

"Let's be clear," I said. "If we don't make it back with your witches in tow, you'll what? Sacrifice her?"

"This one?" Morgan asked, eyes wide in surprise. "No, of course not. Beneath all that Catholic guilt and repression, she is quite powerful, but unfit for sacrifice all the same. She does not worship as we do. No, if you fail, I will gather the coven and we shall seek out this mad doctor ourselves. But if you succeed in rescuing the Fae without also saving our sisters, her life will be mine. She will serve me, serve us, until the day she dies."

"Deal," I said, shrugging.

"Quinn!" Max hissed. "What are you saying?"

I shrugged. "Look, we don't have time to negotiate." I gave Morgan my full attention. "When she thaws out, tell her what I agreed to, and why. And let her know she can shoot me when I get back, if she gets pissy about it." Of course, what I didn't say was that Maria's life expectancy here was a hell of a lot better than it would be if we went after Frankenstein and his people. Sure, Maria had some juice. But she wasn't bulletproof, she wasn't immortal, and she refused to use her powers. In a fight like this, she'd be a liability.

Max gave me a long, steady look that I couldn't decipher, although he didn't seem particularly pleased. Morgan, meanwhile, nodded. "As you like. Now, come. I'll find this man you are looking for." She beckoned us to follow her.

I spared one last glance over my shoulder at the ice sculpture that was Detective Maria Machado and grinned, wondering if Morgan had any clue what she'd just done. Asking *me* to trade Maria's freedom for Max's, as if that was some kind of moral dilemma? Please. Maria was as likely to put a bullet in the High Priestess as she was to "serve until the day she died." If there was one thing I could count on, it was the fact that Maria Machado was the biggest pain in the ass I'd ever known.

And Morgan wanted to keep her around indefinitely?

Good fucking luck with that.

CHAPTER 22

*I*t turned out Morgan's plan to find Frankenstein required scrying for him—pinning his location down using a faintly pink crystal tied to a braided rope. She spun the new-aged relic in slow circles over a map of the area, explaining that she could use the scrying crystal to pinpoint his location, as it was drawn to his magical signature. When I'd asked why she hadn't simply done the same to track down her witches, she'd rambled off some archaic shit about how witches were often hard to track—how persecution had trained them to hide their powers, their auras, from the rest of the world.

Including, it seemed, each other.

"So, how d'ye find Max and his sister?" I asked. Then a question occurred to me, one I should have thought of it a long time ago. "Wait, what put ye onto their scent in the first place? Why go after 'em, at all?"

"They were easy to find. The siblings are tainted with something—a darkness—that we sensed at the homes of the missing," Morgan explained. "It was this we tracked. Besides, the magic of a brujo and a bruja is very different than ours. They aren't as practiced at hiding themselves."

"What's the difference?"

"We commune with the spirits of the dead," Max interjected. "We do not belong to a coven. Many of us practice alone, in secret. We do not draw as much attention this way."

"Does that mean ye can call ghosts? Get 'em to talk to ye?" I asked.

"It is possible, but—"

"Found him," Morgan interrupted. "Here. He's not far. Sixty miles inland, or so."

I arched an eyebrow. "Sixty miles isn't far? Are ye jokin'?" My feet ached at the very thought of walking another ten feet, let alone the distance it would take to get to town, get a car, and drive out into the middle of nowhere—assuming there were roads.

Morgan glanced at Max. "Does this Doctor practice magic, himself?"

Max shook his head.

"Then all you need to do is create a Gateway," Morgan said, as if it was that simple.

"Well, I hope ye can create one, then," I said, rolling my eyes.

"You can't?" Morgan asked, eyes wide with surprise.

"Should I be able to?"

We stared at each other for at least thirty seconds before a wide smile spread across Morgan's face, her eyes twinkling with amusement. "Oh, yes. This should be fun."

I held my hands out in front of me, willing a magical Gateway to form for perhaps the thirtieth time, muttering obscenities under my breath.

The three of us had left the cave and stood bathed in the dying light of the diminished bonfire, its embers smoldering, the large pile of wood that had once fed it turning slowly to ash. Still, it gave off the faintest heat, pressing at my back like a spooning lover. Max, who'd begun shivering the moment we left the cave, stood by that fire, warming himself, while Morgan taught me how to create a Gateway.

Or tried to, at any rate.

"Listen, why don't ye make it and be done with it?" I pleaded, dropping my hands yet again. Despite Morgan's insistence that I should be able to do this, I hadn't felt even an inkling of power, and we'd been at it for almost an hour. "Besides, I'd rather not be here when Maria dries off," I muttered.

"She won't break free of my spell until I wish her to," Morgan said, matter-of-factly. "Now concentrate. Remember, visualize your power in front of you, and use it to pull at the fabric of space. You'll have to learn how to do this or you won't make it back here."

"I could just give ye a call to come get us when we're done?" I suggested.

Morgan frowned. "I can't tell if you're being lazy or stubborn."

I sighed, then raised my hands the way she'd shown me, trying to visualize my power—whatever that meant. Truthfully, I had no idea what my power looked like. Hell, I only had the vaguest notion of what it *felt* like. Telling me to visualize it sounded like some Zen meditation shit, like imagining someone's aura, or having an out of body experience—crazy mental cartwheels so abstract you could damn near talk yourself into believing they really happened. "It's not workin'," I growled.

"What is the problem?" Max asked, the sound of his voice close enough that I knew he must have stepped away from the fire to join us. I realized I'd been closing my eyes, so I opened them. I found the big man standing close by, running his hands up and down his bare arms for warmth.

"She is closed off from her power," Morgan said, sounding miffed. "I've never met a practitioner with less experience accessing their raw potential. Who was your teacher?"

"Teacher?" I asked, arching an eyebrow.

"Yes. Who instructed you on how to use your gifts?"

"I...no one. I only found out I had magic of me own recently. When I broke into Fae, met me aunts, and found out whose daughter I was." I saw Max giving me a sidelong look and waved it away. "It's a long story."

Morgan, meanwhile, was busy staring at me, her mouth hanging open. She'd pulled her cloak closed, secure behind that blood red robe. "What has he done?" she whispered.

"What d'ye mean?"

"Who? Who was your mother?" Morgan demanded.

I seriously considered lying, or simply telling Morgan it was none of her business, but something about the way she held herself, the way she stared at me, made me want to say it. "Her name was Morrigan, sister to Macha and Badb."

"The Crow Goddess? No...no, no, no! That idiot!" Morgan reached for the sky with both hands and the bonfire suddenly blazed to life. In fact, somehow it grew taller than it had been before, the flames licking up the sides of the cauldron, scorching the base of its bowl. "What was Merlin thinking bearing a child with one of them?!" she hissed, clearly not paying attention to Max and me. I stepped back, putting some distance between us, just in case.

Max settled a hand on my shoulder. "My guess is you are overthinking it," he said, casually ignoring the raving High Priestess. "Magic is as much a part of the world as it is part of us. Try not to think of it as your power. Think of it as the power around you. The power that binds all living things."

"Are ye seriously tellin' me to use the Force, Obi-Wan?" I asked.

Max chuckled. "Whatever works for you. But try it. I'll keep an eye out in the meantime."

I sighed, but did what he asked, largely ignoring Morgan; she was muttering in an unfamiliar language, stomping her feet into the ground as if that might help. With every kick, the bonfire blossomed, spewing flame. It was actually kind of neat, in a batshit crazy sort of way.

I shook my head and closed my eyes, concentrating not on my power, but on the world around me. I could hear it, beyond Morgan's voice and the roaring crackle of the bonfire. Beyond the valley, the night was full of music: insects whirring, the fluttering of an owl's wings, the cracking of an overladen branch, the biting wind whistling through the trees. I lost myself in those sounds for a moment, and that's when I felt it. A gentle tug at the center of my being, and a voice whispering in the back of my mind.

Let me show you, it said.

And, suddenly, I knew what to do.

I called my power forth. Not the power I'd put on display earlier, but more an extension of myself, almost as familiar as my arms and legs. It was the same power I'd used to push against the invisible bars of my magical cage. A power that seemed to hover over me, like a cloud of magical energy I could only now see. I took that cloud and made it real. Solid. I envisioned two hands tearing into the night, fingers like claws, and watched as they shredded the fabric of space.

"*Dios mio*," Max said, his voice startlingly close.

I opened my eyes. A Gateway stood before me, perhaps twenty feet away. It was small, too small for us to fit through, and beyond was a bright, sunlit beach. Definitely nowhere near us. Still, it was a start. Except there was something else not quite right with it. I'd seen Gateways before—both those created by GrimmTech and those used by friends.

But I'd never seen any quite like this.

"Is it supposed to look like that?" I asked.

SHAYNE SILVERS & CAMERON O'CONNELL

"No," Morgan replied, close enough to make me jump. She must have stopped throwing her tantrum and joined us. "But then, I think very little with you will be as it is supposed to," she added, studying me. "What Merlin has done, what you are...it has not been done since the Old Ones walked the Earth. I simply don't understand."

"Don't understand what?"

"Why he would have taken such a risk."

"What risk?" I asked.

Morgan pointed to the Gateway I'd created, its edges lined with green flames that seemed to be cauterizing the very air. A green haze spread from it like a fog spilling out over a lake, illuminated by brief bursts of light as if electricity played in those murky depths. I noticed that whatever it touched, grass or tree limb, seemed to wither on contact. It was eerie, not to mention chilling. "The risk of awakening a creature with the power of a god and none of the limitations."

I wasn't sure what to say to that, so I decided to change the subject and focus instead on the task at hand. "Well, any chance ye could help this 'creature' make that damn t'ing bigger? Otherwise, I'm goin' to have to use me power to make meself shrink," I joked.

Morgan's eyes narrowed. "So, you've learned to change shape as well, have you?"

I simply gaped at the woman, wondering how in the hell I was supposed to keep rallying mentally considering all the shit that had been thrown at me in the last couple hours.

"Only kidding," Morgan said, grinning. Then frowned. "I hope."

CHAPTER 23

The sun was rising over the crest of the horizon by the time I mastered opening a Gateway large enough for Max and I, the light creeping in between the trees in slow increments. I should have been exhausted, but I wasn't. If anything, I felt better than I had in hours, as if using my newfound abilities had rejuvenated me somehow. The small scratches had faded, healing several times faster than they would have had I been human, little more now than pink lines crisscrossing my otherwise pale skin. I took a deep breath of the chilly morning air and let it out slowly, relishing in the feeling of being alive. I always felt this way in the early mornings. It was as if time were standing still, the entire world holding its breath, anticipating what would come next—and I, content to wait with it, if only for a little while.

"You ready?" Max asked, coming up alongside me from behind. He and the High Priestess had gone back into the cave while I worked, searching for a change of clothes for the poor, shivering man. I had to admit I was impressed by Max's willingness to tag along with his former captor; if he felt any ill will towards Morgan and her coven for carving him up, he seemed able to keep it to himself. I turned to find she'd found him a thick, woolen button-up which rode his shoulders so close that the tails of the shirt hovered on top of his jeans, high enough that he'd flash skin whenever he raised his arms. But at least he wasn't shivering anymore.

"Aye, as ready as I can be," I replied.

I cast a hand out and focused, the energy curling around a single point in the distance, welling up from inside me. The rush that came with it brought a sudden heat to my cheeks, as if I'd sprinted across the clearing at full speed. Green flames began to writhe in mid-air, surrounded by a cloud of green fog that spread wider and wider as the Gateway grew. After almost a full minute, I released the magic and stared at the result—a little taller than I was, the shimmering Gateway had opened to reveal a dark meadow, accompanied by the sound of swaying grass and the stench of cow manure.

"That was well done," Morgan said, peering over my shoulder.

"T'anks, but ye should see me friend Callie do it. She can call one up like that," I said, snapping my fingers for emphasis. "Hers is all silver flame, though. Very Biblical."

"Is it, now?" Morgan asked, brow furrowed, lips pursed. She tapped one finger to her lips, seemingly lost in thought. "Callie...that's a little coincidental..."

"What is?"

"Nothing, nevermind. You should get going. Once the sun rises, you'll be exposed. Best to sneak in and save your people under the cover of night, don't you think?"

"And your people," I added.

"Oh, of course," Morgan said. "Of course."

I narrowed my eyes, but decided not to comment; she was right, we'd have better odds of moving around undetected if we hurried. I waved to Max. "Come on, let's go."

Max hesitated.

"Gettin' cold feet?" I asked, teasing. But the serious look on Max's face stopped the smile on my face from spreading. I studied the brujo, realizing for perhaps the first time that Max had the least stake in this game than any of us. Between agreeing to help find the missing Fae and the promise of securing some answers for once, I had plenty to motivate me. But with Max's sister safe and his own freedom guaranteed, what did he have to gain by coming with me? Had I really signed the poor guy up for something so dangerous without considering what it might mean for him? What if he never made it back? Who would tell Camila what had happened to her brother?

And why had it taken me so long to consider his point-of-view?

"No, that is not it," Max replied, locking his eyes on mine. "The truth is I am tired of running from Victor and his monsters. Before you take me with you, I want you to know my priority is not to save your people. I intend to kill Victor Frankenstein, if I can find him. I will help you if I am able, but the Doctor must die if my sister and I are ever to find peace."

"You're worried ye won't make it out of this alive," I guessed.

"That is not true," Max said, shaking his head. "Death no longer frightens me. But if Victor catches me, alive, I will pray for death. I am sure of it."

"I'll make ye a deal," I said, stepping close enough to the broad, muscular man that I could feel the heat radiating off his body. "No matter what happens, I won't let him get his hands on ye. I won't leave ye behind, even if it means draggin' your lifeless body through the Gateway meself." I tried to make it a joke by lightly punching his arm, but Max didn't so much as smile.

"And what if you, too, are captured?" Max asked, his voice almost a whisper.

"Then I will intercede," Morgan replied, watching the two of us with cool, calculating eyes. "I will leave neither of you to become playthings of this man. I have no desire to see what fresh horrors he might fashion from your bodies. But," she raised a warning finger, "I would much prefer it if you simply came back in one piece. Much more convenient, that way."

I grunted but smiled. "Well, we wouldn't want to inconvenience ye."

"I should hope not. Now, hurry."

I took hold of Max's wrist and led him towards the Gateway, though not by force. I couldn't blame the guy for being reticent; he'd seen what the Doctor did to his victims, whereas all I could do was imagine—and even that made me want to reconsider what we were about to do. Still, when Max didn't fight me, I resolved to do what I could to help him. If he could afford to be brave, I could afford to be a little selfless. Besides, Max was right. Saving the Fae and the witches was a priority, sure, but someone like Dr. Frankenstein roaming about, playing God by manipulating magic and science? By enslaving people against their will? He had to be stopped.

And we'd be the ones to stop him.

CHAPTER 24

*M*ax and I stood outside the only structure in sight, the rising sun at our backs like a ticking alarm clock, threatening to go off at any moment. I reached out and pressed a hand to the slick plastic surface in front of me and pushed, marveling at the lack of support as the glorified shithouse wobbled back and forth. "Ye know, this doesn't seem right," I said, eyeing the Porta Potty dubiously.

Max squatted low and studied the ground, running his hands along the dying grass. "Things are rarely as they appear with Victor. Ah, here." Max dug into the dirt with his bare hand until he held a black wire as thick as my finger. He pried it free and rose, tearing up the dirt in the process as more of the wire was exposed. "We should follow this."

I arched an eyebrow. "Follow it where?"

Max turned a slow circle, though there was nothing in sight. "I am thinking down." He tugged on the wire more forcefully until enough was revealed to see where it led. "He always liked building underground laboratories. Less conspicuous. This," Max jerked his chin towards the portable outhouse, "was probably for the men he contracted to build his lab."

"Then what's that?" I asked, pointing to the wire.

"Video surveillance."

I must have made a disgusted face, because Max laughed. "He often had cameras installed during a job. That way, if any of the workers saw anything, he would know." Max's smile faded as quickly as it had come. "I had to get rid of a few bodies over the years. Men I had met and joked with who saw or heard too much. Who might have talked."

"Does that mean he's watchin' us right now?" I asked, scanning the horizon for signs of life. "Does he know we're here?"

Max shook his head. "I doubt it. He is careful, but not paranoid. Once the job was done, he would have turned the cameras off. But we should still be careful. There may be others." Max pointed in the direction the wire ran. "I think we should go that way. Wherever this leads, hopefully we can find an entrance nearby."

I shrugged, having no better ideas, and followed as the big man took off, tracking the slight bulge in the dirt that led from the outhouse. We walked in silence for a while, until at last I felt compelled to break it. "Your sister lied to me, ye know," I said, casually.

"What?"

"About who kidnapped the missin' Fae. She blamed the witches, hopin' to get me to go after 'em and rescue ye. But she knew right away who had really done it, didn't she? Same as ye."

Max sighed but didn't take his eyes off the path of the wire. "Camila was once a powerful bruja. She could summon the spirits of the long dead and hear them clearly. They told her secrets they never uttered while they were alive, so glad were they to taste life once more. But when she was captured, Ygor broke her. Somehow, he turned her power to commune with the dead into something else. Now, whenever she feels she is in danger, she loses control." Max glanced back over his shoulder, locking onto my face with his one blue eye.

"How so?"

"Did you see our shop? What was done to it?"

I nodded. "Aye, it looked like a bomb had gone off."

Max winced but nodded. "That was Camila."

I shook my head, not content to merely leave it at that. "And that makes it alright for her to lie, is that it?" I demanded.

"No, it does not. But guilt often makes liars out of us all."

I clamped my mouth shut, my response dying on my tongue before I could say anything else. Was Max right, had Camila felt guilty about lying to me? I thought back, recalling how she'd refused to meet my eyes, how she'd flinched whenever I mentioned her burns. What would I have done, if someone I loved were in danger, and the only solution I could offer was wholesale destruction? Would I have sent someone else in my place? No, of course I wouldn't have; I'd never have trusted anyone else with something that important. But that was my hang-up, not Camila's. "Just make sure she apologizes once this is all said and done," I said, at last.

Max grunted.

"What?" I asked.

"I figured you for the type to hold a grudge," he admitted. "Especially after what you did to Maria, leaving her there." He looked away, and I realized he was disappointed in me. And that—for some reason—it stung.

"It's not that simple," I said, defensively. "Maria is a Regular." I held up a hand before Max could argue with me. "I know she's a witch. But she hates her power and refuses to use it, which means, for all intents and purposes, she's a Regular."

"So, what? You left her behind because you think she's weak?"

"No, I left her behind because Maria is walkin' on the edge!" I hissed. "Trust me, I know what it looks like when someone has a death wish."

Max halted suddenly, turning so abruptly we almost collided. "What is that supposed to mean?"

I looked away, kicking at the dirt in frustration. "It means I'm startin' to realize I don't know meself quite as well as I once did," I replied. "A year ago, I'd never have agreed to find a bunch of missin' strangers. Or risked me neck tryin' to save 'em."

"What changed?" he asked, searching my face. I marched past the man rather than answer his question, and we walked in silence. Frankly, I wasn't avoiding the question because I didn't have an answer, but because I wasn't sure I felt up to talking about it. Finally, against my better judgment, I broke the silence for a second time.

"Someone I loved died," I said, staring at the ground in front of me, but not really seeing it. "She died because I was too busy t'inkin' about meself, about what I wanted. I took her, took our time together, for granted. Now I've got almost nothin' left in this world to care about. No family. Very few friends." I huffed, breath pluming. "I know what Maria has gone through. Is goin' through. But she has to find somethin' to care about. Somethin' to keep her goin'. Otherwise, I don't know how either of us—"

But I never got to finish, because that's when the ground gave out beneath our feet.

And darkness swallowed us whole.

CHAPTER 25

I groaned, rolled over, and collided with a fleshy mass. Someone grunted in pain. Max, judging by the voice, which meant he was alive, at least. That, or we'd died together and were simply waiting to be processed. I sat up, woozily, and found we were at the bottom of a sloped shaft, some thirty feet below the meadow above, the opening visible through the hole we'd fallen through. Max and I must have tumbled down, I realized, slamming into the sides and each other on the way, which would likely explain why I felt so banged up. "Where are we?" I asked, coughing.

"Ventilation shaft?" Max suggested, clambering onto all fours. It was darker this far below the surface, the air thick and heavy and cloying. I reached out with both arms, hands brushing metal on either side. An air vent. We'd fallen through an air vent.

"We're either the best spies in the world, or the worst," I said, shaking my head.

"What do you mean?"

"We go lookin' for a secret underground lab and fall into the ventilation shaft. What are the odds of that, d'ye t'ink?" I ran a hand through my tousled hair and tossed it over one shoulder, marveling at the series of coincidences which had led me here. "Anyway, what d'ye reckon we see where this leads?" I said, deciding to focus on the task at hand.

Max paused to study the shaft as if wondering whether he could make it back up, but apparently decided against it. "After you," he said with a sigh, shuffling to give me enough room to pass by.

"Tryin' to stare at me ass, is that it?" I teased, trying to lighten the mood.

Max chuckled. "No, although I probably will, now that you mention it." He shifted his weight from side to side, shoulders bumping against the walls. "This way, if the vent gets too narrow, I will not block the way forward."

"See, and here I thought ye were just a handsome face," I muttered as I sidled past.

"*Por favor,*" he said, placing a hand against his chest. "There is a body here, too."

I rolled my eyes. "Any chance ye have a light? Otherwise I'll be crawlin' blind."

"What about your phone?"

"Dead," I replied. Max nodded, reached into his pocket, and passed something over to me. A Zippo. "I didn't realize ye smoked."

"It belonged to my father. I keep it as a reminder from when I was a little *niño*. But it should still work."

I flicked the lid open, let it fall back on its hinges, and flicked the wheel with my thumb. A small flame illuminated the darkness, casting a faint orange glow that extended far enough down the shaft ahead that I could make out a slight curve leading off to the right. I snapped the Zippo shut. "This should do."

I felt Max's hand on my arm, less visible now that I'd ruined my night vision. He squeezed, gently, then let go. "If we live through this, you should let me take you out for a beer," he said.

I scoffed. "Screw that." I started forward on my hands and knees, letting the silence build for just a moment before glancing back over my shoulder. "If we make it out of here in one piece, we're takin' shots."

"And then will you marry me?" Max asked, his tone playful.

I turned back, ignoring the rush of heat his comment had sent to my cheeks, and started worming my way through the air vent. "Shut up."

His masculine laughter chased me down the ventilation shaft.

Still a cocky little shit.

CHAPTER 26

*T*rue to Max's fears, the ventilation shaft narrowed as we went, gliding along on our knees and elbows like we were in a warzone, me checking our progress every so often with Max's Zippo heirloom. Fortunately, it remained wide enough for both of us to move, though so slowly that soon all I could focus on was the next few feet and the sound of our combined breathing, my brow stained with sweat from the effort. Unfortunately, I wasn't sure what I expected to find; I'd never crawled through an air vent before and had nothing to compare it to. In the movies, there was always an air duct to look through—something to give us a sense of where we were or, better yet, a way to spy on one's enemies. But at this point, we'd been moving for what felt like hours, and still had found nothing.

Then, at last, I saw the light.

Not metaphorically, thankfully—at this point I wasn't sure I had anything to look forward to on that front—but literally, a faint blush of luminescence creeping in around the bend. I moved forward gingerly, trying not to make any noise, until I could see the source. But, when I finally found it, I realized it wasn't an air duct, or an opening of any kind, really. It was a tiny camera with a mounted light attached to a white rat by a black leather band. The rat froze and stared at me, it's red eyes gleaming, then skittered off into the darkness beyond.

"Well, shit," I said.

"What was that?" Max asked.

But he never got his answer, because that's when whoever had sent the rat to find out who was traipsing through the air vents made their move. The vent shook so violently, so suddenly, I screamed, the sound of my voice lost among the shrieking of metal being ripped apart. In a matter of seconds, our section of ventilation was torn away, and Max and I were flung at least ten feet to the ground. I landed hard on my back, so hard it took my breath away. In fact, I was so busy trying to relearn how to breath, it took me a solid minute to concentrate on what I was seeing.

A creature stood above us holding the large metal vent it had torn from the ceiling, the box partially crumpled between its hands. But there was something wrong about how the creature held it, something off. One arm, I realized, was smaller than the other—and a different color. Both flexed as the creature tossed the air vent down the hallway, skidding along the floor with an awful, nails-on-chalkboard squeal. Then, with nothing obscuring my view, it turned to face me, and I could see the monster in its entirety.

And it was indeed a monster.

The thing's head was stitched together, its scalp barely visible, but the face bisected, two-toned, the jaw not quite lining up. The result was a face from my nightmares, teeth exposed here and there—lips, eyes, and nose not quite aligned. My eyes traveled down its body, too fascinated to stop, although a voice in the back of my head was screaming, telling me not to look. For some reason, its massive torso was all one piece, and—although mismatched—his arms seemed oddly functional; it stood with the knuckles of one hand pressed to the ground, the other held out for balance. The legs were bowed, giving the creature a humpbacked gait as it shuffled towards me, almost like a gorilla.

It wasn't the monster's appearance that made me scream, however—not even the slight drool emerging from one side of that shattered mouth, or the goop spilling from one of its lidless eyes. It was the skin-prickling, nauseating aura the creature gave off, like what I'd felt in that house with Robin, but worse. Magnified. It wasn't evil, as Max had claimed. I'd seen evil, felt it. This was simply wrong. An aberration, an abomination. Something that shouldn't exist in nature.

"Get away from me!" I yelled, struggling backwards, too horrified to get up and run.

But the creature didn't want me; it loped past me down the hallway, oblivious, breath coming in short grunts as if its lungs could hardly support all that mass. I fell back, my own breathing heavy, my heart racing. What the hell was that thing? Frankenstein's monster? And yet for some reason, I didn't think so. There had been something familiar about it. Something awfully familiar.

I shoved the thought away, not willing to dwell on it just yet.

"Well, look what we have here," a woman said, leaning over me. She had short blonde hair which didn't do her too round face any favors and wore what amounted to the attire of an elementary school teacher: frumpy dress slacks and a loose-fitting blouse.

"This one's a man," another woman added, pressing her boot against Max's face. I sat up and saw he was unconscious, bleeding from a head wound. The woman above him, a tall, thin brunette dressed head to toe in black leather, leaned over and sniffed. "A witch. But not one of ours."

The two women shared knowing glances.

"Dolores and Pearl?" I guessed, finding my voice at last, the horror of seeing that monster fading, but still present.

The two women's heads snapped around as one, and they stared at me like dogs who've heard a whistle. So, I'd been right. "Listen," I said, trying to get to my feet, "we've come to save ye. Morgan, your High Priestess, sent us."

"Just the two of you?" the blonde asked.

I bobbed my head as the brunette approached, smiling in relief.

"Good." The brunette lashed out, striking me in the head with the steel reinforced toe of her boot before I could think to dodge it. I had a moment, just a moment, to think before it all went dark...and all I could come up with as I lay on the floor, staring at the feet of the two witches we'd come to save, was that even the blonde's shoes were tacky.

Someone needed to call the fashion police, I thought.

And then maybe the *actual* police.

I woke up in a dim hallway, my wrists pinned above my head, shoulders on fire, head aching from the blow I'd taken. It was cold, made worse by the stone walls and floor, and I wondered how much more my body could take on this particular trip before it simply called it quits. Not much, I decided. Of course, ordinarily a kick like that—even to the temple—wouldn't have done me in right away, but a steel-toed boot could do a lot of damage to anyone, Fae included. Hell, if I'd been human, it might have killed me, which meant the witches Morgan had sent me to find were definitely not on our side.

That thought, combined with the chill, sent shivers up my spine.

Sadly, the instant I shifted my weight, another wave of pain—not my head this time—hit me. My wrists burned. Like literally burned, the stench of grilling flesh riding the air. I struggled, trying to get away from the insanely painful sensation and the sizzle of my flesh against the iron manacles. God, it hurt.

And the fact that I smelled vaguely like bacon only made it worse.

"Stop moving!" A tiny voice cried out. "It'll only hurt worse otherwise."

I gritted my teeth and froze, letting the manacles touch only the smallest piece of skin, a thin tendril of smoke wafting up into the air. Tears welled at the corner of my eyes. "Who's there?" I asked, voice laced with pain.

A light welled up further along the corridor, strobing once, then twice. "Over here," the voice said, softly. "Keep your voice down, or they'll come for you. The dark witch was convinced she put you in a coma, but she'll come back to finish the job if you keep screaming."

"Who are ye?"

"I'm Petal. Who are you?"

"Quinn MacKenna," I replied, too rattled to consider withholding my name. A series of titillated whispers spilled out down the hallway. Petal shushed them, and—now that I could see her better—I realized she was a pixie. What's more, she was a pixie I recognized from the files Robin had given me. "Petal. I remember ye," I said. "You're one of the missin' Faelin's."

"Then they *are* looking for us," Petal said, as if to herself. She strobed again, and I realized she was wearing manacles identical to mine, if only a dozen times smaller. "Which means Ariel was right."

"Ariel?"

"She's unconscious now," Petal explained. "But she swore she could sense someone looking for us. She even used her lifeforce to try and help you find us."

"Help me how?" I asked, grinding my teeth as I struggled to my feet, which at least took some of the strain off my shoulders. Of course, that still left the matter of the iron cuffs. Fortunately, I had an idea; I tore off pieces of my borrowed cloak with my teeth through my tears, wrapped the fabric around the manacles until the iron no longer touched my skin, and fought to control my breathing before I blacked out a second time.

"She sent you luck," Petal replied, once I'd recovered.

"Excuse me?"

"Luck. Ariel is a sylph, an air spirit. She said can bestow luck on other people, even from afar, though it tires her. Didn't you notice?"

I almost said no, but hesitated, realizing there might be some truth to what Petal was saying; I had noticed a series of remarkable coincidences lately. First, I happen to stumble upon the one witch's shop who coincidentally knows *exactly* who I'm looking for, a witch I call right as he's being abducted. Then, my brand-new rental car breaks down on the side of the road and no one picks us up, which ends with Maria and I being "magically" drawn to a valley occupied by the very witches we were hoping to find. And of course, there was the fact that Max and I had practically stumbled on this place by falling through a ventilation shaft in the middle of nowhere. I shook my head, wondering if it was truly possible. "Somehow I doubt this is what she was hopin' for," I said, raising my manacles for Petal to see.

"She passed out about an hour ago," Petal replied, mournfully.

I grunted. "So, that means our luck has run out, does it?"

Petal strobed again but said nothing.

"Who else is in here?" I asked.

"There aren't as many of us, now. Ariel, Eleanor, me, Jameson, Gilly, and...Ennis."

The way she said the ogre's name made me frown. "Where's Ennis?"

A low growl down the corridor caught my attention. I looked past the pixie and saw someone, something, move in the shadows, too big to be a man. Too late, I remembered the man I'd come with. I cursed myself for forgetting and turned to Petal. "Did the witches bring someone else down here with me?" I asked, hopeful. "A man?"

"No manlings," a deep, dull voice replied.

"He's right. There wasn't anyone else with them," Petal insisted, then caught sight of my face. "I'm sorry."

I shook that off. I'd have time to worry about Max later. "Ennis, is that ye back there?"

"Ennis," the voice confirmed.

126

"Listen, Alby sent me. He asked me to help ye." In actuality, the Pooka had asked me to tell Ennis to get his ass back to work, but it didn't seem the time to relay that particular message.

"Alby?" The ogre moved away from the wall and into the light. I gasped. Honestly, I would have taken a step back if I'd have enough give in my restraints, but instead I was forced to stare at the ogre's ruined body. Or what was left of it; one of Ennis' arms were missing, as was his right eye. They'd cauterized the wounds, leaving them unbandaged—blackened but not bleeding. I cringed, unable to stare at his ravaged face any longer. Granted, ogres were rarely the most attractive creatures to begin with, but what had been done to Ennis was truly awful, all the same.

And, what's worse, I knew where his missing appendages had gone.

"Aye, Alby," I said, voice breathless, doing my best not to flash back to the monster's long, knuckle-dragging appendage or that gunked-up eye.

"They brought him back like that," Petal said, quietly. "We tried to help, but there was nothing we could do."

I nodded dumbly but noticed something odd about Ennis' restraints in the process. I leaned forward, peering into the dimness. "Ennis, can ye raise your arm?"

The ogre raised his good arm, his one eye staring as if baffled by the limb itself. But it was enough for me to confirm what I'd seen: they'd chained him to the wall with the wrong manacle. The iron cuff rode tight around his wrist and must have been agonizingly painful, but I was beginning to suspect they'd drugged the poor ogre. That, or ogres had an inexplicably high pain tolerance. Otherwise, he'd probably still be screaming.

Of course, in this case that also meant the chains holding him were weaker, smaller, than they might have been—meant for a weaker, smaller creature.

Which gave me an idea.

A horrible, awful idea.

"Petal, I'm sorry for this," I said. Then, before she could respond, I called out to Ennis. "Oy, ye big lout! What the hell is wrong with ye?" Ennis blinked owlishly at me. "Alby said to come get ye. It's time to get off your big, stupid ass and get to work!"

"Work?" Ennis echoed.

"Aye! Come on, ye moron! This way!" I jerked my head.

Ennis—still looking puzzled—frowned, shrugged, and started walking towards me. Petal started to warn him not to pull at his bonds, but I shushed her. "Let him come," I growled under my breath. The ogre barely managed to take a step before the chain on his wrist drew taut. He tugged at it, scowling.

"Hurry up!" I urged. "We don't have all mornin'!"

Ennis grunted, then tugged harder, the muscles in his good arm bunching, purple veins throbbing under the faintly lime-colored hue of his skin. He growled, then groaned, inching forward. Petal covered her ears as the metal shrieked, the links of his chain stretching until at last, with an audible snap, they gave way. Ennis was free.

The one-armed ogre fell to one knee, breathing labored. "Work," he said, nodding to himself. He rose and began shuffling down the hall towards me, occasionally bumping into the walls in the process, clearly unaccustomed to walking a straight line with only one eye.

"Ennis!" I said, drawing his attention back to me. "Ye have to take me with ye."

The ogre slowed, but didn't stop, and soon he was nearly past me.

"I owe Alby money!" I said, desperately.

Ennis froze. "Owe?"

"Aye. I owe him lots of money. He'll want to deal with me, himself," I suggested. Honestly, I had no idea what sort of arrangement Ennis and Alby had, but at the moment my only shot at freedom was getting the ogre to break me out. Once I managed that, I could figure out how to rescue everyone else, Max included. Hopefully.

"Deal with," Ennis replied, nodding. He took two steps towards me, reached out, and grabbed me by the collar of my cloak, lifting me off the ground with that one obscenely strong arm.

"Oy! Let me go!"

"Owe," he grumbled. He yanked, hard, drawing me away from the wall, pulling my own chains as far as they would go and forcing my arms back as a result. I struggled, screaming in pain, but he ignored me, too focused on the fact that he couldn't seem to drag me away with him. By the time he finally realized it was the chains holding me in place, I was seconds away from rearing back and kicking the miserable fucker in the balls. But, before I was forced to, he dropped me unceremoniously onto my butt.

"Goddammit, ye stupid—"

But that was as far as I got before I had to duck the ogre's haymaker—an ugly punch that took a chunk out of the stone above my head. One of my chains fell limp in the process, no longer secured to the wall, though when I tried to lift my arm I found it attached to a block of mortar the size of my torso. The other chain Ennis simply pulled out of the wall the way you'd draw out a dipstick, forcing me to cover my unprotected head as rubble and debris fell around my shoulders. I shook the dust out of my hair and kicked at the dumb brute with everything I had. "Stay back!" I yelled.

Ennis took the blow on his side and slipped, unable to balance with only one arm, collapsing to the ground. Once on the ground, he made a pitiful sound—a keening wail that reminded me what had been done to him. Hell, what *I'd* made him do. My anger fled as I rose to my feet, struggling with the cumbersome weight attached to my wrists. Of course, now that I had some leverage, that wasn't as problematic as it might have been; I wound one of the chains around my boot, stepped on one of the links, pressed my heel into the metal, and curled my arm until the chain links squealed, then popped loose. It took a good deal of huffing and puffing, but eventually I was left with two manacles and only a foot or so of chain dangling from either hand. It wasn't ideal, but at least I could move.

I hurried to Ennis' side and propped him up, ignoring the stench of seared flesh that radiated off the ogre, not to mention the whimpers. Once he was solidly on his feet, I stepped away, putting as much distance between us as I could manage. "I paid Alby," I said between labored breaths.

"Paid?" Ennis echoed.

"Paid," I confirmed.

The ogre nodded and turned away, staring down the hallway as if listening to a song I couldn't hear, perhaps waiting for me to insist he return to work. The guy certainly seemed to have a one-track mind; no wonder Alby liked having him around.

"That was reckless," Petal whispered, once she realized the excitement was over.

I stumbled towards the pixie, reached out, and snapped two of the links in quick succession. Sure, her restraints might have been made out of iron, but they were also as thin as the chain of a tasteful necklace and—for someone my size—ridiculously easy to break. "Let's find the others and get the hell out of here," I said.

Petal stared down at her shackled wrists, frowning. "I don't think it's going to be that easy."

I slumped against the wall, a small headache threatening to burst over one eye. "Why not?"

"Because that won't work on Jameson." Petal said, pointing down the hallway, coincidentally the same direction Ennis was currently facing. I peered into the gloom, took a step forward, and groaned, palming my face. Jameson. Of course. I remembered now. He'd been the first to reportedly go missing—though perhaps only because his absence had been the most obvious.

Jameson the giant.

You know, maybe it was about time to wake that sylph the fuck up.

Because I was beginning to suspect my luck was shit without her.

CHAPTER 27

*a*fter freeing the other Fae who'd been taken by Frankenstein and his minions—the rest of whom were fortunately closer to Petal's size than my own—I had Eleanor, another pixie, watch the door while I tried to sort out what in the world I was going to do about the giant problem staring me in the face.

Pun intended.

"How did they even get him in here?" I mused, staring at the gargantuan hand of the largest Faeling I'd ever seen; the shackle encircling his wrist would have made a nice belt for someone Max's size. While Jameson certainly wasn't the largest giant I'd met—that honor went to Skadi, the Norse goddess I'd helped set free while in Russia—he was still ridiculously large, his body folded in on itself as if he'd been shoved into the alcove he occupied at the end of the chamber—an opening far bigger than the doorway Eleanor was guarding. Had they built the lab around him? Shrunk the bastard, then blown him up again?

Christ, magic pissed me off sometimes.

"It was the witches," Petal explained. "Jameson said he woke up here after one of them offered him a drink. I'm sure he's been warned not to take drinks from strange manlings, but giants aren't exactly the sharpest knives in the armory, obviously."

"But they didn't take anythin' from him," I murmured, gesturing. The giant turned his big brown eyes to me, nostrils flaring, the few wispy hairs on his head hanging limp over his bald scalp. But, no matter where I looked, I couldn't see any missing limbs. No signs of amputation or damage of any kind, really. So, what had they been after?

"They took hair and blood," Petal supplied. "We weren't sure why."

I frowned but didn't have time to dwell on what Frankenstein might have wanted with Jameson's DNA, because Eleanor came rushing back, buzzing past her fellow Fae, her tinny voice a high-pitched whine that reminded me of a faulty smoke detector. "Someone's coming!"

Of course they were.

I stared up at Jameson, who seemed relatively unconcerned with his predicament, as if being trapped underground were another day in the life of a giant. That, or giants were super chill by nature. Sadly, there was nothing I could do for him at the moment, and I think we both knew it. "I'll come back for ye, I promise!" I called up. Jameson smiled and flashed me a thumbs up, his two good teeth poking out of his lower gums like sunbleached tombstones.

I grimaced but returned the gesture before hurrying back to the others and reminding them of the plan we'd come up with, should we be interrupted. Together, the six of us pressed ourselves against the hallway on either side of the door and waited—even Ennis managed to meld into the shadows. The clatter of footsteps sounded as someone, maybe several someone's judging by the racket, approached the door. Muffled voices. The ding of a keycard.

The door hissed open.

"Now!" I yelled.

The pixies took off first, blasting past the two shocked witches. I had no idea which witch was which—try saying that five times fast—but at this point it didn't matter; I owed both an ass whooping for knocking me out and leaving me to rot in a glorified dungeon. Ennis came next, barreling through the doorway as the witches turned to pursue the pixies. That was pretty much the whole plan, if I was being honest. Distract and conquer. The ogre easily bowled over the blonde, but missed the brunette, who dove to safety on the other side of the door. Gilly—twin sister of the web-footed selkie I'd met back at Christoff's bar—carried Ariel through the gaping doorway, her bare feet slapping against the tile floor as she bolted to safety.

Which, as I'd hoped, meant I was batting cleanup. Of course, without my guns or my Fairyville Slugger, may he rest in peace, I was going to have to make do with what I had—a whole lot of pent-up frustration and a penchant for violence.

"Get off—" the brunette began to shout, holding out one hand towards Ennis, who had basically done all he could by falling on the blonde, letting his weight do the rest. But I didn't let her finish; if I'd learned one thing about witches over the last couple of days, it was that I didn't want them casting spells.

So, I resolve to break her jaw.

Thankfully, I'd practiced this and was careful not to snap her neck with the kick I fired off, holding back enough so I wouldn't inadvertently kill her. The leather-clad brunette spat blood as she toppled, eyes fluttering closed. "Aye, that's right. Payback's a witch!" I declared as I stood over her limp body.

I turned to find Ennis and the blonde looking up at me, neither struggling. I rolled my eyes. "Fine, no more puns." I bent down and hauled the blonde out from underneath the ogre, clamping a hand over her mouth before she could start leveling curses at me.

"Ennis, grab the dark-haired one," I said, tilting my head towards the witch I'd knocked unconscious.

"Grab," Ennis replied, rising awkwardly to his feet, slowly adapting to his one-armed status. Once upright, the ogre snatched one of the brunette's arms by the wrist, drug her to his side, and looked at me expectantly.

"Close enough." I turned my attention back to the blonde, whose eyes were wide and tear-filled, and shook her. "Knock that shit off," I snarled. "Listen, I'm going to ask ye two questions, and I want ye to answer those questions as fast and accurately as ye can. But if I even t'ink your castin' a spell, I'll hold ye down and let Ennis here eat your tongue." I leaned in until my lips brushed her ear. "Ogres love to eat tongues, especially when they find one still squirmin'," I whispered, intimately.

Not even remotely true, by the way.

That would be hobgoblins.

The blonde made a whimpering noise and I shook her again. "D'ye understand me?" Once I knew I had her full attention, I held up one finger. "Alright. First question, where is Max?" The blonde began to answer, her voice muffled behind my hand, but I pressed that same finger into the flesh of her cheek. "Remember," I insisted, "be very fast, very precise. Or say goodbye to that tongue."

She nodded, hurriedly, tears trailing down her doughy cheeks, and I let go. "He's with Ygor," she said. "Take this hallway, turn right, second door on your left."

I slammed my hand back over her mouth before she could continue and held up a second finger. "Question number two. And t'ink very carefully about this one. Is there anythin' I should know before I knock ye out? Because, and keep this in mind, if I come across any surprises on me way, I may just have to kill ye and leave ye to rot out of spite."

Sadly, the blonde didn't seem interested in answering that question.

Because that's when she fainted, slumping to the floor like a sack of potatoes, her face covered in a sheen of sweat and tear tracks.

"Well shit." I turned to look at Ennis, who shrugged, jerking the brunette off the ground. I sighed. "Any chance ye could take both of 'em and get above ground?"

"Shit," Ennis echoed, cocking his head quizzically.

I nodded, cursing. "You're right. Too much to hope for."

Thankfully, it turned out my luck wasn't complete shit after all, because the other Fae hadn't run off like I'd told them to; Petal and Eleanor came buzzing around the corner with Gilly and Ariel taking up the rear. "The way is clear ahead," Petal said. She took one look at my current predicament and actually smiled, her teeth razor sharp like that of a shark's. "Don't worry. Go save your friend. We can take care of the witches."

"Ye can't kill 'em," I instructed. "I mean it. I have to get 'em back to their coven, or else a...well, not a friend. More of a frenemy, really…" I waved that away. "Whatever. Let's just say someone I know would end up payin' for it."

Petal frowned but bobbed her head. "Fine, but if you find any of the others—"

"Oh, they're all dead." I glanced at Ennis' wounded face, at Ariel collapsed in Gilly's arms, and thought of those poor witnesses I'd met who would never see their loved ones again. I clenched my fists. "Trust me. They simply don't know it, yet."

"Glad to hear it," Petal said, flashing those honed incisors once more. "Come on, let's go!" The other Faelings fell in line as Ennis wrapped his huge hand around the wrists of both witches, dragging them across the tile floor like bags of trash. Given his prodigious strength, they'd probably end up with dislocated arms when they woke up.

Excellent.

Unfortunately, it wasn't until Petal and her cohort turned the bend and left my line of sight that it occurred to me to ask what the pixie had meant by "others." At this point, my hit list included Frankenstein, his monster, and Ygor...but were there more of these bastards down here?

I considered calling her back, but suspected I'd be wasting time Max didn't have; no matter what they had planned for the brujo, I knew I wouldn't like it, and that I'd blame myself if I showed up even a second too late.

Take the hallway, turn right, second door on the left.

Here's hoping I could trust the witch.

CHAPTER 28

I turned the corner half-expecting to find Frankenstein's monster looming in the corridor in all its grotesque glory, but the hallway was empty. As I ran, I marveled at how clean the underground laboratory seemed, how sanitized; it reminded me of a hospital. So, this was why Camila had refused to seek medical treatment, I realized. Guess I couldn't blame her; spending years in facilities like these, prying off butterfly wings in the name of science, had to take its toll.

Sadly, it turned out the lab had other things in common with a hospital —like pain-fueled howls tearing throughout its polished halls. I bolted forward, urged on by the sudden clamor of what I could only assume were Max's tortured screams. By the time I made it to the second door on the right and peered through the window—a thin slit like you might see in a doctor's office—I couldn't make out much except a man's bare, brawny arm, spasming. I snarled, stepped back, and kicked the door in, blasting the lock to bits.

The screams stopped so suddenly I thought I might have imagined them, and a tall, bespectacled man poked his head around the corner. He reached up and pushed his glasses further up his nose, lenses catching the light so I couldn't see his eyes. "I'm busy. Go away, and shut the door on your way out," he said, ducking back out of sight.

I stepped into the doorway, preparing to free Max and snap the bossy bastard's neck, but it wasn't Max in the hospital bed. It was someone else entirely—a stocky man with a buzz cut so short you could see skin beneath. "What the hell were ye doin' to him?" I asked, turning to the man in the glasses.

"I don't see how that's any of your business," the man replied, fiddling with a handful of instruments on the other side of the gurney. I frowned, studying the victim for clues of torture...but he didn't seem to bear any marks. In fact, he seemed peaceful, perhaps even asleep. But if that were the case, then who had been screaming?

The man in the glasses continued adjusting a tray full of tools—none of which looked particularly friendly. It was then I noticed he wore a white lab coat, like what you might expect from a mad scientist. "Are ye Dr. Franken-stein?" I asked, prepared to pounce; no matter what he was up to, if this was Frankenstein, he needed to die.

"No," the man replied. "I'm just a lab assistant. The Doctor's in surgery, working on a man we found trespassing. Lucky for us, he turned out to be a perfect match for a donor operation."

I blanched. "Surgery?"

"Yes. If you hurry, you might be able to stop him. Assuming that's what you're here to do. Surgery is upstairs, on the east wing. Hard to miss." The lab assistant picked up a scalpel and waved it at me over his shoulder.

I froze, glancing down at the sleeping patient, unsure what to do. "What are ye plannin' to do to him?" I asked.

"Does it matter?" he replied. "It's not like you know him. Shouldn't you be running off to save your friend?"

I ground my teeth. He was right; Max was my priority. For all I knew, this guy was some sort of murderous mob boss here for a tune-up. Or a lowlife who beat his wife and kids. Basically, a worthless, no-good piece of shit human being who wouldn't stick out his neck for a stranger.

"Get away from him," I growled.

The lab assistant looked up at the ceiling imploringly. "I thought you said she'd leave?"

"Who are ye talkin' to?" I demanded, edging around the gurney, inching closer to the lab assistant.

He held up a finger as if asking me to give him a minute before speaking to the ceiling once more. "Well then, what would you like me to do?" he asked.

I reached out and slapped at that hand, planning to knock the damn guy out and take my chances saving the stranger. But the instant my hand connected with his, something shattered, and I was left touching the outstretched hand of a tall, black-skinned elf in a tailored three-piece pinstripe suit, glaring at me from over one shoulder, his yellow eyes seething with disdain.

"Well, so much for that," he said.

Of course, it was hard to hear him over the screams, which were suddenly as audible as they'd been before I stepped into the room. I whirled to face the hospital bed and nearly fainted at what I saw: where the stocky man had been only a moment before, Max lay, his chest bare, skin blistered and so red it physically hurt me to look at it—as if he'd suffered the worst possible sunburn. But, before I could so much as reach out for him, the elf slapped my hand away.

"It's too late. The change has already begun." The elf smirked, flashing black teeth.

"Who the hell are ye?" I asked, grabbing the bastard by his lapels and whipping him over onto my side of the room. I slammed him against the wall so hard the nearby cabinets shattered, spilling medical supplies—mostly gauze and bandages—onto the small counter below.

"My name is Ygor," he replied, seemingly unperturbed. "It's a pleasure to meet you, Miss MacKenna. I've heard a lot about—"

I shoved the fucker against the wall again, harder this time. His head bounced off the wall and he looked a little dazed. "What's happenin' to Max?" I demanded.

"It seems his sister was the stronger of the two, after all," Ygor said, staring over my shoulder at Max, who was writhing in pain. "I was always curious, but she at least could control her gift. Better than we ever expected, I'll admit, or else she'd never have escaped." He shook his head, mournfully. "They were such fun to torment, those two. Oh well."

"How do I fix it?" I snarled.

Ygor started to laugh.

I snatched up the scalpel he'd brandished earlier and held it to his throat. "Tell me."

Ygor smiled and pressed his throat against the blade, the blade bending against his skin. "Steel? You'll have to do better than that."

I tossed the scalpel and watched as his eyes brightened with triumph.

Then I took a step back, cocked one arm, and jabbed at his face, fingers splayed. I pierced the meaty pulp of his eye, scooped out the orbital socket, and drew the fleshy mass out between my middle and index fingers before flinging the whole mess to the ground with a splat.

Ygor howled and clutched at his ruined face.

"Tell me how to fix him, or you'll be blind in under a minute," I swore. And I meant it.

"Too...late..." Ygor replied. He collapsed, his tar-like blood dripping onto the tile, and felt about for his missing eye as if he might shove it back into place.

I clenched my fists in frustration and turned to Max only to note the burns had gotten worse, somehow. The skin redder, practically pulsing with heat. His eyes bulged while I watched, and he began seizing on the table. I reached for him, hoping to hold him down, to keep him from hurting himself further, but it was too late.

Because that's when everything went up in flames.

CHAPTER 29

I was blown back by the unexpected eruption, landing flat on the tile floor, which is all that saved me from being consumed by flames—an inferno which soared improbably towards the ceiling like a waterfall in reverse, defying gravity as it spilled across its surface. I shielded my eyes from the light but managed to peer over my arm long enough to see Max at the epicenter of the conflagration, his back bowed, mouth open so wide it made my jaw hurt, the muscles of his arms straining.

I tried to get my bearings, but the heat was so intense the best I could manage was to get to my knees and scrabble towards the gurney, which had not yet caught on fire, somehow. Honestly, I had no idea what I was going to do—what I could do—but I knew I couldn't leave Max like this. At this rate, he'd either burn the whole lab down around us or die of a magic-induced stroke. Which meant he had to be stopped, and soon. Of course, when I finally thought to look around, I found no sign of Ygor; a trail of oily liquid led to the door and beyond. I cursed and crawled closer until, at last, I was within touching distance.

But I hesitated, fingers hovering inches above the brujo's skin, steam billowing off his body from the heat he radiated. I clenched my jaw, closed my eyes, and pressed my palm against that blistered flesh. And screamed. Not from pain—though that was what I'd expected—but from the rush of power that swept over me. Filled me. It raged inside my body, wracking my bones, my nerves on fire—nothing like the ritual magic I'd manipulated before. This magic was wild, untamed, directionless. In fact, it was all I could do not to lose myself in it, to fall back writhing, as Max had, as it seared my soul.

Consume the power, that voice in the back of my head urged. *Before it consumes you.*

But how? I realized I was still screaming and snapped my mouth shut so hard my teeth ached. I opened my eyes. The flames danced above us both now, the effect doubled. The ceiling above would be a blackened husk, I suspected. Charred to a crisp, unless I could do something. But what could I do? Before, the magic had answered a need. I'd been a conduit, not an outlet.

But why couldn't I be both?

I thrust my hand into the air.

I willed the magic to come to me. I called to that roiling power, eager to embrace it, to let it find a home in me. In seconds, the swirling flames began to rotate in the opposite direction, like a tornado touching down, the inferno funneling towards my outstretched fingertips. Then, mere inches from my skin, the flames disappeared, converting to pure, raw energy I could cup in my palm. Heat spread up my arm, but it was the kind of heat that thaws you out on a cold winter night after shoveling snow, not the kind that leaves you twitching on the floor in agony. There was a blinding flash of light as the iron shackles around my wrists snapped free, landing on the floor, the metal white hot. I almost closed my eyes, hoping to blink away the spots in my vision, but that's when I caught sight of the sundial on my wrist, the silver surface gleaming beneath the light.

It was spinning inexorably backwards.

At last, the flames died completely, and I was left kneeling on the floor, one hand in the air, the other pressed to Max's tan, unblemished skin. I rose, using the gurney as a crutch, and sought out the brujo's face, dreading the damage the flames must have done. Max—his face unmarred—gazed at me with heavy-lidded eyes, looking exhausted, but nothing like the over-cooked lobster I was expecting, which was definitely an improvement. Before I could say anything, he reached out and slid my hand from his hip to his chest and let it rest there.

I didn't pull away.

"What happened?" he asked.

"Ygor got away."

Max winced. "I meant, what did I do? Did I hurt you?"

"No. I...I managed to stop it from spreadin'. The flames, I mean." I frowned, hoping he'd refrain from asking me *how* I'd done that; I really had no idea. The best I could come up with was that I—somehow—had the ability to consume and convert energy. But into what? I glanced down at my watch, wondering what Darling and Dear had intended for me when they'd passed it along. Just what the hell was I?

"*Gracias*," Max said, looking visibly relieved, eyes pinched shut.

"Don't mention it," I replied. I rapped my knuckles on his bare chest good-naturedly, far more aware now of his nudity than I had been before. "Can ye stand?"

"I can try."

"Good, because if ye still want to kill Victor and his piece-of-shit lackey, we have a blood trail to follow. But we'll have to hurry." I jerked my head towards the doorway for emphasis.

"A blood trail?"

"I took Ygor's eye," I explained. "Matter of fact, it's probably around here, somewhere."

"You took his eye?"

"Is there an echo in here?" I asked, playfully. I leaned in close, splaying my fingers against the firm swell of the Hispanic man's chest. "Don't ye t'ink a woman should be allowed to get real nasty when she wants to?" I whispered, grinning peevishly.

Max visibly gulped but nodded.

I patted his chest. "Good lad."

And who says foreplay is a lost art?

CHAPTER 30

*T*he trail of blood, black as pitch, led down the corridor in splashes and smears, marring the once virginal hallways. Max and I moved quickly, accompanied by the sound of our clomping steps against the smooth tile floor. Luckily, it seemed Max had recovered from his little ordeal; were it not for the fact that he was topless, the muscles of his upper body bunching as he jogged, I'd never had known anything remotely life-threatening had happened. Ordinarily, I'd have loved to pause and take in the view, but I wasn't in the mood. Truthfully, all I could think about was ending this and going the fuck home. It'd been an exhausting two, maybe three days—depending on how long I'd been out. Between the repeated beatings, the lack of sleep, and the life-altering revelations, it was all I could do to put one foot in front of the other.

In fact, I was so focused that I almost missed Max wheeling off on his own. "Oy! Where are ye goin'?" I asked, pointing down at the diminishing trail of blood in front of me.

Max paused and pointed to his own trail, which lead off to the left, opposite mine. We stared at one another for a moment before I cursed. "Bastard must have created a false trail," I said. "Now what?" I muttered to myself.

"We split up," Max insisted.

I shook my head, uncomfortable with the idea; this was the rookie mistake made in every horror movie, and I wasn't fond of how those turned out. "I really don't like that plan."

"Do not worry. He could not have gone far. If I do not find Ygor, I will hurry back."

"And if ye do find him?"

"I will kill him," Max said, a fierce look in his eyes.

Well, at least he had his priorities straight. But I still didn't like it. Logic dictated that Max was right; one of us would stumble upon the wounded Ygor before long, and the other would likely realize their mistake and quickly turn back. But it didn't make me feel any better. Not with Victor Frankenstein and his monster still unaccounted for. "What if ye run into more than just Ygor?"

"I will not go rushing in foolishly, I swear. But you must trust me," Max said, imploringly. "I can take care of myself."

I frowned but refrained from saying anything scathing about what a bang up job he'd done so far. To be fair, Max hadn't exactly had much of an opportunity to shine; getting ambushed in one's own shop—not to mention being knocked unconscious and unable to defend oneself—would bruise anyone's ego. Maybe Max was right. Maybe I was underestimating him. "Aye, well, be sure that ye do," I said.

"You will wait for me, yes? If you run into Ygor, first?" the brujo asked.

"Not a chance. But I'll be sure to bring ye his other eye as a souvenir?"

Max grunted. "Good enough."

I grinned, gave him a curt nod, a quick salute, and took off down the corridor—praying I wasn't making a mistake. "See ye soon!" I called back as I ran.

"*Hasta la vista*, baby!" Max replied.

I rolled my eyes, though I had to admit I was secretly pleased to have met someone who could quote movie lines at me. But now wasn't the time; I quickly returned my attention back to the blood spatter. Evidence of Ygor's passing had diminished considerably—little more than a few drops here and there—which meant either Ygor had covered his wound or it was healing awfully fast. Regardless, I had to slow somewhat to make sure I didn't lose the trail; I tracked the blood down one hallway, then another. Just how big was this place, anyway?

Before I could speculate, I heard a loud, resounding crash further down the hall, like the metallic cacophony a cymbal makes. I picked up speed, spotting a pair of steel double doors like you might find leading into a restaurant kitchen. A black, bloody handprint was smeared across its surface. Looked like I'd found Ygor, after all. Poor Max.

Guess he wouldn't get to kill the Faeling after all.

I burst through those double doors and skidded to a halt. "Jesus Christ," I whispered.

Smack dab in the middle of what was indeed a kitchen floor lay Frankenstein's monster, its great fleshy body flopped out on the floor, unmoving, surrounded by a pool of viscous liquid that had congealed into something red and firm, like the jelly inside a donut. Its mismatched eyes lay open and staring, glazed over, its tongue lolling out of its mouth. Without moving the body, I couldn't see a wound, but it didn't make much difference; I knew dead when I saw it.

Next to the body of the monster, I discovered a small, silver-haired gentleman, dressed casually in a polo and jeans, propped upright against one of those metal carts chefs use to wheel food around, its edge pushed up against the kitchen's prepping station. A knife jutted out of the man's gut, hilt deep, blood spreading from the wound, staining the man's clothes to form a puddle between his legs. His eyes, unlike the monster's, were closed.

I spotted Ygor last, the Faeling sprawled out on the carving station, his mouth open in a silent scream, his chest a pitch black, bloody mass. His ribs were exposed, as if someone or something had torn out his still beating heart. The contrast of white bone jutting out from so much tar made me sick to my stomach.

For at least a solid minute, I simply stood there, trying to make sense of what I was seeing. What had happened here? Was that Frankenstein with the knife in his stomach? Who or what had taken Ygor's heart? Had they attacked each other, for some reason? A falling out? Hell, a suicide pact? But, the longer I looked on, the more I realized there were a few other things which didn't add up. Why were we in a kitchen? And, what's more, why did that kitchen look so familiar?

But that wasn't the biggest question.

I stepped over to the carving station and examined the Faeling's body, staring into that gaping wound as if it were some sort of code to be deciphered. The blackened meat inside was mangled, barely recognizable, but it also looked exactly how I'd have expected it to look—like a slick, three-dimensional anatomical model, heart not included. Except there was something missing. Something that couldn't be seen. The smell. There was no smell.

Why was there no smell?

In a room full of dead bodies, even the freshly dead, you'd expect there to be a stench of some kind. An odor. The slightest hint of blood's peculiar, copper penny aroma. But there was nothing. If anything, the whole place had an antiseptic quality to it—the faintest whiff of bleach.

Which could only mean one thing, as far as I was concerned.

This wasn't real.

I reached out towards Ygor, tentatively at first, then with more assurance, plunging my hand inside that fleshy wound, gritting my teeth and closing my eyes. I wasn't sure what I'd expected to feel, but I certainly hadn't expected to encounter the smooth, cool surface of the station beneath. I opened my eyes. No, not a station. A lab table.

I turned in circles. The bodies were gone. I no longer stood in a kitchen; I was in a tidy lab, complete with the scientific apparatuses you'd expect to find: several microscopes, mounted beakers, test tubes, and so on. I shook my head, feeling silly for not figuring it out sooner. It had all been merely an illusion—a misdirect. But wait, did that mean Ygor had worked up some grammerie to throw me off his scent? If so, did that mean Max was in danger? The thought made my blood run cold. Shit. I took off towards the exit, determined to backtrack and find the brujo before something truly awful happened.

I thrust open the swinging doors and stepped out into the hallway.

Except the hallway wasn't there.

CHAPTER 31

*I*nstead, I found myself in Dez's living room.

I nearly ran into the sofa, slowing in the nick of time to avoid knocking over the end table and the lamp which sat on top of it. I cursed and wheeled around, taking in this newest illusion with no small amount of shock. Everything looked as it should have. As it would have, had that fire not taken out the kitchen and half the living room. Except this time, even the smell was right; there was a slight wood smoke tinge to the air, intermingled with the mouth-watering fragrance of pumpkin pie and carved turkey. I meandered throughout the room, too taken aback—or perhaps too taken in—by the illusion to consider forcing my way out. Not yet.

I edged around the couch and approached the fireplace, running my fingers over the mantle, marveling at the rough, brittle stone that grazed my fingertips. It felt so real. So wonderfully, awfully real. Hell, even the floorboards creaked as I headed for the stairs, the hardwood slightly bowed in places. But I never made it to the stairs. Instead, a voice called out to me from the kitchen—a kitchen that shouldn't exist.

"Quinn MacKenna! Get in here and help me with this cookin' or I swear I'll tan your hide!"

My hand went to my mouth before I could help it, tears welling, threatening to spill over into my cheeks. I shook my head so forcefully it felt like my brain was rattling away inside my skull, and the tears were suddenly gone. Not real, I reminded myself. Not. Real.

But then her face appeared, poking out of the kitchen doorway, her silver-streaked hair tied back in a severe bun—the way she preferred it when she was cooking, always complaining about how it got in her way because "it was always so thick and got everywhere," her complaint somehow self-congratulatory. I'd always teased her about that, about how she hid her vanity behind a thin veneer of humility. "Quinn, what is it?" Dez asked. "What's wrong?"

I took a step back, willing the apparition to disappear. "No, no, no..."

She couldn't be real. She couldn't. But...what if she was? What if I'd dreamt all the rest: my adventures in Fae, my trip to Russia, Wortcunning Corner, the Salem witches, and the underground laboratory? Thinking about it, about how utterly preposterous that all sounded—meeting Peter Pan, fighting alongside Captain Hook, defeating Rasputin, learning how to make Gateways with Morgan le Fay, chasing after Dr. Frankenstein and his newly-fashioned monster—how could it have been anything else but a dream?

And yet...something told me *this* was the dream. No, not a dream; it was too real to be a dream. This was something else, something that surpassed a mere illusion. It was more like a memory. Replayed just for me. But, as I studied Dez's face, I considered where we were—especially given Dez's appearance and the smells—and realized it wasn't my memory.

But I did know whose it was.

"How could ye?" I whispered.

Dez smiled, looking past me as if I were the ghost. "Well, then, tell him to come on in and help," she said. She tilted her head quizzically and then laughed. "Ryan! Come here."

I turned and found a man standing behind me, his blonde hair curling artfully away from that too handsome, leading man face. Ryan—whose memory this was—grinned and rubbed at the shaggy mane, doing his best to appear charming. "You know, I'm much better behind the bar than behind the stove," he said.

"Nonsense," Dez replied, snapping the hand towel she always carried tucked into the pocket of her apron when she cooked. "Get in here, Ryan O'Rye. If Quinn says you're to eat Thanksgivin' dinner with us, then you're goin' to earn your keep."

"Stop," I murmured. "Please…"

"Alright, if you insist," Ryan said, as if I hadn't spoken. "Just don't blame me if it all comes out tasting like a bad dream."

"A bad dream…" I muttered, anger stirring within me. I shuffled towards that figure, hands balled into fists at my sides. "Ryan! Ryan, come out! Where are ye?!"

The imposter in front of me strolled past, headed for the kitchen with slumped shoulders, pantomiming his reticence. But that left someone, something, in his place—a vaguely man-shaped, grainy figure with indistinguishable features. I stared at the newest apparition, then pressed a hand to my head, as if I could will myself to see clearer. "Is that ye, Ryan?" I ground out. The figure moved, reaching for me, brushing my arm with one smudged hand.

Suddenly, I was left in a burning living room—my memory this time.

Up the stairs, Dez screamed.

I was running before I could help myself, tearing up the stairs. Except, the instant I made it to the top, I fell, tripping over some unseen object. When I scrambled to my feet, I found myself no longer in my old house, but in a bar; it was almost as if someone had changed the channel, plopping me in a different show altogether.

"It is pleasure to see you again," Christoff said, drawing my attention. The bar owner was artfully cutting up fruit, a small pile of limes in a plastic dish beside him. He glanced up at me, smiling. "Are you here to close tab? You forget last night."

I walked warily towards the barkeep, casing the room as I went. None of the movie monsters lined the walls. In fact, judging by the decor and Christoff's comment, this had to be another memory. Today was the day I was introduced to Christoff, back when his bar had been just a bar, when he still spoke broken English, before I found out he was a former spy, before I even knew he was actually a werebear. Hell, Ryan hadn't yet started as bar manager, even; it had been his idea to start using themes to draw in bigger crowds. "I know you're not real," I hissed. "And I know you're out there, Ryan! Knock this off, or I swear I'll—"

"Ryan!" Christoff said, waving a hand. "Come, look. The woman you brought in last night has returned! It is a first, no?"

"I told you it wasn't a date," Ryan said, smirking, turning to look at me from the end of the bar. He tipped an imaginary hat at me. "This one is bad news."

Christoff's booming laughter spilled out of his mouth, which was surrounded on all sides by a thick, greying beard he rarely ever wore. "And I think you say this because she drank you under table. Is expression, yes? Under table."

"Under *the* table," a woman said, coming down the stairs that led to the office. Elena, Christoff's wife. She cradled their son in one arm, the boy not even a year old, yet. "The expression is 'under the table', dear."

Christoff grinned, shrugged, and flashed me a wink. Ryan turned away as Elena approached, nursing his beer, smile dimming just a hair. But if either Christoff or his wife noticed, they declined to comment. I remembered how Ryan had always kept his distance from the barkeep's stunning wife, as if there were some history there he didn't like to talk about.

"She's dead, too," I whispered. "Elena is dead."

This time, when the illusion shattered, I felt more than saw it. It was like stepping onto the roiling deck of a boat at sea, the motion making my stomach roll. I was about to collapse from the sensation when a frigid gust of air hit me, splashing across my skin as if I'd leapt into the Atlantic. My gasp came out in a cool burst, misting as it drifted into the air. I wobbled and closed my eyes, fighting the chills threatening to rack my body.

"You lie!" Ryan hissed. "Tell me you're lying!"

I opened my eyes and stared, unable to help myself.

"Say it!" he commanded.

But I couldn't.

Because what I saw had left me speechless.

CHAPTER 32

*T*he creature before me had Ryan's voice, even his face, but that was where the similarities ended; it stood a few inches taller than Ryan, with a rangier build, as if Ryan had been stretched and then whittled down. Oh, and his whole body consisted of various shades of blue. His bright, fluorescent blue eyes swam in a teal sea, so eerily familiar it took me only seconds to recognize where I'd seen them before—in a different face.

The face of a Faeling I'd killed.

"Jack?" I asked, squinting as if I could find that Faeling's features lurking behind Ryan's. Yet another illusion, maybe? But this was real. Somehow, I knew it was.

"Really, Quinn? You don't recognize me?" Ryan said, disdainfully.

"Of course I do, Ryan, but..." I showcased his body with one hand. "But since when have ye been, ye know, blue? D'ye have a growth spurt, too?"

"Something like that," Ryan replied, running both hands through his hair, tousling it a bit.

Oddly enough, the fond memories that gesture brought back reminded me why I'd been so pissed only a moment before. I took a step forward and pointed an accusing finger at the Faeling. "Alright, if ye really are Ryan, why don't ye explain why ye put me through that just now?" I demanded.

Ryan cocked his head, folding his arms over his chest. "Through what?"

"What d'ye mean, 'through what'? Ye made me see Dez!"

"I was trying to distract you," Ryan replied, cocking an eyebrow. "To throw you off the scent for a while."

Tears pricked my eyes, and I rubbed at them fiercely, unwilling to break down now. Was it possible Ryan hadn't known? That he'd shown me Dez on a whim? "Me aunt is dead, Ryan."

Ryan's lips, the color of black ice, parted in surprise. He gasped like a fish for a moment before stammering, his tone shifting back to that soft, caring version of Ryan I remembered. "I—I'm sorry, Quinn. I didn't know." He hung his head, blue locks spilling across that snow-white face like paint on drywall. "How did it happen?"

"It was Dobby."

Ryan's head shot up. "What?"

"He was workin' for Balor and the Fomorians. A spy." The truth was a bit more complicated, but I didn't feel like going into it. Of course, it had been Ryan who introduced me to Dobby in the first place, so perhaps he'd known what Dobby was all along. I searched for the truth in his eyes, willing him to be honest with me.

"I don't..." Ryan drifted off, total shock written all over his face. "Quinn, I had no idea. I'm so sorry."

"Whatever ye say," I replied, too upset—too angry—to blindly accept Ryan's apology. "Listen, why are ye tryin' to stop me? Matter of fact, what the fuck are ye even doin' here?"

Ryan uncrossed his arms and shoved them into the pockets of his dress slacks, refusing to meet my eyes. "Is it true? What you said about Elena?"

I just stared at him for a moment, then nodded.

Ryan's face crumbled, and he buried it in his hands. "How?" he asked, voice tight. He wasn't sobbing or anything, but—before he'd covered up—I'd seen real pain there. Real anguish. Loss.

"She was taken," I replied. "Christoff, too."

Ryan jerked his hands away from his face, staring at me wide-eyed.

"We got Christoff back," I reassured him. "Rescued their wee ones. But Elena...Elena we couldn't save. She caught somethin' while she was in prison. I'm not sure what. Christoff doesn't like to talk about it."

"Who?" Ryan asked, through gritted teeth. As I watched, a large swath of ice began to form beneath his feet, spreading until it reached frost-licked walls. A draft of chilly air blew through the corridor, sending shivers down my spine.

"What?"

"Who did it? Who took her?"

I shook my head. "The man responsible is dead, Ryan. Him, and all his men. Everyone who had anythin' to do with it, to the best of me knowledge, is gone."

Ryan's shoulders slumped, and the draft subsided. "I loved her, you know."

"I know."

He glanced up at me in surprise.

"No one gets that worked up, not unless they loved the person," I said, shrugging. "Did Christoff know?"

Ryan grunted. "Of course. They both knew. It wasn't exactly a secret, though I kept it to myself. I knew better than to get between them. Besides, Christoff is...was...my friend."

Wait, was?

"Ryan, what has happened to ye?" I asked, approaching the Faeling. "Why are ye here, now?"

"Stay back, Quinn."

The anger in that voice stopped me cold. I narrowed my eyes. "Since when have I ever let ye tell me what to do, Ryan O'Rye?"

"Times change." Ryan slashed at the air with his hand and a shard of ice appeared. A spear, by the looks of it. Ryan caught the shard before it fell to the ground and leaned on it, casually. "Listen, Quinn, I can't let you past. I can't have you interfering."

"Let me what?" I shook my head. "For fuck's sake, Ryan, what's goin' on?"

Ryan sighed. "Do you remember the last time we spoke?"

I thought back, flashing to a memory of Ryan staring at me through the bars of a cage, threatening me, his anger a white-hot thing I couldn't cool no matter how I tried—his hatred so all-consuming I'd hardly even recognized him. In the end, that obsession—not to mention his reckless pursuit of vengeance—had driven a wedge between us. Ironically, it had all been aimed at one man. A man I didn't even like. Nate Temple.

"Aye, but what does that have to do with anythin'?"

"And how about the promise you made to the Winter Queen?" Ryan replied, seemingly refusing to answer my question directly. "Can you recall what you swore to do?"

I frowned. Back in Fae, pressed for time and in desperate need of a weapon capable of defeating Balor and his Fomorian army, I'd brokered a deal with one of the Fae queens. The terms? To confront Temple and—if necessary—kill him. Under normal circumstances, I would never have agreed to something so rife with potential mishaps, but at the time I'd run out of options. Of course, back then it had seemed like Temple and I were already on a collision path, the clash inevitable, so I'd agreed without much thought.

A problem for another time, in essence.

Except that months had come and gone since then, and Temple and I still hadn't hashed things out. Partly because, between mourning Dez and saving Christoff, I'd been busy, but also because Temple had recently gone missing. At this point, our impending confrontation had become more of an indefinite possibility. "I remember," I said, blushing slightly. "I just haven't gotten around to it."

Ryan slammed the dull end of his spear into the ground and a dozen icicles as long and thick as my leg shot out from the ice at his feet, angled towards me; in an instant, I was facing a low wall of deadly spikes, only Ryan's upper body visible. "Oh? You've been too busy, is that it?" Ryan hissed.

"Aye! Not that it's any of your business," I added, getting well and truly angry at this point. No one threatened me, even passive-aggressively, without paying the consequences. No one—not even Ryan. I held out my hand and felt the magic within me well up. I dipped into that reservoir of power I'd stolen from Max and stepped forward, willing time to spin backwards as it had in the valley outside Salem. Except it didn't. Not really. Instead, as I approached, the ice retreated—icicles diminishing until the frozen surface was smooth once more. Ryan, however, seemed completely unaffected.

"What are you doing?" he challenged, eyes panicked.

Honestly, I wasn't sure how to answer that; I'd apparently learned how to access my newfound abilities, but not how to properly employ them. Still, I'd achieved my goal: no more pointy wall between Ryan and me. That, and I'd freaked the Faeling out in the process. Bonus. "Ye don't want to threaten me, Ryan," I growled. "Ye really, really don't."

Ryan's eyes flashed, but not with fear this time. More like anticipation. Not good. "When you failed to go after Temple," Ryan said, changing subjects so abruptly it left me floundering, "the Winter Queen took new measures. Do you know where she found me?"

I scowled. "A brothel?" I deadpanned.

"I was searching through Oberon's records. And, wouldn't you know, I'd found something strange. A report regarding who broke in to steal from the King, the burglars who put me to sleep and got me exiled." Ryan's grin grew manic. Crazed, even. "Nate Temple's parents."

"Wait, what?"

Ryan barked a laugh. "Exactly! You know, I was as shocked as you were. I mean, how could one family cause me this much suffering? His parents responsible for my exile, the man himself responsible for my father's death, and now he's even managed to drive a wedge between us." Ryan reached for me, but I leaned away, wary of his icy touch; I'd seen what it could do.

"I don't understand," I began. "Why—"

"She came to me. The Winter Queen saw how much I was hurting; how much I hated that bastard. And then, what's more, she gave me the power to do something about it." Ryan drew his hand back, closed it into a fist. "I have become the new Jack Frost. And I will do what the old one failed to do."

"Murder innocent women for fun?" I asked, completely baffled by the reference; Jack had been a demented psychopath, content to carve his way through history—literally.

"Of course not," Ryan said. "No, I will shatter the boundaries between our two worlds. As we speak, Temple is lost somewhere in Fae, which means now is my chance to tear down all the gates between our realms. I will leave him stranded in Fae, unable to return to his world, to ever see his friends again. I will take everything from him, as he has taken everything from me." A single tear slid down Ryan's face, freezing on his snow-white cheek like a dermal piercing.

"Ryan, what has happened to ye?" I asked, raising one hand, planning to brush away that tear. But the Faeling caught my wrist, instead. Pain radiated down my arm, my very bones so chilled I would have done anything to be rid of the sensation. I screamed.

"The Winter Queen sends her regards," Ryan said, leaning close. "We will deal with Temple, ourselves. No thanks to you." He released me, tossed my arm away, and straightened. "We've already begun. We will parade this monster of Frankenstein's throughout your world. We will prove the Fae are real, and that they should be stopped. Forced out. We'll make the humans fear us, and then they'll take care of the rest."

"Jesus, you're talkin' about what? Genocide?" I said, cradling my aching arm, too shocked by the audacity of Ryan's plan to even consider lashing out.

"I'm talking about an exodus!" Ryan snarled. "A liberation, Quinn. The Fae here will return home, and we'll accept them with open arms. We'll give them asylum, even as we close our borders and fend off the human menace. By any means necessary."

"But wait..." I said, a horrific idea forming in the back of my mind. "Then, that means ye were a part of this? Ye knew they were goin' to take the Chancery members? To experiment on 'em?"

Ryan looked away, flicking that tear off his cheek with disdain. "Knew? Please. Who do you think took them?"

My jaw dropped as I realized what Ryan was saying. But of course, it all made sense, now; I knew how the Fae had been taken under everyone's noses. It had been Ryan, with his knack for illusion magic, who had stolen the Chancery members away. Though not entirely without notice; some had felt his cold presence lingering afterwards. I raised both hands, balling them into fists, anger making my blood boil. "Ryan O'Rye, d'ye have any idea what you've done?"

"Only what you wouldn't," he spat, expression contorted into a rictus of hate. "Now, turn and walk away. Keep out of this and keep your head down, Quinn. Otherwise you won't survive what's coming."

I laughed, but it was bitter. Catty. "If ye t'ink I'm goin' anywhere, that I won't try to stop ye from doin' somethin' so moronic, then ye never knew me at all."

Ryan leveled his spear, looking me up and down. "Maybe you're right. Or maybe I was hoping you'd try. I've been looking forward to this."

"*Hola, amigo,* may I cut in?" a voice I recognized called out on the other end of the hall. But then, before either of us could respond, Max yelled, "Quinn, duck! Now!"

I dove to the floor.

And who says I don't listen well?

CHAPTER 33

*a*t this point, I had to admit I was really tired of ending up on the floor for one reason or another. But, for once at least, I seemed to have the best view in the house; from the chilly linoleum, I was able to watch as Ryan took a massive fireball directly to the chest. It hit him like a battering ram, sending the Faeling flying well over my head to crash through the double doors that led to the lab beyond. A thunderous crash sounded—mostly that of shattered glass—and I cringed. That had to hurt. But at least the coast was clear; I scrambled to my feet, searching the hallway for signs of the fire-wielding brujo.

When I finally spotted him, my eyes widened. Max strode down the hall towards me, his skin covered in what looked like tribal tattoos forged in fire, spilling along the rippling muscles of his massive upper body in runnels, like lava. They seemed to writhe as I watched, molding into familiar patterns, mimicking those magic circles I'd seen in spell books. But, before I could ask about the makeover, Ryan came racing out from between the doors, hoarfrost coating his entire body, his chest blackened and exposed beneath his t-shirt, but whole.

"You really think a little fire could stop me?" he asked.

"I had hoped so," Max said, shrugging. The brujo flicked a hand out and spoke a word three times—a word I couldn't decipher. Not because it was unfamiliar, but because, no matter how many times he'd said it, I couldn't seem to recall what it sounded like, as if the word itself were sand, slipping through my fingers. The tribal tattoos swirled once more, and suddenly Ryan was slammed into the wall by some unseen force. Then to the other wall and back again, leaving a man-shaped dent on either side of the hallway.

Ryan slid to the floor with a sigh, looking more annoyed than pained, his remarkably resilient body not the least bit damaged despite the force of the blows he'd taken. The Faeling straightened and dusted off his shoulders. "Well, that was fun. Are you done, yet?"

But it seemed Ryan wasn't interested in waiting for an answer; the Faeling cocked his arm and mimed a throw. The instant Ryan's arm fell, however, I realized he'd created a new spear in the space of time it would have taken to draw a breath; the icy javelin sped straight for the brujo, who was forced to dive to the right, which was all that saved him from being impaled. I, meanwhile, pressed my back flat against the wall, eager to stay out of the crossfire.

"Quinn," Max said, "get the others and get out of here! I will handle this."

I stared into those two-toned eyes from across the hall and grinned. "As if I'd let ye do this alone."

"This is your last chance, Quinn," Ryan said, another javelin already in hand. "Go, now, or—"

But this time it was *my* turn to interrupt someone. "Ye know, I'd say I'm sorry about this, but I'm really not," I said, turning my attention to the Faeling. I thrust both hands forward and concentrated, visualizing what I wanted the way Morgan had shown me, urging my magic to play along—just this once.

Thing was, if this kept up, I knew at least one of us was bound to end up dead. No matter what Ryan had done, I didn't want that. But if what the Faeling said was true, if their end goal was to parade Frankenstein's monster around the country, then they had to be stopped. The creature would have to be killed—preferably before it made its debut.

Which meant it was about time Ryan took a trip.

But hey, maybe I'd see him next fall?

"What do you think you're—" Ryan began.

Before he could finish, I opened a Gateway below Ryan's feet. The heir apparent to the mantle of Jack Frost had an instant—perhaps less than a second—to react, but he wasn't able to stop his descent; I listened to the sound of his screams for several seconds before I heard the tell-tale sound of a splash. I willed the Gateway out of existence and watched it close before my very eyes, those green flames hissing and sparking as the circle shrunk and—finally—disappeared.

Max rose to his feet, groaning. "Where did you send him?" he asked.

"No idea," I said, shrugging. "I was aiming for somewhere in the Pacific. I'm sure he'll be fine. Ryan just needs to cool off a bit, that's all." Of course, that wasn't all. Never in a million years would I have thought Ryan capable of selling out his own people, even going so far as to kidnap them. Which meant he'd changed. That he'd become something he, himself, would one day come to hate. Of course, the threat he represented as the Winter Queen's newest agent was the bigger concern. His plan, to essentially create a rift between the two worlds, to start a war between humankind and Faelings, would only lead to pain and suffering.

Part of me wanted to dwell on how it had come to this, to review Ryan's descent into madness, maybe even determine if there'd been something I might have done or said differently—some kindness I'd denied my former friend that had facilitated his transformation. But the rest of me knew better; what's done is done.

And I had more important shit to worry about right now.

"Does ye comin' back to find me mean ye lost Ygor?" I asked.

"*Nada*," Max replied. "I found Ygor. But it seems Victor got away."

Well, that wasn't the best news we could have hoped for. What would Frankenstein do now, with Ryan gone—at least for the moment—and his henchman dispatched? "He is dead, aye? Ygor, I mean."

Max gave me a curt nod, eyes flinty—the eyes of a killer. But I was glad. One less monster out there. Of course, that still left the *actual* monster. Ryan's would-be show pony. Once we found and destroyed it, I could focus on returning the witches we'd caught and getting the Faelings back home safe and sound. One step at a time.

"I don't suppose there's any chance ye saw a hideous monster runnin' around while ye were goin' about your business?" I asked, hopeful. "Maybe ten-feet-tall, all patched together?"

"No," Max replied, "but I did see a large creature on one of the video screens in the control room where I found Ygor. Unfortunately, it was above ground, and a lot bigger than ten feet. I hoped it might be one of your missing Fae, at the time."

I frowned; unless Jameson had broken free somehow, it was unlikely to be any of the Faelings I'd freed. Had the creature grown since I'd seen it last? I cursed, then glanced sidelong at Max. "If ye were in the control room, then d'ye know how to get out of here?"

Max nodded, and I realized his tattoos were fading, dimming like the dying embers of a fire.

"Let's go, then," I insisted. "And on the way ye can tell me all about those nifty tattoos of yours."

Max glanced down at himself as he turned to lead the way, shaking his head. "I have absolutely no idea what these are," he replied. "Never seen them before in my life."

I cocked an eyebrow at that but declined to comment. Hell, if Max's new, metaphysical ink was the biggest unanswered question that remained by the end of the day, I could live with it.

As if.

CHAPTER 34

$\mathcal{W}$e emerged from one of the laboratory's service entrances ten minutes later, the bright sunlight almost blinding after spending so much time in what amounted to a dimly lit underground bunker; Max had taken a picture of the building's schematics and used it to guide us out, insisting the structure might very well span an entire acre. When I'd asked how Frankenstein could afford to have something like that built, Max had become uncharacteristically taciturn.

My guess? Not legally.

I held up a hand to shield my eyes and scoured the meadow, searching for any sign of the monster. But instead, I spotted the Faelings I'd helped rescue running towards us, too far to make out their faces, but I could tell they were panicked. Even Ennis seemed in a hurry; he'd tucked the two witches under his one arm as if they were footballs, managing somehow to keep his balance, though the witches were being flung about like rag dolls in the process. Of course, when what was chasing them broke through the tree line in the distance, any concern I might have had for the wellbeing of the witches vanished, replaced by awe and dismay.

Frankenstein's monster—a hideous amalgamation of various Faelings—had doubled in size, although its proportions were only slightly altered from when I'd last seen it. As I watched, it thrust what had once been Ennis' arm into the ground and propelled itself forward, loping across the clearing like a hundred-pound mastiff chasing field mice. Unfortunately, next to that gargantuan thing, we were all tiny rodents. Easily exterminated rodents.

"Ye thought *that* was one of us?" I asked, giving Max a flat, level stare.

"I have not met that many Fae. Do they not get that big, usually?"

I started to open my mouth to comment on the fact that they weren't all that *ugly*, then closed it. The truth was some Fae were pretty hideous, and a few were nearly that big. But that's not why I stopped myself; what Max had said had given me an idea. "Give me that schematic," I said.

Max passed over the phone he'd stolen off Ygor, and I adjusted the image on his screen until I could see where we were in relation to the laboratory. Meanwhile, the Faelings drew close enough that I could hear them shouting, their voices indistinct, but audible. Of course, I didn't need to hear them to know what they were saying; even the thin, warbling voices of the pixies would be urging us to run. But I wasn't interested in running. Besides, I'd hit my step count for the day, and my poor boots were pretty much done for.

"Here." I tossed Max his phone.

"Do you have a plan?" he asked.

"Aye, but if it doesn't work, I'm out of ideas."

"What can I do?"

I waved that off. "This one's on me. If it falls flat, do your best to get the other Fae to safety. I'll lead it off." Of course, what I didn't say was the obvious; as big as the monster was, I'd be hard pressed to outrun the damn thing. In reality, my only contribution as a distraction would be if the creature decided it wanted to toy with me. Or if it slipped and fell when it squashed me flat beneath its foot, like a gag reel involving a banana peel.

Ugh. That visual was going to stick with me.

I took a deep breath and held out both hands. I had no idea if using two hands would help or not but figured it couldn't hurt. I closed my eyes, ignoring the approaching screams and the sound of a lumbering monstrosity coming to squash me flat. I pictured the schematic and overlaid it on the meadow. Then, once I was as sure as could be, I opened my eyes, created the Gateway, and stepped through into relative darkness.

*T*he alcove was exactly how I'd left it, including Jameson, who I found hugging his knees, unable to move beyond occasionally adjusting himself. The giant swung his head around to look down at me, his miserable face barely visible beneath the eerie green light of the Gateway flickering behind me. "Oy! Ye ready to get out of here?" I yelled.

The giant scratched at his cheek and coughed so loudly that I felt it reverberate in my chest, as if I were standing in front of a subwoofer. "Out." Jameson nodded. "Yes."

"Good. Now then, when I tell ye to, I want ye to try and stand up, alright?"

Jameson started to stand and banged his head against the ceiling—a shower of debris falling around his shoulders. He made a pained sound and rubbed at his scalp, looking at me accusatorily.

"I said when I tell ye to!" Of course, that was assuming I succeeded; what I was planning wasn't exactly a sure thing. I mean, sure, I'd successfully created a few Gateways since learning I was capable of the feat. Hell, I'd managed to create a Gateway under someone's feet earlier. Thing is, not only had that someone happened to be an average-sized person, but I'd been fairly imprecise regarding his destination. Making a Gateway large enough for Jameson, not to mention getting the target right, would require a lot more concentration...assuming it was even possible. But I had to try.

I was plum out of other ideas.

I shut my eyes and felt the Gateway behind me snap shut as I visualized another, larger Gateway above Jameson's head. I poured energy into it, making it bigger, focusing on the intended destination—the meadow above. But, for some reason, I found it significantly more taxing. Draining. In fact, I felt my energy waning with every passing second, until at last I knew I couldn't continue.

I opened my eyes, groggily. "Jameson, now!" I called, voice weakened.

The giant rose creakily, like an old man getting out of his hospital bed. But he did rise, shoulders nearly brushing the edges of the Gateway I'd created—a Gateway so wide that sunlight spilled into the chamber and the hallway beyond. The giant raised his hands to his face, shielding his eyes from the light, then took a tenuous step forward as if climbing up the stairs, and ascended beyond the chamber onto the surface. Once he'd cleared both legs, I slammed the Gateway closed, reopened the one behind me, and stumbled through.

"Did it work?" I asked, breathing labored.

"Did what work?" Max asked, whirling to face me, turning his attention from the Faelings and the monster beyond for a moment. Both were much closer than they had been only minutes before, although it seemed the Faelings had shown a little ingenuity by splitting up to keep the monster from hunting them all down at once. Max's eyes widened, and he pointed over my shoulder. "Please tell me he is part of your plan?" Max asked, breathlessly

I spun in time to see Jameson lumbering towards us, hands still bound together by chains, but otherwise free. The giant waved one massive hand, and I returned the gesture. "Aye, that's the one." I turned to Max. "Help the others get clear, if ye can. Tell 'em you're with me."

"And what are you going to do?"

"What I do best...pick a fight." I slapped Max's bare shoulder, grinned, and made a beeline for Jameson. Or tried, anyway. I was so exhausted the best I could manage was a beleaguered jog. Once I was within earshot, however, I began shouting. "Jameson! That t'ing is tryin' to hurt your friends!" I pointed at the monster, who'd begun spinning in circles, trying to decide which Fae to hunt down first.

Jameson lifted his eyes beyond me and a strange look passed over his face. Disgust, maybe? Contempt? Either way, it seemed Jameson was smart enough to be repulsed by the thing Frankenstein created and wouldn't need telling twice; his gait went from a casual jog to a sprint, tearing up the ground as he went, huge clods of earth flying. I ducked as a shower of dirt spewed over me, covering my head, leaving me hissing and spitting.

A slight tremor rocked the ground beneath my feet, and I poked my head out to find Jameson had collided with Frankenstein's monster. The two creatures were grappling, Jameson hooking the monster's longer arm, using his hips to twist and pull the creature off balance. The giant roared and, in an impressive display of strength, hip threw the monster, flinging the massive, misshapen behemoth end-over-end to land flat on its back. I fell to my knees as the ground shook, a cloud of dirt flying into the air.

But Jameson wasn't done.

The giant wrapped his chains around the monster's throat as it struggled to sit up, its upper body so heavy it could barely manage. Ironically, it seemed that in their effort to make the monster as hideous as possible, Frankenstein and his crew had created something uncoordinated, daunting only in that it was so much larger than all the other bipeds on this planet. In essence, they hadn't counted on the abomination taking on a giant.

And Jameson was taking advantage of that.

The giant pulled, forearms straining, his chains burying themselves so far inside the monster's flesh that they began to disappear, swallowed by the skin that protected its throat. I watched as those mismatched eyes bulged, its tongue lolling, and yet it didn't seem to matter; the monster reached around with its long arm, scrabbling for Jameson, while its shorter limb clawed at the chain. It refused to die, and I could see Jameson's strength fading.

"You won't beat that thing with brute force," a sultry voice said. I spun about and found Morgan le Fay watching the ensuing battle, still cloaked in red, her raven-hair billowing in the slight breeze.

"What are ye doin' here?"

"You were taking an awfully long time," Morgan replied. "Thought I'd come see what was holding you two up." The witch scanned the horizon. "Where is the brujo?"

"Off makin' sure your backstabbin' witches survive long enough to get Maria back," I snapped.

"So, they were turned, after all," Morgan replied, lips pursed.

"Wait, ye knew?" I rose to my feet, glaring at the High Priestess, but she didn't seem to notice, or care.

"You have a bigger problem," Morgan said, tilting her head towards the fight, where Jameson had fallen to one knee, his grip on the monster's throat looser than it had been a moment ago. "That poor creature..." Morgan shook her head. "Dolores and Pearl will not be forgiven for this."

"Why won't it just die?" I muttered.

"It cannot." Morgan's voice was tinged with sadness, and I realized she was crying. "It was forged from pieces of nigh-immortal beings, animated through unforgivable means, then bound and sanctified by witches. It must have taken days, even weeks, of preparation. But to conceive of such a thing, to even entertain the idea, I don't understand..."

"They wanted to use it to expose us all to the world. To terrorize the Regulars and prove the Fae existed," I explained.

"To what end?"

"To start a war," I replied, paraphrasing what Ryan had told me. "Eventually, to destroy what few gates still exist between our world and theirs."

Morgan snorted. "Then they are fools."

"Why?"

"Because that would only bring the two worlds closer! The Fae influence has been waning in this realm for a long time. Believers are few and far between. In another hundred years, the gates will not exist. The Old Gods will be forgotten, no longer idolized. Magic will die, replaced by science. What they have done here is guaranteed to slow that process, perhaps even reverse it."

"Then why..." I shook my head. Ryan had seemed so certain, but what if he was wrong? What if he'd been lied to, convinced that *this* was the way to get back at his nemesis. What if the Winter Queen had different goals in mind? After meeting the catty bitch, I was more than willing to buy that. Still, none of that wouldn't solve the immediate problem. "What can we do?" I asked, grabbing at Morgan's cloak.

Morgan sighed. "I can do nothing. With time, and a plan, perhaps. But for now, this creature is beyond me. It is filled to bursting with magic. Volatile magic."

"We can't just leave it here," I insisted. "What about a Gateway? We could drop it into the ocean? Or leave it to die in a desert?"

Morgan frowned at me. "Would you do such a thing, Merlin's daughter? Would you condemn that poor creature to a fate worse than death? Look at it. Really look."

I did, facing the combatants once more. Jameson was on his back, now, digging into the earth with his heels to keep the monster from rising, as it was trying to do. I stared at the monster's horrific face, the offsetting patches of skin, and saw something I'd missed before. An almost imperceptible emotion skittering across that hideous visage. Fear. The thing was terrified. And what's worse, now that I could see it, I could feel it, too.

In an instant, the monster's fear became a palpable thing, skittering over my arms like spiders, slithering up my thighs like snakes, blinding, choking. I let go of Morgan's robe and stumbled forward, reaching out towards that poor, suffering creature.

"What is it?" Morgan asked. "What do you feel?"

But I was beyond talking, now. It was all I could do to ride those waves of terror and not drown, not give in. It was as if part of me—a part I'd never realized existed—was suddenly bound to this thing. Linked, somehow. Within seconds, I felt another wave of something—concern. I glanced down and saw Morgan's hand on my arm, helping to keep me upright. I locked eyes with the legendary enchantress and felt her draw away, yanking her hand back so forcefully it made me stagger.

"What are you?" she whispered.

"Ye mean ye don't know?" I replied sarcastically, straightening.

"I've never seen anything quite like you," Morgan admitted. "You can move yourself through time as Merlin did, but it's as if you have a great, gaping hole where your mother's power should be. And it's as if it will take whatever is at hand to fill itself." Her eyes widened, and she put a hand to her mouth. *"That's* why you were able to subvert the ritual. That's what the remarkable device on your wrist tracks. The energy you devour."

I glanced down at the silver sundial, recalling that crystalline moment when I'd absorbed the heat of Max's all-consuming fire. After opening the Gateways, it seemed the gnomon had cycled back to its original position. "A hole..." I whispered. The hole where my mother's power should be. But I knew where her power was, didn't I? I'd spoken to it. To my mother's ghost, the last remnant of her power.

Another tremor brought me back to the present moment. I whirled and saw Jameson on his side, bleeding from his mouth, eyes closed. The monster loomed over him, panting, torso expanding and contracting so visibly with every breath it seemed like a massive, pumping heart with limbs attached. It raised that long arm and made a fist, preparing to bring it down.

Preparing to finish off its assailant.

"No!" I yelled. I held out my hand, arm outstretched, and the monster hesitated. I could feel it again, feel its rage. It wasn't scared now. It wanted the giant to pay. It wanted the giant to die and never, ever hurt it again. The creature's thoughts were primitive, even animalistic. But this anger, this righteous need to destroy, *that* I understood.

I latched on to those emotions, drawn to them. I strode forward, letting that rage dance along my skin, bathing in its heat, relishing in it. But the closer I got, the more I realized this wasn't merely emotion, it was power. The power that animated the monster, that gave it life, that made it *need.* Made it want. With every step I could sense more of that magic, until at last

I stood only a few feet away, staring up into the bitter, angry eyes of a creature who could not die.

I pressed my hand against its flesh, and it was as if everything I'd felt before had been tucked safely away behind bulletproof glass; emotions swirled violently through me. Anger and fear, yes. But also sorrow. Confusion. This creature was an infant, abandoned by its caretaker, too young to understand its place in the world, and too powerful to have one.

I reached out to that wild, volatile magic. At first, it rebuked me, slapping me away like an errant fly. But I wasn't so easily dismissed; I thrust my own dwindling energy into that maelstrom of power, prying it open like a kitchen drawer which refused to budge.

The ensuing rush of power hit me like a closed fist, sending me to my knees. But I kept my hand on the creature's flesh, even as it shifted under my palm—a roiling sensation that reminded me of a snake curling beneath my hand. And yet, as the creature shrunk, I felt my own blood boil, my skin flush. Energy coursed through me, and I fed on it. I let it fill that empty hole Morgan had brought to my attention, although I knew it wouldn't be enough, knew I wouldn't be complete—not even with this much power. My mother had been a goddess once, one of the mightiest beings in existence, and without that power I was an empty vessel.

Still, a meal's a meal.

Once the creature had diminished to eye level, I rose to my feet, cradling the side of its face in one hand. It was crying out of one eye, knowing somehow—despite its tumultuous, chaotic thoughts—that it was dying. That I was killing it.

"I'm so sorry," I whispered. And I was. Sorry to end its miserable existence before it could grow, before it could be allowed to think for itself. Sorry it had ever been fashioned in the first place. Sorry that I was the one who had to kill it, to bear that burden—because it would be a burden. I stayed there, cradling the creature's face, until the last light flickered in its eyes—one final surge of suffering, then nothing.

It went limp and toppled to the ground, lifeless.

The others found me standing beside its corpse, gathering around over the next several minutes. I could feel them at my back—literally. All their emotions. Their gratefulness. Their joy. Their guilt. Their fear. I knew I could turn this hunger on them, that I could feed on their life-force as I had this creature's. Had my mother intended for this to happen? Was this the power of the Tuatha de Danann? The power to strip everything from their subjects on a whim?

"You'll never be whole," Morgan warned, as if she could sense what I was considering. The sound of her footsteps crunching on dead grass enough to make me turn. "Not this way," she insisted.

"Worried I'll gobble ye all up?" I asked, giving her a flat stare.

Morgan chuckled. "The others, perhaps. But you'd be biting off a bit more than you can chew with me."

I stared at the woman and flexed my burgeoning power. A flock of birds soaring overhead froze in mid-flight, their wings unfurled. Sun motes stood still. I strolled forward, circled the High Priestess, and put my hand on her shoulder. I leaned in and felt something inside me give as time reasserted itself. "Wanna bet?" I whispered.

Morgan jumped, dancing away from me so quickly she actually tripped and fell back on her ass. She glared up at me and began to say something, but I held up my hand.

"No threats, please." I shook my head. "That was childish, I know. I apologize."

Morgan looked taken aback, then suspicious. She glanced at the gathered Faelings, then back at me. "Something tells me that doesn't happen often," she said, warily.

"It doesn't. Ennis!" I called. "Drop the witches!"

Ennis did as I asked; two thuds and a moan accompanied their unceremonious fall. Morgan glanced back, sighed, and made to get to her feet. I helped her, drawing the High Priestess up with very little effort; it seemed my strength and stamina had returned in full force after consuming the creature's magical energy.

Morgan held my hand a moment longer than necessary, searching my eyes. "Your father never would have apologized, you know."

I released her hand. "Is he alive?"

"I don't know," Morgan admitted. "He was always a mystery, even to those closest to him."

"Well look, me da was never part of me life to begin with," I said after a moment's silence, sounding more tired than bitter. "Why should I have inherited anythin' from him, anyway? Me stubbornness is me own trait. Aren't I entitled to change, if I want?"

Morgan smiled. "I'm beginning to see why Merlin chose as he did. The power of a god, with none of the limitations. But with the heart, the conscience of a mortal."

I rolled my eyes. "Don't read too much into it. I'm still pissed ye let us walk into this mess without warnin' us about your witches, first."

"I wasn't certain. But it's true, I did suspect these two had opted to join another faction. They are young. Ambitious. Part of a splinter group, you might say, trying to make their marks on the world."

"Ye used us," I said, a sudden realization registering even as I spoke. "This way, ye can say ye had no part in takin' 'em down. Ye won't even have to get your hands dirty."

Morgan had the grace to look embarrassed. "Please understand. Being powerful is not the same as being a good leader," she said. "Not all of my people believe as I do, or would rule as I do, although I have seen more rebellions, more betrayal, than anyone I know. I have become well acquainted with what actions foster hate, and how to avoid them." She sighed. "But you're right. It did seem easier to point fingers at outsiders and lay the blame at your feet. It was a cowardly decision. But a necessary one."

I nodded, comprehension dawning. In her own way, Morgan was as fixated on protecting her people as I was—with the added hindsight provided by several centuries of experience, be those successes or failures. "Where's Maria?" I asked, deciding to change the subject.

Morgan grinned, shaking her head. "She came to not long after you left. I've never heard such language. I had to bespell her to keep her from trying to shoot me." Morgan snapped her fingers, and a Gateway appeared. Through it, I saw Maria lounging on a recliner, sipping a beer.

She saw me, smiled, and hopped up. "MacKenna!" she said excitedly, leaping through the opening to land in my outstretched arms; I'd been too shocked to step aside. "How are you?"

I fumbled my words, at a loss as to how to respond. "Livin' the dream," I replied, finally. "Or *a* dream, anyway."

"It should wear off in a couple hours," Morgan added, patting my shoulder. She fetched her two coven members and marched them towards her Gateway. I noticed the brunette glaring at me, a bruise running the length of her face. Meanwhile, the blonde refused to look at me, whimpering whenever I glanced in her direction.

"Does it have to wear off?" I asked, studying the exuberant face of the detective I'd come to loathe.

Morgan laughed. "Yes. It is impossible to change anyone permanently against their will. We all revert to who we were meant to be, eventually."

I met the woman's gaze. "And just who am I meant to be?" I asked, only half-teasing.

"That remains to be seen." Morgan cocked her head. "But, if you ever want help figuring it out, come to Salem. I'll be waiting." She winked as she thrust her two charges face first through the Gateway, letting them fall—squealing—to the cave floor. "Until then."

The High Priestess stepped through, leaving myself, two witches, and a handful of Faelings in a meadow in the middle of nowhere.

There was a joke in there somewhere.

But, for once, I wasn't in the mood.

CHAPTER 35

Fortunately, it seemed Maria had jokes enough for all of us. The Hispanic detective, flush with a youthful energy I'd never seen her display before, spun a slow circle, staring at the vast array of Faelings in the immediate vicinity, including the unconscious giant, and burst out laughing. She slapped my shoulder. "Only you, MacKenna. Only you would have such ridiculous friends." Then, before I could comment, she began jumping up and down. "Max! Max, over here!" Maria called, waving.

I plucked her from mid-air and settled her on her feet before she went and sprained an ankle. "Max!" I called. "Come keep Maria company while I sort out where we go from here."

Max obeyed, weaving through the Faelings and linking his arm in Maria's, leading her away from the carnage, chatting in Spanish. I sighed. "Ye know, in hindsight, I think I prefer the bitchy Maria," I muttered under my breath. At least that version I could relate to. Vapid, bouncy Maria had no place in my life.

Hell, vapid, bouncy *people* had no place in my life.

"Did you say something?" Petal asked, hovering just past my shoulder.

"Just talkin' to meself," I replied, rubbing at the bridge of my nose. "So, did everyone make it out? No casualties, right?"

"All accounted for. Even Ariel is up and about, now."

I snorted. "Is that right? Is that how we managed to survive all this?"

Petal cocked her head. "Ariel had nothing to do with it. She was too weak to lend you anymore luck. We're alive, and free, because of you, Lady Quinn."

"That's not—" I began.

"Lady Quinn," Ennis barked, his ravaged face sporting a grisly grin. The ogre bent at the waist, listing slightly to his heavier side.

"Don't—"

"Lady Quinn," Eleanor chimed in, curtsying in mid-air, a move which Petal mimicked. The title was repeated by the remaining members, each bowing or curtsying as was appropriate. I felt my cheeks burning but didn't turn away. To do so would be to reject them, and something told me they wouldn't recover from a casual dismissal of their feelings. Not after everything they'd been through.

"I'm just glad you're all safe," I replied, at last, bowing awkwardly, tossing my cloak aside in the process.

"What now, Lady Quinn?" Petal asked.

"Please, no more of that," I insisted, straightening. Petal gave me a small shrug and an almost imperceptible smile that said she'd do as she pleased. I let it go. "Now...now we get ye lot home," I declared.

"All of us?" Eleanor asked, sounding surprised. "Even Jameson?"

Oh, right. The giant. I frowned, considering what to do. I could create another Gateway, but to where? Of course, that was assuming I could even make another large enough for Jameson to pass through. After I'd nearly keeled over making the last one, the thought didn't exactly appeal to me.

"I will guard him," a woman said. Ariel floated forward, little more than an errant twist in the wind, shaped vaguely like a person—similar to the waves you sometimes see bending the air on hot summer days, or rising up from a manhole. The thought made me wonder how many of her kind I'd seen before without realizing it, hiding in plain sight.

"But Ariel—" Petal began.

"We'll travel at night," Ariel interrupted, placatingly. "Remember, giants can turn to stone to avoid detection, and I am all but invisible to mortals. It shouldn't take long."

I glanced at Petal, who seemed reticent, but finally nodded.

"Very well," she replied.

"Ariel," I said, earning the Faeling's attention. "I want ye to know I'd never have found ye all if it weren't for what ye did. T'anks for that."

173

"We can all use a little luck sometimes, Lady Quinn. You, I think, more than most," she chided.

I coughed out a laugh. "Ain't that the truth."

"Quinn," Max called, waving, Maria riding piggyback, her legs wrapped around his naked waist, tugging on two ends of his shoulder-length hair as if they were handlebars. The look in his eyes screamed for help.

I waved back, laughing. "Just a few more minutes!" I called. He sighed and began shuffling away, urged to a trot by Maria's insistent squeals. I turned back to the Faelings, grinning.

"Is there anything left to discuss before we leave?" Petal asked, frowning.

"Nope."

Petal glanced at the cheering detective and her broad, muscular mount, raised both eyebrows, and flashed those sharpened teeth. "Nice."

CHAPTER 36

$\mathcal{H}$ ansel's office was as I remembered it: dark and stately, the walls lined with books bound in the same cast of brown leather, lit by sconces and small, tasteful lamps. I occupied one of Hansel's ornate chairs, opposite the two German siblings once more.

"I was wrong to doubt you," Hansel said, breaking the silence that had welled up since they'd invited me to sit.

"No, you weren't," I replied.

Hansel's eyebrows shot up in surprise, Gretel's as well; I think they'd expected me to agree. I sighed and ran my fingers along the robe I'd essentially stolen from Morgan's people. It was frayed and dirty, as was the rest of me; I hadn't had time to shower before my audience with the Chancery's lawyers. I almost felt bad, sitting in their fancy leather chair; they'd definitely have to get it cleaned after I left.

"Listen," I began, "I didn't save your people. Not really. I had help, and a lot of luck on me side. All I did was follow the breadcrumbs."

The Germans pursed their lips but let that particular turn of phrase slide. In the end, it was Gretel who spoke, her tone wary. "I'm glad you succeeded, but I worry this is false modesty."

"Ye mean I don't seem the humble type," I ventured. Hansel coughed, covering up a small laugh. I nodded, smiling. "You're right. I'm not. But, this once, I want to try t'ings a different way." I stared down at my hand, flexing it. "Ye know, ever since I was a wee girl, I've always liked havin' people owe me." I glanced up, meeting their eyes in turn, marveling at how different two shades of blue could be.

They each nodded. "We understand," Gretel added, for emphasis. "What is it you want from us as payment for our people's safe return?"

"No, see, that won't do. Not this time." I leaned forward, clasping my hands together. "T'ing is, as far as I'm concerned, ye owe me nothin'." The siblings shared surprised glances. "But," I amended, holding up a finger, "ye do owe your people. Without 'em, after all, the Winter Queen would have brought a war to your doors."

"A what?" Hansel asked, eyes wide.

I waved that off. "That's not the important bit. Her plan failed. But I t'ink we can all agree it didn't have to happen like this. That it should never have gotten this far." I gave them both knowing looks.

"What is it you want?" Gretel asked.

"I want ye to name Scathach and Robin as the new Adjudicators." I held up a hand before either could speak. "I want ye to plan for more attacks. For bigger threats. Because I have a feelin' they're comin'. And soon, too soon to wait around on help that may never arrive."

Gretel crossed her legs, staring me down, rapping her nails sequentially on the arm of her chair. "Have you considered applying?" she asked, promptly ignoring her brother's shocked expression.

"Me?" I found myself shaking my head before I could even think up a response. "Look, I'm no good at politics, and I know next to nothin' about the Fae. No, Robin and Scathach are your best options. Besides, I'm goin' to be busy, soon, I t'ink."

"Busy?" Gretel echoed.

"Aye," I replied, though I didn't elaborate; now wasn't the time to discuss my travel itinerary.

"I see."

"What makes you think the Huntress will agree?" Hansel asked. "She's turned down the position before. Numerous times."

"Because she will have no choice," I answered. "Because, if she doesn't, the war that's comin' may bleed over, may affect the ones she cares about. If she refuses to see that, tell her it was me idea. I'll talk some sense into her."

Gretel gave me yet another considering look. "You seem to have changed in a rather short span of time, if you don't mind the observation, Miss MacKenna."

I shrugged. It was true, though not entirely accurate. I hadn't changed all that much; I'd simply decided which path I was going to take, moving forward. Honestly, there's a lot to be said for finding one's intended destination. For years, I'd played things by ear. Dealing in magical artifacts by necessity, then because I felt I was better at it than I'd ever been at anything else—except maybe drinking. And all the while I'd been searching for that sense of belonging I'd always felt was missing. Until Dez died, that is, and I'd realized I'd belonged all along. But now? Now, I finally had my answers. I knew I who my mother was. Who my father was. Sure, it wasn't as satisfying as I'd hoped, but it was closure, of a sort. Enough that I could start looking to move on, at least. To build a life of my own, whatever that looked like.

Plus, I was dogshit tired.

"We'll see if it sticks," I said, smiling wryly.

A knock at the door interrupted whatever Gretel had been about to say next, and a small, elderly gentleman poked his head in. He had the same fine blonde hair as his siblings, though he wore it short, and his thick bifocals took some of the shine away from his blue eyes. But still, there was no mistaking the resemblance.

"Ah, Hans," Gretel said, waving him forward. "Come in. We were just finishing up with Miss MacKenna."

Hansel the Younger—Hans—turned to me, his mouth open in surprise, though that quickly gave way to a broad smile. "It is a pleasure, Quinn MacKenna! Niece of Desdemona Jones, once Desdemona Flaherty before fleeing Ireland. Daughter of Morrigan MacKenna, once Morrigan McNair, once Morrigan Malloy. She did like her alliteration, your mother," Hans said, jovially.

I simply stared at the man.

"Our brother is a bit of a genealogist. He does background work for us from time to time," Gretel explained.

"I investigated you quite some time ago," Hans added. "I even went to your aunt's home to discuss the matter of your sibling once. But you weren't home, of course. I'd planned to visit your apartment but was told to leave you be." Hans leaned in conspiratorially, and I realized he had a brace on one leg, making his otherwise casual movement awkward and ungainly. "Came directly from the top, or so I'm told." He winked.

"I'm sorry," I said, after a long, uncomfortable silence, "but d'ye say somethin' about a siblin'? And what's this about me ma havin' three different last names?"

Hans straightened and glanced back at his brother and sister, both of whom had buried their heads in their hands. "Did I do it again?" Hans asked.

Hansel nodded, wordlessly.

"Our brother means well," Gretel assured me. "But when he investigates, he tends to find out more than most. I'm sorry."

"I don't understand..." I started to laugh, though it was strained. "Listen, I don't have a brother or sister. Ye must be mistaken."

Hans thrust his glasses up his nose. "Well, technically—"

"Hans," Gretel hissed. "Enough."

"No, tell me," I insisted.

Hans glanced back and forth between the two of us before finally meeting my eyes. "Technically you have a half-brother, or sister. It is unlikely you share the same father. Your mother and your aunt came to this country long after she gave birth to her first child, back in Ireland, and there was no reason to suspect she was joined by the same man. That, and the baby she bore was given away, according to the paperwork I was able to obtain."

I sat, mute, unable to process what he was telling me. Finally, Gretel took pity on me. "Listen," she said, "you've had a long few days. I'll have Hans send over everything he found first thing in the morning. But you should keep in mind that he may have gotten it wrong." Hans started to protest, but Gretel interrupted him, "For example, I doubt he knew one of your parents was, in fact, Fae, or he'd have disclosed that to *us*." She stared her younger brother down, daring him to contradict her.

Hans looked surprised, then brightened. "Oh, this makes so much more sense! I must go back over everything!"

Hansel groaned.

"Do it," I said.

Everyone turned to look at me.

"Go over everythin'. I want to know everythin' there is to know about 'em, about this child ye mentioned. All of it. I'll even tell ye who me da is, if ye t'ink it'll help."

"Oh, it will!" Hans insisted.

"Merlin," I said. "Me da is Merlin."

Now it was their turn to stare at me, the silence building until you could hear a wand drop.

Guess even lawyers end up speechless sometimes.

Good to know.

CHAPTER 37

*M*ax, Maria, and I took an Uber to Christoff's bar; I enjoyed the convenience of using a Gateway, but the thought of using one so frivolously simply didn't appeal. I mean, it was *magic*. Surely you should appreciate it enough not to go using it to make your life more convenient.

Right?

Sadly, the instant we stepped outside the offices of *Hansel, Hansel, & Gretel*, I wished I'd opted to do just that; the street was crowded with people milling from one place to the next, drivers blasting their horns, traffic in a total gridlock. I reached out to tap the shoulder of a passerby. "Oy! What's goin' on here?" I asked, gesturing at the crowd.

"Seriously, lady?" the man asked, his rough Southie accent reminding me instantly of home. "It's the World Series. Game 5." He shook his head at me as if I were some sort of alien.

Which, to be fair, I sort of was.

"Let's go say hi to all the people!" Maria yelled, eyes shining with excitement.

"Alright, new plan," I said, cancelling the Uber. I glanced over at Max, who looked as excited as I did about the massive contingent of people we'd have to fight through to get anywhere on a night like tonight, especially wearing the ill-fitting button-up Hansel's secretary had loaned him while he and Maria occupied themselves in the waiting room. "Let's find an alley. Preferably a deserted one."

"Ooh, MacKenna. That's naughty," Maria chimed in, elbowing me gently in the gut.

Max and I shared a look over her head.

"Come on, Maria," Max said, drawing her to his side. "Before Quinn strangles you."

"Don't go threatening me with a good time," she quipped, giggling.

*C*hristoff's bar was oddly busy for a place that wasn't supposed to open for another day. It seemed he'd agreed to let his staff throw a shindig in celebration of the grand opening, which just so happened to coincide with Game 5. TVs lined the bar, many of them haphazardly mounted, with small crowds gathered around each. Most wore various shades of patriotic colors, supporting The Sox—though a brave few had opted for the regalia of the opposing team and were currently defending their choice while tossing back mugs of beer.

The three of us found Robin and Camila cozied up next to one of the smaller TVs, their barstools pressed so close together the backs overlapped. Camila had her head on Robin's beefy shoulder, running her fingers through his beard.

Guess she'd gotten over her Fae-phobia.

"Camila!" Max shouted, eyeing Robin with suspicion. I laughed, dodged Maria's request that I dance with her, and headed for the bar. I needed a drink more than I needed to see the happy reunion—as fun as that was guaranteed to be.

I found Christoff watching one of the screens absentmindedly as he polished glasses, restocking them one at a time. He spotted me and hurried over, smiling. "You made it! Robin was worried."

"Oh, was he, now? Worried I'd catch him pawin' at the bruja, more like," I teased.

Christoff chuckled. "She likes his beard, I think." The barkeep rubbed at his smooth cheeks. "Maybe I will grow mine back. Elena used to hate it, but I thought it made me look manly."

"It made ye look old," I said, smirking. I flashed to the memory of him behind the bar, Elena coming down the stairs, how they'd looked at each other, and felt my smile fade.

Christoff grunted. "That's what Elena said. She grew up in this city, you know. Loved this sport. We watched it together, the last time they went to this World Series of theirs." His smile was wry. "I should have taken her to that game, I think. She would have liked that."

I reached out and squeezed Christoff's hand. "She loved ye, ye know that."

The Russian man nodded, but slowly. "This is true. But maybe it would have been better if she had loved someone else. Safer, at least."

I thought about Ryan, about his confession, the pure misery on his face when I'd told him about Elena's death. I shook my head and drew Christoff's hand to me, clutching it with both of mine. "If love was all about safety, it wouldn't be love," I said, earnestly.

"*Da*," Christoff said, his smile sad, but genuine. "You are right. You know, Elena always said you were a smart girl."

I scoffed at that, but Christoff raised a hand. "I swear it. She always knew you had potential, even when I came home complaining about having to throw you out time and time again." He chuckled. "Elena would say, 'One day that girl will figure out how to forgive people for not meeting her expectations. When that happens, she will prove herself worth all the trouble.'"

"Christoff!" a small, blonde staffer called from further down the bar, holding up her empty mug, drawing his attention. Christoff patted my hands and withdrew. Which was good, because I wasn't particularly in the mood to have him see me cry, or to have to explain why I was crying.

✦

*M*ax found me a couple minutes later, sporting Robin's Red Sox jacket. I thought it fit pretty well for what amounted to Camila's dowry. The brujo sat down on the barstool beside me, slid a snifter of whiskey across the bar top, then made to cheers me. I smirked, raised the glass, and tapped it against his beer. "So, was that Robin's peace offerin'?" I asked, tilting my head towards the jacket after tossing back some of the whiskey, relishing in that sweet burn.

"Camila said I looked like shit," Max replied, lips pursed. "Her new...friend...offered me his jacket." Max grinned, shaking his head. "But still, I am glad to see her happy."

"D'ye tell her about Ygor?"

"Now is not the time," Max replied, face darkening. "It would upset her. Later, when we are alone, perhaps."

I sipped my whiskey, then studied the big man. He'd swept his hair back behind one ear, leaving his face bare, his jawline so masculine it made everyone else look like they had a glass jaw. I nudged him. "I t'ink it's about time I head home," I said, slipping off my barstool. I threw back the rest of the whiskey and squeezed his arm. "T'anks for the drink."

"The game isn't over," Max said, staring up at me. "Do you not want to see how it ends?"

I smiled. "That's the beauty of livin' in Boston. We're always winnin' one t'ing or another. I'm sure I'll get another shot. Besides, I haven't slept or showered in two days. Plus, I need to water me plant. She gets temperamental when left alone too long."

Max grunted and stood, leaving his half-finished beer on the bar. "Let me walk you out," he insisted.

I thought about it. Really thought about it. "Alright," I said. "But keep in mind, if ye try anythin', I can always drop ye into an ocean on a whim."

Max gazed into my eyes, his height advantage slight enough it made the stare that much more intimate. "That is a risk I am willing to take, *señorita.*"

I felt a blush creep up my cheeks, but turned before he could see it, and headed for the door. Out of the corner of my eye, I spotted Maria chatting up Robin and Camila, both of whom looked amused, if not a little annoyed. Robin happened to spot me and raised a hand, saluting me from across the bar. I rolled my eyes and flashed him a thumbs up. All in all, it was the best exchange of shoddy sign language I'd ever had; most of the time it ended with me giving someone the finger.

Once outside, Max removed Robin's jacket and draped it over my shoulders before I froze to death; I'd left the cloak with Christoff, unsure what else to do with it. I snuggled into that warmth and sighed. "Won't ye be cold?" I asked, turning to the brujo.

He stepped into me, slid one hand around to the small of my back, and rested his fingers along my cheek. It was smoothly done, like a perfectly executed dance move. "With you, I am never cold," he said, grinning.

"Liar," I said, my own hands resting on his chest, smirking.

Max shrugged. "*Si*, but it was a good line, right?"

I laughed. "Aye, it was."

"Warm me up?" Max suggested, eyes hopeful.

This time, when I gazed into that face, I saw something else besides all that masculinity. I saw a man, vulnerable, waiting for me to make a move. Ordinarily, I'd have preferred a man to take charge, to take the risk. But for some reason—in the circle of Max's arms—I found it charming. I nodded, once, then rose just a hair to press my lips against his. The kiss was chaste, our lips moistened by the drinks. Then, suddenly, it wasn't. Max drew me close, pressing the line of our bodies together, and kissed me the way you so often see leading men do it. Max kissed me as if I were the last woman he'd ever kiss, so thorough that when he finally leaned back to look at me, I was breathless, eyes closed.

"I feel much warmer," he said, his voice low.

I opened my eyes, then pushed myself away. "Christ!"

"What?" Max asked, surprised, then hurt.

I pointed. "Look at ye," I hissed. The big man looked down and cursed, finally seeing what I'd seen the instant I opened my eyes: those flaming tattoos spiraling all over his face and arms, so bright they even shone beneath his t-shirt. I hurriedly removed Robin's jacket and tossed it to the man. "Cover up!" I insisted, glancing out into the street to see if anyone had noticed. Fortunately, on a night like tonight, everyone's attention was elsewhere.

Max threw on the jacket, zipping it over his throat, leaving only his face shining in the darkness, an arc of flame curling over one eye and down his cheek like a question mark. I wanted to reach out and caress that cheek, I realized. To run my fingers along that bright flame. I huddled into myself, worried about what would happen if I did.

"I am sorry," Max said. "I had no idea—"

"It's alright. Not your fault," I said, shaking my head.

"Then why do I have a feeling I am about to be punished?"

"Because ye aren't stupid," I said, sighing. I reached out and squeezed his arm. "It's time I head home. Goodnight, Max." I left him there, watching me with serious eyes, the fiery tattoos fading, and headed downtown, looking for the nearest darkened alley.

"I will call you tomorrow!" Max yelled, finally, causing half the street to look back at him. I glanced back and saw him grinning, unperturbed by the attention, arms folded across his chest.

I rolled my eyes but found myself smiling back. "*Hasta la vista*, baby," I muttered.

CHAPTER 38

*I*t's been months now since I last dreamed of my mother's ghost. Which is a real shame, because I've got questions. Primarily about this hole inside me, and how I can fill it before I start inadvertently feeding off my friends and neighbors. Oh yeah, and let's not forget whether or not I have a half-sibling running around out there somewhere.

Of course, that doesn't mean I'm out of options; I know where she lives, after all. The Otherworld. Home to the Tuatha de Danann, to the Fae Royals, sort of like what Valhalla is to the Norse Gods, or Mount Olympus to the Greeks, I gather. I've been there before, but my stay had been brief to say the least...not to mention troubling. Still, if I'm not given answers soon, I may have to seek them out myself.

Speaking of answers, I still haven't given Max mine. He's asked me out twice, and I've put him off both times. Partly because I've been busy, but also partly because I'm worried about what might happen if our contact upgrades from incidental to intentional. Neither of us knew what to make of his little light show, but I could admit—at least to myself—that I'd felt a connection. I simply wasn't sure how much of that connection was meta-physical, and how much was straight physical.

So, for now, I was keeping my distance.

Ironically, it seems the brujo is the only person I can keep my distance from in this city; ever since returning to Boston, I've been fielding off calls left and right from members of the Chancery to attend this or that event. I've managed to turn down most, but not all. Sadly, my preferred date for these politically motivated invitations—a certain Redcap—seems a little preoccupied with his new bruja girlfriend. Camila and I get along well enough now, though, that I don't mind the intrusion—especially since she apologized. She keeps dropping hints about her brother's undying devotion to me, religiously attempting to set up double dates. It's almost cute. Almost.

Halloween is just around the corner, and Eve is already begging me to let her sit outside my apartment and greet people, like some sort of prop. I think I'll veto the idea, but I am looking into taking her to Fae like I'd promised—hence my travel plans. In fact, I've gotten so wrapped up in research that I've forgotten all about buying a costume. Frankly, while I once loved to dress up, to throw on a goofy onesie, or slip into something skintight, I'm not sure I'm in the mood to pretend to be something I'm not, at the moment. Feels a lot like I've been doing that my whole life. Besides, I have no idea what I'd go as.

I'm the daughter of the world's most infamous wizard and a Celtic goddess, a time-defying, magic-devouring half-breed, and—apparently— still growing the fuck up, one day at a time.

With all that shit to work with, who even needs a fucking costume?

*Q*uinn MacKenna returns in SALTY DOG. Get your copy online!
http://www.shaynesilvers.com/l/533506

VIP's get early access to all sorts of Temple-Verse goodies, including signed copies, private giveaways, and advance notice of future projects. AND A FREE NOVELLA! Join here: www.shaynesilvers.com/l/219800

*Turn the page to read a sample of **OBSIDIAN SON** - Nate Temple Book 1 - or **BUY ONLINE (It's FREE with a Kindle Unlimited subscription**). Nate Temple is a billionaire wizard from St. Louis. He rides a bloodthirsty unicorn and drinks with the Four Horsemen. He even cow-tipped the Minotaur. Once...*

TRY: OBSIDIAN SON (NATE TEMPLE #1)

There was no room for emotion in a hate crime. I had to be cold. Heartless. This was just another victim. Nothing more. No face, no name.

Frosted blades of grass crunched under my feet, sounding to my ears like the symbolic glass that one would shatter under a napkin at a Jewish wedding. The noise would have threatened to give away my stealthy advance as I stalked through the moonlit field, but I was no novice and had planned accordingly. Being a wizard, I was able to muffle all sensory evidence with a fine cloud of magic—no sounds, and no smells. Nifty. But if I made the spell much stronger, the anomaly would be too obvious to my prey.

I knew the consequences for my dark deed tonight. If caught, jail time or possibly even a gruesome, painful death. But if I succeeded, the look of fear and surprise in my victim's eyes before his world collapsed around him, it was well worth the risk. I simply couldn't help myself; I had to take him down.

I knew the cops had been keeping tabs on my car, but I was confident that they hadn't followed me. I hadn't seen a tail on my way here but seeing as how they frowned on this kind of thing, I had taken a circuitous route just in case. I was safe. I hoped.

Then my phone chirped at me as I received a text.

I practically jumped out of my skin, hissing instinctively. "Motherf—" I cut off abruptly, remembering the whole stealth aspect of my mission. I was off to a stellar start. I had forgotten to silence the damned phone. *Stupid, stupid, stupid!*

My heart felt like it was on the verge of exploding inside my chest with such thunderous violence that I briefly envisioned a mystifying Rorschach blood-blot that would have made coroners and psychologists drool.

My body remained tense as I swept my gaze over the field, fearing that I had been made. Precious seconds ticked by without any change in my surroundings, and my breathing finally began to slow as my pulse returned to normal. Hopefully, my magic had muted the phone and my resulting outburst. I glanced down at the phone to scan the text and then typed back a quick and angry response before I switched the cursed device to vibrate.

Now, where were we?

I continued on, the lining of my coat constricting my breathing. Or maybe it was because I was leaning forward in anticipation. *Breathe,* I chided myself. *He doesn't know you're here.* All this risk for a book. It had better be worth it.

I'm taller than most, and not abnormally handsome, but I knew how to play the genetic cards I had been dealt. I had shaggy, dirty blonde hair—leaning more towards brown with each passing year—and my frame was thick with well-earned muscle, yet I was still lean. I had once been told that my eyes were like twin emeralds pitted against the golden-brown tufts of my hair—a face like a jewelry box. Of course, that was two bottles of wine into a date, so I could have been a little foggy on her quote. Still, I liked to imagine that was how everyone saw me.

But tonight, all that was masked by magic.

I grinned broadly as the outline of the hairy hulk finally came into view. He was blessedly alone—no nearby sentries to give me away. That was always a risk when performing this ancient rite-of-passage. I tried to keep the grin on my face from dissolving into a maniacal cackle.

My skin danced with energy, both natural and unnatural, as I manipulated the threads of magic floating all around me. My victim stood just ahead, oblivious to the world of hurt that I was about to unleash. Even with his millennia of experience, he didn't stand a chance. I had done this so many times that the routine of it was my only enemy. I lost count of how many times I had been told not to do it again; those who knew declared it *cruel, evil, and sadistic.* But what fun wasn't? Regardless, that wasn't enough to stop me from doing it again. And again. And again.

It was an addiction.

The pungent smell of manure filled the air, latching onto my nostril hairs. I took another step, trying to calm my racing pulse. A glint of gold reflected in the silver moonlight, but my victim remained motionless, hopefully unaware or all was lost. I wouldn't make it out alive if he knew I was here. Timing was everything.

I carefully took the last two steps, a lifetime between each, watching the legendary monster's ears, anxious and terrified that I would catch even so much as a twitch in my direction. Seeing nothing, a fierce grin split my unshaven cheeks. My spell had worked! I raised my palms an inch away from their target, firmly planted my feet, and squared my shoulders. I took one silent, calming breath, and then heaved forward with every ounce of physical strength I could muster. As well as a teensy-weensy boost of magic. Enough to goose him good.

"*MOOO!!!*" The sound tore through the cool October night like an unstoppable freight train. *Thud-splat!* The beast collapsed sideways onto the frosted grass; straight into a steaming patty of cow shit, cow dung, or, if you really wanted to church it up, a Meadow Muffin. But to me, shit is, and always will be, shit.

Cow tipping. It doesn't get any better than that in Missouri.

Especially when you're tipping the *Minotaur.* Capital M. I'd tipped plenty of ordinary cows before, but never the legendary variety.

Razor-blade hooves tore at the frozen earth as the beast struggled to stand, his grunts of rage vibrating the air. I raised my arms triumphantly. "Boo-yah! Temple 1, Minotaur 0!" I crowed. Then I very bravely prepared to protect myself. Some people just couldn't take a joke. *Cruel, evil,* and *sadistic* cow tipping may be, but by hell, it was a *rush.* The legendary beast turned his gaze on me after gaining his feet, eyes ablaze as his body...*shifted* from his bull disguise into his notorious, well-known bipedal form. He unfolded to his full height on two tree trunk-thick legs, his hooves having magically transformed into heavily booted feet. The thick, gold ring dangling from his snotty snout quivered as the Minotaur panted, and his dense, corded muscles contracted over his now human-like chest. As I stared up into those brown eyes, I actually felt sorry...for, well, myself.

"I have killed greater men than you for lesser offense," he growled.

His voice sounded like an angry James Earl Jones—like Mufasa talking to Scar.

"You have shit on your shoulder, Asterion." I ignited a roiling ball of fire in my palm in order to see his eyes more clearly. By no means was it a defensive gesture on my part. It was just dark. Under the weight of his glare, I somehow managed to keep my face composed, even though my fraudulent, self-denial had curled up into the fetal position and started whimpering. I hoped using a form of his ancient name would give me brownie points. Or maybe just not-worthy-of-killing points.

The beast grunted, eyes tightening, and I sensed the barest hesitation. "Nate Temple...your name would look splendid on my already long list of slain idiots." Asterion took a threatening step forward, and I thrust out my palm in warning, my roiling flame blue now.

"You lost fair and square, Asterion. Yield or perish." The beast's shoulders sagged slightly. Then he finally nodded to himself in resignation, appraising me with the scrutiny of a worthy adversary. "Your time comes, Temple, but I will grant you this. You've got a pair of stones on you to rival Hercules."

I reflexively glanced in the direction of the myth's own crown jewels before jerking my gaze away. Some things you simply couldn't un-see. "Well, I won't be needing a wheelbarrow any time soon, but overcompensating today keeps future lower-back pain away."

The Minotaur blinked once, and then he bellowed out a deep, contagious, snorting laughter. Realizing I wasn't about to become a murder statistic, I couldn't help but join in. It felt good. It had been a while since I had allowed myself to experience genuine laughter.

In the harsh moonlight, his bulk was even more intimidating as he towered head and shoulders above me. This was the beast that had fed upon human sacrifices for countless years while imprisoned in Daedalus' Labyrinth in Greece. And all that protein had not gone to waste, forming a heavily woven musculature over the beast's body that made even Mr. Olympia look puny.

From the neck up, he was now entirely bull, but the rest of his body more closely resembled a thickly furred man. But, as shown moments ago, he could adapt his form to his environment, never appearing fully human, but able to make his entire form appear as a bull when necessary. For instance, how he had looked just before I tipped him. Maybe he had been scouting the field for heifers before I had so efficiently killed the mood.

His bull face was also covered in thick, coarse hair—he even sported a long, wavy beard of sorts, and his eyes were the deepest brown I had ever seen. Cow-shit brown. His snout jutted out, emphasizing the golden ring dangling from his glistening nostrils, and both glinted in the luminous glow of the moon. The metal was at least an inch thick and etched with runes of a language long forgotten. Wide, aged ivory horns sprouted from each temple, long enough to skewer a wizard with little effort. He was nude except for a massive beaded necklace and a pair of worn leather boots that were big enough to stomp a size twenty-five imprint in my face if he felt so inclined.

I hoped our blossoming friendship wouldn't end that way. I really did.

Because friends didn't let friends wear boots naked…

Get your copy of OBSIDIAN SON online today!
http://www.shaynesilvers.com/l/38474

Shayne has written a few other books without Cameron helping him. Some of them are marginally decent—easily a 4 out of 10.

Turn the page to read a sample of **UNCHAINED** *- Feathers and Fire Series Book 1, or* **BUY ONLINE (FREE with Kindle Unlimited subscription)***. Callie Penrose is a wizard in Kansas City, MO who hunts monsters for the Vatican. She meets Nate Temple, and things devolve from there...*

(Note: Callie appears in the TempleVerse after Nate's book 6, TINY GODS...Full chronology of all books in the TempleVerse shown on the 'Books by the authors' page)

TRY: UNCHAINED (FEATHERS AND FIRE #1)

The rain pelted my hair, plastering loose strands of it to my forehead as I panted, eyes darting from tree to tree, terrified of each shifting branch, splash of water, and whistle of wind slipping through the nightscape around us. But... I was somewhat *excited*, too.

Somewhat.

"Easy, girl. All will be well," the big man creeping just ahead of me, murmured.

"You said we were going to get ice cream!" I hissed at him, failing to compose myself, but careful to keep my voice low and my eyes alert. "I'm not ready for this!" I had been trained to fight, with my hands, with weapons, and with my magic. But I had never taken an active role in a hunt before. I'd always been the getaway driver for my mentor.

The man grunted, grey eyes scanning the trees as he slipped through the tall grass. "And did we not get ice cream before coming here? Because I think I see some in your hair."

"You know what I mean, Roland. You tricked me." I checked the tips of my loose hair, saw nothing, and scowled at his back.

"The Lord does not give us a greater burden than we can shoulder."

I muttered dark things under my breath, wiping the water from my eyes. Again. My new shirt was going to be ruined. Silk never fared well in the rain. My choice of shoes wasn't much better. Boots, yes, but distressed, *fashionable* boots. Not work boots designed for the rain and mud. Definitely not monster hunting boots for our evening excursion through one of Kansas City's wooded parks. I realized I was forcibly distracting myself, keeping my mind busy with mundane thoughts to avoid my very real anxiety. Because whenever I grew nervous, an imagined nightmare always—

A church looming before me. Rain pouring down. Night sky and a glowing moon overhead. I was all alone. Crying on the cold, stone steps, an infant in a cardboard box—

I forced the nightmare away, breathing heavily. "You know I hate it when you talk like that," I whispered to him, trying to regain my composure. I wasn't angry with him, but was growing increasingly uncomfortable with our situation after my brief flashback of fear.

"Doesn't mean it shouldn't be said," he said kindly. "I think we're close. Be alert. Remember your training. Banish your fears. I am here. And the Lord is here. He always is."

So, he had noticed my sudden anxiety. "Maybe I should just go back to the car. I know I've trained, but I really don't think—"

A shape of fur, fangs, and claws launched from the shadows towards me, cutting off my words as it snarled, thirsty for my blood.

And my nightmare slipped back into my thoughts like a veiled assassin, a wraith hoping to hold me still for the monster to eat. I froze, unable to move. Twin sticks of power abruptly erupted into being in my clenched fists, but my fear swamped me with that stupid nightmare, the sticks held at my side, useless to save me.

Right before the beast's claws reached me, it grunted as something batted it from the air, sending it flying sideways. It struck a tree with another grunt and an angry whine of pain.

I fell to my knees right into a puddle, arms shaking, breathing fast.

My sticks crackled in the rain like live cattle prods, except their entire length was the electrical section — at least to anyone other than me. I could hold them without pain.

Magic was a part of me, coursing through my veins whether I wanted it or not, and Roland had spent many years teaching me how to master it. But I had never been able to fully master the nightmare inside me, and in moments of fear, it always won, overriding my training.

The fact that I had resorted to weapons — like the ones he had trained me with — rather than a burst of flame, was startling. It was good in the fact that my body's reflexes knew enough to call up a defense even without my direct command, but bad in the fact that it was the worst form of defense for the situation presented. I could have very easily done as Roland did, and hurt it from a distance. But I hadn't. Because of my stupid block.

Roland placed a calloused palm on my shoulder, and I flinched. "Easy, see? I am here." But he did frown at my choice of weapons, the reprimand silent but loud in my mind. I let out a shaky breath, forcing my fear back down. It was all in my head, but still, it wasn't easy. Fear could be like that.

I focused on Roland's implied lesson. Close combat weapons — even magically-powered ones — were for last resorts. I averted my eyes in very real shame. I knew these things. He didn't even need to tell me them. But when that damned nightmare caught hold of me, all my training went out the window. It haunted me like a shadow, waiting for moments just like this, as if trying to kill me. A form of psychological suicide? But it was why I constantly refused to join Roland on his hunts. He knew about it. And although he was trying to help me overcome that fear, he never pressed too hard.

Rain continued to sizzle as it struck my batons. I didn't let them go, using them as a totem to build my confidence back up. I slowly lifted my eyes to nod at him as I climbed back to my feet.

That's when I saw the second set of eyes in the shadows, right before they flew out of the darkness towards Roland's back. I threw one of my batons and missed, but that pretty much let Roland know that an unfriendly was behind him. Either that or I had just failed to murder my mentor at point-blank range. He whirled to confront the monster, expecting another aerial assault as he unleashed a ball of fire that splashed over the tree at chest height, washing the trunk in blue flames. But this monster was tricky. It hadn't planned on tackling Roland, but had merely jumped out of the darkness to get closer, no doubt learning from its fallen comrade, who still lay unmoving against the tree behind me.

His coat shone like midnight clouds with hints of lightning flashing in the depths of thick, wiry fur. The coat of dew dotting his fur reflected the moonlight, giving him a faint sheen as if covered in fresh oil. He was tall, easily hip height at the shoulder, and barrel chested, his rump much leaner than the rest of his body. He — I assumed male from the long, thick mane around his neck — had a very long snout, much longer and wider than any werewolf I had ever seen. Amazingly, and beyond my control, I realized he was beautiful.

But most of the natural world's lethal hunters were beautiful.

He landed in a wet puddle a pace in front of Roland, juked to the right, and then to the left, racing past the big man, biting into his hamstrings on his way by.

A wash of anger rolled over me at seeing my mentor injured, dousing my fear, and I swung my baton down as hard as I could. It struck the beast in the rump as it tried to dart back to cover — a typical wolf tactic. My blow singed his hair and shattered bone. The creature collapsed into a puddle of mud with a yelp, instinctively snapping his jaws over his shoulder to bite whatever had hit him.

I let him. But mostly out of dumb luck as I heard Roland hiss in pain, falling to the ground.

The monster's jaws clamped around my baton, and there was an immediate explosion of teeth and blood that sent him flying several feet away into the tall brush, yipping, screaming, and staggering. Before he slipped out of sight, I noticed that his lower jaw was simply *gone*, from the contact of his saliva on my electrified magical batons. Then he managed to limp into the woods with more pitiful yowls, but I had no mind to chase him. Roland — that titan of a man, my mentor — was hurt. I could smell copper in the air, and knew we had to get out of here. Fast. Because we had anticipated only one of the monsters. But there had been two of them, and they hadn't been the run-of-the-mill werewolves we had been warned about. If there were two, perhaps there were more. And they were evidently the prehistoric cousin of any werewolf I had ever seen or read about.

Roland hissed again as he stared down at his leg, growling with both pain and anger. My eyes darted back to the first monster, wary of another attack. It *almost* looked like a werewolf, but bigger. Much bigger. He didn't move, but I saw he was breathing. He had a notch in his right ear and a jagged scar on his long snout. Part of me wanted to go over to him and torture him. Slowly. Use his pain to finally drown my nightmare, my fear. The fear that had caused Roland's injury. My lack of inner-strength had not only put me in danger, but had hurt my mentor, my friend.

I shivered, forcing the thought away. That was *cold*. Not me. Sure, I was no stranger to fighting, but that had always been in a ring. Practicing. Sparring. Never life or death.

But I suddenly realized something very dark about myself in the chill, rainy night. Although I was terrified, I felt a deep ocean of anger manifest inside me, wanting only to dispense justice as I saw fit. To use that rage to battle my own demons. As if feeding one would starve the other, reminding me of the Cherokee Indian Legend Roland had once told me.

An old Cherokee man was teaching his grandson about life. "A fight is going on inside me," he told the boy. "It is a terrible fight between two wolves. One is evil — he is anger, envy, sorrow, regret, greed, arrogance, self-pity, guilt, resentment, inferiority, lies, false pride, superiority, and ego." After a few moments to make sure he had the boy's undivided attention, he continued.

"The other wolf is good — he is joy, peace, love, hope, serenity, humility, kindness, benevolence, empathy, generosity, truth, compassion, and faith. The same fight is going on inside of you, boy, and inside of every other person, too."

The grandson thought about this for a few minutes before replying. "Which wolf will win?"

The old Cherokee man simply said, "The one you feed, boy. The one you feed..."

And I felt like feeding one of my wolves today, by killing this one...

Get the full book ONLINE! http://www.shaynesilvers.com/l/38952

MAKE A DIFFERENCE

Reviews are the most powerful tools in our arsenal when it comes to getting attention for our books. Much as we'd like to, we don't have the financial muscle of a New York publisher.

But we do have something much more powerful and effective than that, and it's something that those publishers would kill to get their hands on.

A committed and loyal bunch of readers.

Honest reviews of our books help bring them to the attention of other readers.

If you've enjoyed this book, we would be very grateful if you could spend just five minutes leaving a review on our book's Amazon page.

Thank you very much in advance.

ACKNOWLEDGMENTS

From Cameron:

I'd like to thank Shayne, for paving the way in style. Kori, for an introduction that would change my life. My three wonderful sisters, for showing me what a strong, independent woman looks and sounds like. And, above all, my parents, for—literally—everything.

From Shayne (the self-proclaimed prettiest one):

Team Temple and the Den of Freaks on Facebook have become family to me. I couldn't do it without die-hard readers like them.

I would also like to thank you, the reader. I hope you enjoyed reading *WITCHES BREW* as much as we enjoyed writing it. Be sure to check out the two crossover series in the TempleVerse: **The Nate Temple Series** and the **Feathers and Fire Series**.

And last, but definitely not least, I thank my wife, Lexy. Without your support, none of this would have been possible.

ABOUT CAMERON O'CONNELL

Cameron O'Connell is a Jack-of-All-Trades and Master of Some.

He writes The Phantom Queen Diaries, a series in The TempleVerse, about Quinn MacKenna, a mouthy black magic arms dealer trading favors in Boston. All she wants? A round-trip ticket to the Fae realm...and maybe a drink on the house.

A former member of the United States military, a professional model, and English teacher, Cameron finds time to write in the mornings after his first cup of coffee...and in the evenings after his thirty-seventh. Follow him, and the TempleVerse founder, Shayne Silvers, online for all sorts of insider tips, giveaways, and new release updates!

Get Down with Cameron Online

f facebook.com/Cameron-OConnell-788806397985289

a amazon.com/author/cameronoconnell

BB bookbub.com/authors/cameron-o-connell

twitter.com/thecamoconnell

instagram.com/camoconnellauthor

g goodreads.com/cameronoconnell

ABOUT SHAYNE SILVERS

Shayne is a man of mystery and power, whose power is exceeded only by his mystery...

He currently writes the Amazon Bestselling **Nate Temple** Series, which features a foul-mouthed wizard from St. Louis. He rides a bloodthirsty unicorn, drinks with Achilles, and is pals with the Four Horsemen.

He also writes the Amazon Bestselling **Feathers and Fire** Series—a second series in the TempleVerse. The story follows a rookie spell-slinger named Callie Penrose who works for the Vatican in Kansas City. Her problem? Hell seems to know more about her past than she does.

He coauthors **The Phantom Queen Diaries**—a third series set in The TempleVerse—with Cameron O'Connell. The story follows Quinn MacKenna, a mouthy black magic arms dealer in Boston. All she wants? A round-trip ticket to the Fae realm...and maybe a drink on the house.

He also writes the **Shade of Devil Series**, which tells the story of Sorin Ambrogio—the world's FIRST vampire. He was put into a magical slumber by a Native American Medicine Man when the Americas were first discovered by Europeans. Sorin wakes up after five-hundred years to learn that his protege, Dracula, stole his reputation and that no one has ever even heard of Sorin Ambrogio. The streets of New York City will run with blood as Sorin reclaims his legend.

Shayne holds two high-ranking black belts, and can be found writing in a coffee shop, cackling madly into his computer screen while pounding shots of espresso. He's hard at work on the newest books in the TempleVerse—You can find updates on new releases or chronological reading order on the next page, his website, or any of his social media accounts. **Follow him online for all sorts of groovy goodies, giveaways, and new release updates:**

Get Down with Shayne Online
www.shaynesilvers.com
info@shaynesilvers.com

facebook.com/shaynesilversfanpage
amazon.com/author/shaynesilvers
bookbub.com/profile/shayne-silvers
instagram.com/shaynesilversofficial
twitter.com/shaynesilvers
goodreads.com/ShayneSilvers

BOOKS BY THE AUTHORS

CHRONOLOGY: All stories in the TempleVerse are shown in chronological order on the following page

PHANTOM QUEEN DIARIES

(Set in the TempleVerse)

by Cameron O'Connell & Shayne Silvers

COLLINS (Prequel novella #0 in the 'LAST CALL' anthology)

WHISKEY GINGER

COSMOPOLITAN

OLD FASHIONED

MOTHERLUCKER (Novella #3.5 in the 'LAST CALL' anthology)

DARK AND STORMY

MOSCOW MULE

WITCHES BREW

SALTY DOG

SEA BREEZE

HURRICANE

NATE TEMPLE SERIES

(Main series in the TempleVerse)

by Shayne Silvers

FAIRY TALE - FREE prequel novella #0 for my subscribers

OBSIDIAN SON

BLOOD DEBTS

GRIMM

SILVER TONGUE

BEAST MASTER

BEERLYMPIAN (Novella #5.5 in the 'LAST CALL' anthology)

TINY GODS

DADDY DUTY (Novella #6.5)

WILD SIDE

WAR HAMMER

NINE SOULS

HORSEMAN

LEGEND

KNIGHTMARE

ASCENSION

FEATHERS AND FIRE SERIES

(Also set in the TempleVerse)

by Shayne Silvers

UNCHAINED

RAGE

WHISPERS

ANGEL'S ROAR

MOTHERLUCKER (Novella #4.5 in the 'LAST CALL' anthology)

SINNER

BLACK SHEEP

GODLESS

CHRONOLOGICAL ORDER: TEMPLEVERSE

FAIRY TALE (TEMPLE PREQUEL)

OBSIDIAN SON (TEMPLE 1)

BLOOD DEBTS (TEMPLE 2)

GRIMM (TEMPLE 3)

SILVER TONGUE (TEMPLE 4)

BEAST MASTER (TEMPLE 5)

BEERLYMPIAN (TEMPLE 5.5)

TINY GODS (TEMPLE 6)

SHADE OF DEVIL SERIES

(Not part of the TempleVerse)

by Shayne Silvers

DEVIL'S DREAM

DEVIL'S CRY
DEVIL'S BLOOD

NOTHING TO SEE HERE.

Thanks for reaching the last page of the book, you over-achiever. Sniff the spine. You've earned it. Or sniff your Kindle.

Now this has gotten weird.

Alright. I'm leaving.

Made in the USA
Coppell, TX
11 May 2021